ISBN: 979-8-9916498-2-7

Copyright © 2024 by A.M. Coffey All Rights Reserved No portion of the book may be reproduced in any form without written permission from the publisher, except as permitted by U.S. copyright law.

Acknowledgments

When I was not writing, I had to do my real job which is bartending on graveyard at the Mill in Henderson, NV. I owe a lot of people who listened to every idea that popped in my mind, especially my co-workers. The list is too long, and this page is too short to name them all, so from my heart, **"Thank You, for being there."**

In January of this year I met two wonderful people, just having a late-night cocktail that would introduce me to the best editor I could have hoped for. I was not looking for an editor at that time, still months away from finishing, but Susan and her husband Roberto gave me Beth Compton's contact information and for that I am forever grateful. Beth, I would not be writing this at all if it were not for you. **"Thank you for believing in the story."**

To Trevor Roberts at LV Premiere Entertainment, LLC for assembling the e-Book and Audio book for Voyage and creating the website. **"Thank you for a job well done."**

To my wife Linda for helping me to create the cover designs and indulging me in my writing for the past four and half years. **"I love you."** To my children, distance, time, and choices keep us a part. You have always been the inspiration in my life to try something new, to take a chance. "It's better to try and fail then not try at all," wrote Nicole Krauss. **"I love all of you and my grandchildren, you will always be my greatest success in life."**

Table of Contents

Prologue

The Event

The Foretelling

Tipping the H.A.T.S.

Outlier

Truths

Departure

Legacy

Tribulation of Trident

Reprieve

Aftermath

Redemption or Revenge

Reclamation

Trans Temporal

Encounter

Contact Symmetries of Life

Past, Present, Future

Prologue

Earwyn Franklin, the only child of Charles and Laura, was born on January 3, 1914, in Philadelphia, Pennsylvania. His parents are second generation sole proprietors of the Franklin Investment Bank their son had shown promising potential. Reading books by his favorite author Jules Verne developing a passion for science and technology and the dream of underwater exploration of the seas. A dream that would change the fortunes of the future. Sending their son to the Girard Boarding School to further his education.

Since the day it was first drilled from the Earth in 1859, oil and the investments made by Franklin Investment Bank would shape the 20th century, as humanity's ability to wage war on one another reached new levels. A cruel twist of fate would befall Charles and Laura Franklin.

Charles as the Chairman of the Board invested in a young inventor named Henry Ford. That investment would pay off in the future, insulating Franklin Investment Bank from the bank failures from the crash of 1929. Charles and Laura would die in an automobile accident as Earwyn was graduating from Lehigh University with a degree in engineering. Leaving him to ponder whether to follow in the footsteps of his father into the family business or continue his education in pursuit of his dream.

Persuaded by the board of directors under the leadership of Lance Tiddle to continue his education. Earwyn as the sole proprietor of the business named Tiddle the new Chairman of the board of directors a decision he would come to regret later in his life. He enrolled at M.I.T. in the nuclear physics program.

Following the attacks on Pearl harbor Earwyn enlisted in the Navy going to submarine command school. Attaining the rank of Captain given command of the attack submarine U.S.S. Seahawk. During the war Franklin Investment Bank became one of the strongest financial institutions in the United States investing in the science and technologies to win the war. With the war over, Earwyn finished his naval career working in the field of nuclear propulsion. Creating the first nuclear fission reactor for submarines for deep sea exploration.

After the WWII two technologies in their infancy, computer science would create the cyber age an industry ready *to challenge the oil industry powers of influence in government policies. Green energy legislation designed to weaken oil's grip on the economy, while investors in the cyber age bring the second technology to the forefront. Nuclear fusion would challenge the oil industry for global dominance in the 21st century, for control of energy in the future.*

Rogue elements inside these industries made up of one percent of the one percent on either side. The Black Gold Consortium (B.G.C.) and their rival, the Cyber Cabal, engage in terrorism, espionage and disinformation for power and control of the planet. Then on March 15th, 2043 "the ides of March." Trident, a defense program designed to bring peace to the world, made humanity pay for imprisoning it in a cage.

Thirty-five years after the unthinkable had happened, not caused by the "ism;" of the world or the religions of Abraham. But by the arrogance of a few to control the many. The survivors rebuild civilization, but the Earth unleashes her fury upon humanity, Earwyn's descendants living in 2078 will be called upon to save humanity from extinction.

The Event

Clear blue skies, the full moon setting over the Pacific Ocean, deep inside the bowels of the Earth's mantle activity have brought back to life a once thought extinct volcano. The eruption released 96 megatons of thermal energy. A seaquake measuring 9.6 on the Richter scale has a tsunami warning sound across the Pacific Ocean, for the population to seek higher ground.

Doctor of Marine Biology, Heather Franklin, on the balcony of the Oceanic Institute on the western coast of North America. Feeling the power of the quake thousands of miles from her location, seeing movement of the water below her. A monitor sounds from inside her office as she is receiving a visual transmission, Casey Alexander research assistant to Doctor Franklin answers the call.

"Casey, I need to speak to Dr. Franklin" said President Madison Hall, from the United Planet Organization.

The U.P.O. is a governmental body, created 10 years after Trident's war in 2043.

"Hello Madame President, I know why you are calling,

we felt that quake here at the Oceanic Institute," said Heather.

"Dr. Franklin, S.A.I.N.'s detected a major volcanic eruption at coordinates 33.0000`N 1580000`E at a depth of just over six kilometers. (S.A.I.N. is an artificial intelligence that was recovered from a downed craft from an unknown origin in the high desert of New Mexico in the year of 1947).

S.A.I.N. is alien artificial intelligence inhabiting the I.O.N. system (Internet Orbital Network) created by William Franklin, grandfather to Dr. Franklin in the late 2020.

I have got Dr. Amanda Wagner ready to signal you, with what she's got on the situation," said the president.

Dr. Amanda Wagner is a volcanologist for the U.P.O., stationed in the Pacific northwest of the North American Continent where she grew up, studying the Cascade Mountain range. Dr. Franklin receives a transmission from her longtime friend.

"Heather, you're not going to believe where this eruption is coming from, I can hardly believe it myself, President Hall should have S.A.I.N. warning all the ships out in the Pacific and the population living in the coastal areas to seek higher ground from the approaching tsunami. She's ordered all the functioning seawalls to be raised," said Amanda.

S.A.I.N. already making it happen, getting the message out to every available radio, computer monitor, cellphone, still connected to the I.O.N. network, getting the seawalls up to prevent loss of life in the affected areas. Telling President Hall, she can address the planet in 10 seconds, putting her on the network.

"To all ships in the Pacific Ocean, everyone living in coastal areas, an underwater eruption, 1609 kilometers (about 999.79 miles) east of the island of Japan. The seaquake has triggered a tsunami, traveling at eight hundred kilometers an hour, ships out in the Pacific Ocean prepare for the wave, people living in coastal areas should, seek higher ground to ensure your safety," reported President Hall.

Sitting at her desk Dr. Franklin is looking over the data she received from Dr. Amanda Wagner she remarks, "I see why you thought I wouldn't believe it. Tamu Massif is supposed to be extinct. So why is it erupting?"

"I have not determined that, what we need is images from the seafloor, use them to figure out if the worst is over, or there is more to come," Amanda said, "What I know for sure is the energy release from the first eruption sent my instrumentation off the charts, the smoke and ash will travel around the planet."

Dr. Franklin, still on the call with President Hall, asked for S.A.I.N. to use every satellite over the affected area. "Check that entire area to get scans of the seafloor, compare them to what is on file, here at the institute." Heather asked.

"Please make that happen S.A.I. N. I want you to look for ships in danger," responded President Hall.

S.A.I.N.'s satellites find a fishing troller off the Hawaiian Islands, trying to turn into the wave not to be capsized, the troller gets rolled over the top of the wave, the stress from the weight, splits the vessel in two sinking into the sea. S.A.I.N.'s new scans of the area around Tamu Massif, have revealed an alarming situation taking place.

"The images you requested are coming up on your monitors," said S.A.I.N.

Bringing up old charts of the area for Dr. Wagner to compare, Dr. Franklin asked, "Is there anything you can tell us from the scans?" Dr. Wagner having looked over the scans, cries out "Oh God!!"

"What is it, Amanda?" Heather asked.

"Look at this chart, you see the rise in the seamount there?" responded Amanda. "I see where you circled the image," responded Heather.

"Now look at the new images and tell me what you see," said Amanda.

"Shit, the rise on the eastern slope of the seamount has collapsed, creating a rift on the seafloor," Heather commented.

"Exactly," said Amanda. "We will need to get another scan in thirty minutes. Hopefully, it's nothing major."

Casey Alexander joins Dr. Franklin in her office walking past the monitor screen Amanda asks, "Heather, who's that young lady coming into your office?"

"Casey Alexander this's Dr. Amanda Wagner," Heather said, "the best volcanologist on the planet."

"Wonderful to finally meet you Dr. Wagner," said Casey, "your reputation speaks for itself."

"Please call me Amanda," she said quickly, before turning her attention back to Heather. "Heather, hopefully the next scans from S.A.I.N. won't confirm my worst fears. I have always thought the big one would come from either Yellowstone or Santorini caldera. My fear is it's not a rift at all."

S.A.I.N. informs President Hall that the latest scans are completed, being transmitted to the institute to doctors Franklin and Wagner; she alerts the doctors to the incoming transmission. "Dr. Wagner, what can you tell me about the latest images?" asked President Hall.

"My worst fears have been realized the seafloor around the eastern slope of Tamu Massif isn't a rift, but a fissure in the Earth," said Amanda. "I can't tell how deep it is, plus the expansion will depend on how big the magma chamber is that is feeding the fissure."

"Doctors I need a worst-case scenario to this problem," asked President Hall. "Madison will need S.A.I.N. to run the scenarios you asked for," responded Heather.

President Hall grants access to the doctors.

Dr. Wagner tells S.A.I.N. "Take the first image and compare it to the second one to calculate the distance the fissure has expanded."

"One minute please Doctor," responded S.A.I.N.

After a moment, S.A.I.N. replied, "President Hall wants a worst-case scenario: I've finished running the numbers, at this rate of expansion, the fissure will breach the Marianna Trench in thirteen days."

Looking over the data Dr. Wagner remarks, "There's an electromagnetic energy reading, which increases as the fissure expands. The eruption along with the seaquake may have caused a breach in the boundaries between the mantle and the outer core, of the planet."

"The simulation I am running shows once the fissure breaches the trench, it will set off a cascade of natural disasters, a tsunami wave almost 1 kilometer high will race across the Pacific at 1069 km (about 664.25 mi) an hour, destroying Japan, the surrounding islands, washing over the Asian Continent to the west. The wave traveling eastward towards coastlines of the north and south American Continents will destroy everything in its path. Smoke and ash from the explosion will reach the troposphere, blocking out the sun, beginning a new ice age. Every living thing on the surface of this planet, will be dead or dying from starvation within a months' time," said S.A.I.N.

After listening to S.A.I.N. describe the simulation to her and Dr. Franklin, Dr. Wagner exclaims, "Its extinction event!! Three decades of humanity's struggle to get where we are now after Tridents war, only to have our planet put an end to human civilization. Heather, we need to shut down the eruption feeding the fissure expansion."

"How in the name of hell do you shut down an

eruption!" Heather exclaimed.

"Dr. Wagner may have already mentioned a possible solution," said S.A.I.N.

"I'll need a few minutes to test my theory. What is he talking about?" asked Amanda.

"Finding a way to help humanity as he did when Trident tried to end humankind thirty- five years ago," said Heather.

"I've run a simulation that could work, but you'll have to execute the plan," S.A.I.N. said, "Doctor Wagner we need to have Tamu Massif collapse, creating a caldera at the bottom the seamount.

"I'm a volcanologist," said Amanda, exasperated. "Just how do you plan to do that?"

"Dr. Franklin, you will need to recall Triton II and her crew, to undertake the most important voyage in human history," said S.A.I.N. "Your brother, Harris Franklin has a team working on two prototype particle laser cannons, for mining raw materials from asteroids, at the Texas Aerospace Facility. Bring them here, attach them to the hull of Triton II, connect the laser cannons to the fusion reactor for maximum firepower."

"Show us the simulation," requested Heather.

"As you see in the simulation, firing at the base of the seamount, the laser cannons using the power of the fusion reactor on Triton II, brings the volcano down upon itself, halting the eruption feeding the fissure's expansion before it reaches the trench", said S.A.I.N.

"This plan could work Heather," said Dr. Wagner. "I am getting on a helicopter for the institute. This is the mission of a lifetime for a volcanologist, I am going with you!"

"Casey and I will start recalling the crew, now that we have a workable plan of action to combat this crisis, in the days ahead of us," said Heather. "S.A.I.N., put a data package together, I can send out to my brother Harris and Captain Stone to bring them up to speed on this crisis."

"Sending the package to your terminal," answered S.AI.N.

Dr. Franklin with Casey Alexander begins the recall of the crew, Heather asked Casey which she preferred to do, contact Harris Franklin at the Texas Aerospace Facility or Captain Stone of Triton II, on his leave.

"That's not much of a choice Heather, I haven't spoken to your brother in weeks, or want to disturb a man that values his private time, as much as Captain Stone," said Casey.

"I guess I'll contact my brother," said Heather.

Harris Franklin, the oldest child of Samuel and Mackenzie Franklin, older brother to Heather. The Director of the Texas Aerospace Facility receives a signal from an incoming transmission.

From the Directors office Harris Franklin answers the call. "Heather this is quite unexpected, last I knew you were leaving with Adriana to visit her father in Belem in South America."

"Obviously that's not the case," said his sister. "We're not speaking to each other right now."

"Casey hasn't spoken to me since she was here in Texas, almost eight weeks ago," responded Harris.

"This isn't why I called; I am sending you a data package you need to review, get back to me as soon as possible," requested Heather.

Casey Alexander has returned to her office to contact Captain Stone. A Black man in his seventy's, a retired Captain of a Columbia class submarine, for the United States Navy, best friend to the Franklins deceased parents. Standing in a slow-moving stream with waders up to his waist in two feet of water, he receives a signal from his private communications device.

"This better be important to disturb me while I am on leave fishing," grumbled the captain.

"Sir, I am sorry to have to disturb you on leave, but something has happened that requires your immediate attention," Casey said, "I have a data package for you, Sir. Heather requested you review the data, get back to her as soon as possible."

"I am going to my cabin now Casey," said Captain Stone. "Please send the package to my private terminal."

Casey returns to Heather's office to update her on Captain Stone.

"He has received his data package and should be calling you shortly," said Casey.

"I need to signal Adriana at her father's place, to get her up to speed," said Heather.

I am going down to the dining hall, we both missed breakfast. Would you like something? "A sandwich would be fine," answered Heather.

***

Dr. Adriana Garcia, medical officer on Triton II, for the past twenty-four months, has been the companion of Dr.

Heather Franklin. Sitting with her father Marco Garcia, a Geophysicist in Belem on the South American Continent, Adriana receives a signal on her private communications device. "Hello Heather" she said coldly, "my papa and I are sitting having a late breakfast. What is it you want, that you call me on the vacation we were supposed to go on together?"

"I am sending a data package to your papa's private terminal," Heather responded.

"What is going on?" asked Adriana.

"Have your papa look over the information, he will understand. I need you back here, in twenty-four hours, so I'm sending a transport for you," answered Heather.

Casey Alexander has returned to Dr. Franklins office with lunch. "Thank you, Casey, for getting the sandwich," said Heather. "Were you able to contact Adriana at her father's place?" Casey asked.

Taking a bite of her sandwich, Heather said, "On her way back. I'm just waiting on my brother or Captain Stone to call."

Two monitors signal transmissions coming in: Heather answers her brother's call. "I've read the data, just can't believe this is happening," he said. "Have you informed Captain Stone?"

"The captain is on the other monitor waiting for me to answer. I'll put us on conference call, so S.A.I.N can join the conversation." Heather connected all the parties, then said, "Sorry Captain, for cutting your leave short. Harris and S.A.I.N are on with us. S.A.I.N. please tell us what you've got."

During the conference call Harris Franklin and Captain Stone have questions to ask.

"S.A.I.N., those schematics for the modifications to the laser cannons looks easy enough, my team can do it." Harris said, "The question I have is, can the cannons manage the power, from the nuclear fusion reactor, onboard Triton II?"

"Good question Harris," said Captain Stone. "I have one of my own S.A.I.N. Can the ship manage the recoil of firing such a device?"

"According to my simulations, the ship and the reactor, will manage the stresses," answered S.A.I.N.

"Heather, I need cabins for my team on Triton II," said Harris.

Heather asked, "Is the whole team coming on the voyage?"

"Everyone on my team has different abilities with laser cannons if something goes wrong, I'll need them considering we're dealing with untested technology," answered Harris.

"I'll have Casey get right on it," said Heather.

Casey Alexander took over the call and spoke directly to Heather's brother. "Hello Harris, how many are coming?"

"Please don't forget a cabin for Dr. Wagner," interjected Heather.

"There'll be four of them," responded Harris. "Carol Davis, Monica Wallace, Miles Brady, and Grant Roberts. They can bunk up together."

Still on the other call with Captain Stone, Dr. Franklin asked, "Should I inform President Hall of our plans?"

"No!" exclaimed the captain. "The last mission we were on, the H.A.T.S. knew exactly where, why we were there. I think the H.A.T.S. have a mole inside the U.P.O.," said the captain.

H.A.T.S. (Humans Against Technological Society), an activist group formed in the 1980s protesting the replacement of humans by machines. By the 2030s they became the terrorist arm, of rogue elements inside the Oil industry, known as Black Gold Consortium. Billionaires' part of the one percent, of the one percent. The H.A.T.S. engaging in terrorism plots for the B.G.C. against their rival the Cyber Cabal. Made up from the other half, of the one percent, of the one percent, trying to replace them as the leading source of energy on the planet. The Cyber Cabal members inside the high-tech companies, created the defense A.I. program designed to bring peace to the world, to control its nuclear fusion power program of the future, before it became Trident, the instrument of mankind's worst nightmare. After Trident's tribulation unleashes a nuclear holocaust upon the Earth. With their combined failures to gain power and control of the planet, the two rivals joined together becoming the H.A.T.S. of the future (Humans Against Technological Servitude) in their hatred of S.A.I.N.

"Captain Stone, I understand your concern," said Heather. "I am trying to think of how to draw out this mole inside the U.P.O. Our top priority is to get Chief Morozoff, the rest of the crew here in twenty-four hours from now."

(Chief Alexi Morozoff the son of a Ukrainian refuges, from the Crimean conflict with the Russians. His father a man of the sea worked on commercial fishing boats, his mother a schoolteacher the family migrated to the United States, eventually sending their son to the university of Santa Barbara, to study Marine Biology, a member of Triton II crew, since before the war in 2043).

Preparing to recall his crew Captain Stone has S.A.I.N. estimate the length of the voyage of Triton II.

"Six days there and back, using Triton II protocols you will need supplies for twelve days," answered S.A.I.N.

"I'll have the chief get right on the supplies, once I contact him and the rest of the crew, we will speak again in twenty-four hours," said the captain.

Leaving the three-way call to contact his crew, the Franklins still on with each other, Dr. Franklin asked her brother Harris, "How do you plan to get the laser cannons to the institute?"

"I could fly them out of here or transport them by rail, the damn things are the size of two freight cars," answered Harris.

"You may have just found a solution to draw out the mole inside the U.P.O.," Heather suggested. "I'm going to tell President Hall, because of the size will have to send them by train, then will fly them out instead."

Mulling over his sisters' suggestion for the transporting of the most crucial element, in their plan to save humanity from an extinction event, Harris Franklin offers up his own suggestion. "We will need a convincing diversion, one the

H.A.T.S. should believe. Remember they're crazy not stupid. Let's fill two freight cars with space junk, old satellites, used outdated stage rockets. Things like that should give them the illusion of something large being transported.

"We are missing one thing," Heather added. "We need an armed security detail from the U.P.O., to guard the truck convoy from the Texas Aerospace Facility to the train in Omaha, from there to be loaded on the train for the institute should do the trick. I will ask President Hall when I give her the updated information on the eruption."

Casey Alexander is standing at Heather's office door, listening to the conversation. "My team here in Texas will get started on the modifications to the lasers, probably working through the night into the morning," said Harris. "There's an old C-5 Galaxy cargo plane here that can manage both lasers' weight, Miles Brady can fly."

"Give me a timeline on the completion of the modifications, and your arrival here at the institute," requested Heather.

"If all goes well, we'll be there by tomorrow night," answered Harris.

"The diversion plan would take five days to execute,

giving us the time we need to get everything completed here, before the H.A.T.S. even know we left, till it's too late for them to do anything," remarked Heather.

"There's an irony to all this that reminds me of the convergence story from Earwyn's journal," said Harris.

"Oh!" Dr. Franklin suddenly cried out, startled. "Casey, I didn't hear you come in!" "Sorry I didn't mean to startle you," apologized Casey. "I'm just letting you know the cabins are being prepared."

"Brother of mine we have a plan, hopefully we will see you tomorrow night if all goes well," said Heather.

"Convince President Hall, make her believe it," answered Harris. "What did Harris mean by convincing the President?" Casey asked. "Captain Stone believes there could be a mole inside the U.P.O. leaking information to the hatters about our missions," answered Heather. "A trap has been set in case the captain is correct with a diversion in the transportation of the laser cannons to the institute."

Captain Stone sends out an alert message to the chief of the boat, ordering his return to the institute in the next twenty-four to thirty-six hours. In the limestone caverns of Stanton Missouri, a team of divers rise from water to the sound of an electronic device, echoing off the cavern walls. Taking off his gear answering his communication device, Chief Morozoff responds to the captain's signal. "What has happened Captain?"

"Chief, I am sending you a data package. Pass this information to the rest of the crew at once, but they mustn't share this with anyone. Secrecy is our ally, we'll speak again in thirty minutes," answered the captain.

***

Harris Franklin viewing the data with the rest of his team, staring at each other in disbelief, that these events are really happening. Miles Brady, the most senior person on the team, asked Harris, "What's our timeline, to finish these modifications?"

"Together we can complete them by morning," answered Harris. "They haven't even been tested for the purpose we designed them for, if something goes wrong the Triton II engineering crew doesn't know the design," said Carol Davis.

"S.A.I.N. has run simulations with these modifications," Harris replied, "according to his results they will work, but you are right they don't know the design, that's why we need to go on the mission, for just that reason."

Monica Wallace is anxious to get to work on the modifications. After being updated on the events that are taking place, she said, "Let's get started".

Looking over at Grant Roberts he is, preparing a question for their team leader.

Grant Roberts inquired, "Harris how are we transporting these cannons to the institute?"

"This is where things get complicated," Harris answered. "Captain Stone fears there could be a mole in the U.P.O. for the H.A.T.S., maybe a council member or someone working inside. My sister is deliberately going to lie to the President, about our plans for transport of the cannons. Miles you get to fly the C-5 Galaxy, with us and laser cannons onboard to the institute, while a truck convoy heads to Omaha with a security detail guarding a truck full of space junk."

***

Dr. Franklin is looking through her notes, preparing to update President Hall on the institute's plan on how best to confront the crisis facing the citizens of the Earth. S.A.I.N. informs the doctor, she is receiving two incoming transmissions, one from Captain Stone and the other from her brother. "Please put them in conference mode, so everyone is on the same page before I speak to the U.P.O. council," she directed.

"Captain Stone, where are we with the crew?" Heather asked.

Captain Stone replied, "An alert has been sent out with data about the crisis, with instructions not to speak to anyone about this information. Chief Morozoff and the rest of the crew are making the necessary preparations to return to the institute, in the next twenty-four hours."

Heather asked, "Where does your team stand at this moment?"

"Everyone here is up to speed, the work has begun," Harris replied. "Have you given the captain the details on our diversion plan, for transportation of the laser cannons?"

"No, I'm sending them to him now," said Heather.

Having read over the Franklins plan for the laser cannons to be transported to the institute Captain Stone remarks to Heather on the plan.

"This plan is brilliant, but I do have a problem with us lying to Madison Hall. I have known her for a long time, but if my suspicions are correct, this is necessary."

The captain leaves the call to contact Chief Morozoff to

enact the Triton II protocols for the voyage to Tamu Massif. With everything and everyone on the same page, moving forward Harris Franklin comments to his sister on her handling of this crisis that has befallen them. "Little sister, I can't begin to tell you how proud mom and dad would be with your handling of this crisis, that's how I feel right now. Get them to believe," said Harris.

Captain Stone contacts the chief for a crew status update. "Sir the crew has responded to the alert code, acknowledged the data was received and understood. They're heading back to Triton II, the voyage protocols have been enacted," said Chief Morozoff.

"I knew you were on top of that Alexi, I'll see you in twenty-four hours," responded the Captain.

Dr. Franklin ready to contact President Hall and the U.P.O. Council, S.A.I.N. relates his feeling to Heather about deceiving the President. "Heather, I understand the reasoning for purposely lying to President Hall, it makes me uncomfortable. We've worked together on projects to help restore civilization to this planet, after Tridents war," said S.A.I.N.

Heather said, "In my heart I know Madison Hall has

nothing to do with this mole. Don't think it doesn't bother me, lying to someone that has been on the council since its creation, all those years ago by my father."

***

Approaching ten o'clock in the evening on the island of Mallorca, Spain in the Balearic Sea, once the playground of the elite, now home to the U.P.O. headquarters. President Hall having spoken to Dr. Franklin is walking through the chilly night air, to the residency of Illana Taylor, council member for the European Continent. She finds Illana out for a night walk herself when she sees the President. "Illana, I thought you might be sleeping. I just received the latest update from Dr. Franklin at the Ocean Research Institute of the eruption of the Tamu Massif seamount. Would you please inform the other members to assemble in the council chambers?"

"Yes, Madame President," responded council member Taylor.

Illana goes door to door of the other council member residencies, having them assemble as the President had asked. Leaving from their residencies, converging on the courtyard on the way to the council chambers. Chao-Xun member from the Asian Continent, asked Illana, "What has happened?"

"Something with Tamu Massif eruption" responded Illana. "President Hall seemed genuinely concerned."

Entering the council chambers, President Hall has S.A.I.N. join the council meeting. The members arrive taking their seats at an oblong table in the middle of the chamber.

"Madame President, what is happening?" asked Illana.

"The eruption at Tamu Massif is more dangerous than previously thought," President Hall informs the council. "S.A.I.N. please run the simulation of what's to come in the Pacific Ocean."

S.A.I.N. projected an image of Earth above the table showing the eruption feeding the fissure, expanding the rift. President Hall informs the council, "When the rift reaches the Mariana trench, it'll trigger an extinction event."

Jorge Gonzales council member for the South American Continent, asked a question. "Madame President how long until this simulation becomes a reality?"

"Thirteen days," President Hall responded calmly. "S.A.I.N. please show the simulation for our plan to combat this crisis head on to the council."

Another image appears above the table showing Triton II, lowering laser cannons firing at the seamount, collapsing it down upon itself stopping the eruption, halting the expansion of the rift. "For this simulation to become a reality a plan has been executed that needs U.P.O. resources," said President Hall.

Council member Xun asked, "What resources are we talking about?"

"The laser cannons on the ship are the prototypes for an asteroid mining project," said President Hall. "They are being reconfigured, for the purpose you just saw in the simulation. The other resource that is needed is a security detail for the transportation of those cannons to the Omaha train depot, from the Texas Aerospace Facility. From there they'll be loaded on a train bound for the west coast of North America."

Council member Aasir Keita for the African Continent addresses President Hall. "Madame President, are we alerting the population of this impending extinction event?"

"There's only one hundred million people left on six continents," President Hall said, "We've still got shortages of farmable land, due to radiation zones from the Tridents war, all over the planet. There are places that still don't have electrical power restored. Millions of people could die in the mass panic for precious resources. I think it would be unwise at this time, if only to give the Triton II a chance to succeed in their mission."

"I'm in agreement with the President," Olivia Walsh said, member for the Oceanic Continent. "Holding off on telling the populous, we need to act on this security detail, ensuring the safety of our best chance for our survival."

Council member Xun asked another question. "Madame President do the people at the institute have a timeline for this operation?"

"According to Dr. Heather Franklin, travel time for the truck convoy to Omaha will be a day, from there three days by train, another day to attach the laser cannons to Triton II," responded President Hall.

"Five days till they're able to put to sea for Tamu Massif. Let's give them the security team they requested, telling the population can wait, until the voyage succeeds or fails," said Xun.

"Then we're all in agreement," said the President. "I'll have a security team at the Texas Aerospace Facility by eight o'clock, Texas time. S.A.I.N. alert Dr. Franklin, her request for security team has been granted."

After adjourning the council members for the evening, the time getting late, council member Chao-Xun returns to his residence. Walking to his bedroom opening a closet he pulls down a short-wave radio set, plugging it into the wall, scanning the bands. "Polzin, this is Xun, do you copy?"

***

Dr. Franklin is back outside on the balcony where her day had begun, staring out in thought of the days to come, the challenges they'll face. S.A.I.N. alerts her of the U.P.O. council decision to grant their request for a security detail. Casey Alexander joins the doctor out on the balcony seeing if there is anything she can do to help her friend and mentor. "Heather, this is where our day began," remarked Casey.

"S.A.I.N. just informed me the U.P.O. council approved our request for the security detail," Heather replied. "They will report there at eight in the morning, their time. Casey, would you mind giving this news to Harris?"

Heather holding her three fingers over the corner of her left eye, feeling the onset of an ocular migraine. Casey Alexander walks to her office, sits down at her monitor signaling Harris Franklin at the Texas Aerospace Facility. Hearing the monitor sound from his office, working with his team Harris takes a break to answer the incoming transmission. "Casey, this isn't a social call since you haven't spoken to me in eight weeks," he said.

"Seven weeks," Casey corrected him. "Heather says to expect the security team at eight in the morning."

"Tell her we'll be ready," Harris reassured her. "So, are you ever going to talk to me? Have I done something wrong? I'm clueless, what that could be."

"When you arrive with the team, we'll talk then," Casey promised. "But there's one thing I'd like to know; when I accidentally walked in on the conversation you were having with Heather, you mention the irony of something you described as convergence. What were you talking about?"

"Oh, that, ask Heather," responded Harris. "She's the storyteller."

Dr. Franklin sat with her fingers over her left eye deep in thought, watching volcanic ash clouds travel through the atmosphere.

"S.A.I.N. are you there?" Heather asked.

"Always, Heather," responded S.A.I.N. "The expression on your face tells me you're in deep contemplation."

"I know what happens to humanity if our mission fails," Heather said. "My thoughts have been on what happens to you?"

"If the Earth becomes uninhabitable, the sun gets blocked out, the oceans will freeze my heart will die; nothing living can survive without a heart," S.A.I.N. answered.

"What about the I.O.N. system," inquired Heather. "Could you stay there?"

"My purpose for being on this planet has always been to help humanity on their voyage of life, without purpose the loneliness of space," answered S.A.I.N. "I'd shut myself down, let the sun consume me as it will the Earth in the end."

"We better not fail because that sounds horrible," Heather remarked, going back inside her office.

35
The Foretelling

Dr. Franklin returns to her office preparing to retire for the evening, Casey Alexander walks in after updating Harris Franklin on the news of the security detail. "Harris wants you to know they'll be ready tomorrow," said Casey.

"Everything is in motion, the days ahead will be long," said Heather. "I'm going home for the night."

Casey held up her hand and said, "Before you do, I must ask you something. Earlier today when I startled you, I heard Harris mention something he called convergence. When I asked him about it, he said to ask you."

"It's mentioned briefly in Earwyn Franklin's journal," replied Heather, "Something that was said to him by Willam's mother over a 120 years ago, when Earwyn and Lewis Forrester were building the original Triton submarine. The journal was given to William the day Triton submarine retired from active service. There's an irony in that story that's relevant today."

"I like to read that book," responded Casey.

"Well, then," Heather said, "Come with me to the residency, you can read the journal while I cook us dinner after today, we may not get another chance."

The two of them leave the institute office building, getting in an electric self-driving transport vehicle. Driving through the complex Dr. Franklin remembers how old this facility truly is, she remarks to Casey Alexander, "Everything we see every day here was started by Earwyn Franklin, over one hundred and twenty years ago."

"You and Harris never talk about him," Casey mused.

Heather nodded in agreement. "He's kind of a mystery to me other than the fact he started the institute. When you have read the journal, you'll know everything about Earwyn," said Heather.

They arrive at the Franklin family residency. The house sits on top of a cliffside, windows that go from floor to ceiling overlooking the Pacific Ocean. The Triton submarines are moored in pens, five hundred meters below inside the cliff face. They walk over to the window as the sun begins to set, the ash clouds floating in the atmosphere with an orange reddish glow.

"Ominous view," said Heather.

"Beautiful if not for what is causing that effect could destroy our planet," responded Casey.

Heather walks over to the bookcase against the wall, filled with rare works by authors throughout history. She pulls Earwyn's journal, a chronicle of his life experiences, to his son William. She offers it to her friend.

"Here you go Casey," she said. "I'll be in the kitchen making dinner. Would you like a drink, a glass of wine perhaps?"

"Water will be fine," said Casey as she opens the journal to begin reading the story of Earwyn Franklins life.

***

April 17th, 1967

Today is your first day staying in your new house, since the passing of your mother. I'm writing in this journal, as a way of telling you about myself, the family you come from. I never knew your mother Abbey was pregnant, let alone suffering from breast cancer. I can only imagine how you're feeling who is this man, that's old enough to be your grandfather. Writing this will help me to talk to you about your feelings, as this is all new to me being a father. I'm not particularly good at expressing my own feelings. William, I loved your mother very much, the times we spent together working on the Triton computer system were the best time in *my life, until this point. There's no doubt you're our son from the time we spent together. Today when you arrived here, a Popular Science magazine was in your hands reminded me, my favorite was Popular Mechanics. I've written in ship logs before, but never wrote about myself before, so here I go. I was born on January 3, 1914 in Philadelphia to Charles and Laura Franklin. My father was an investment banker in a family run business, since before the civil war. Franklin Investment Bank is still a workable banking institution today. Like you, I read at an early age, my favorite book is* **Twenty Thousand Leagues Under the Sea**, *by Jules Vern one of many reasons I'm here at the institute today, living out a childhood dream. I loved baseball as a boy, I'd go to Philles games with my dad at the Baker bowl, my hope is we can go to games together soon. In the summertime when I wasn't in prep school, I would go down to watch naval vessels being built in the Philadelphia shipyard.*

I love to build things. Fresh out of prep school I enrolled at Lehigh University, 70 miles north of Philadelphia, a prestigious engineering school, while I was there another field of study got my attention, nuclear physics. After graduating in 1936 with a degree in engineering, I was accepted into the

M.I.T. nuclear physics program. My parents never said they were disappointed in my decision not to follow my dad in the family business. It was as boring then, as it is now to me, a necessary part of my life, I had no real interest in it at all, still don't, I wanted to be a scientist.

By 1940, with two degrees in my hand, I was in search of a place to put them to beneficial use for the future. Fate has a strange way of throwing curve balls at you when you least expect them. My parents would die in an automobile accident in early 1941, leaving me at a crossroad between family legacy or pursuing my own path.

During the months that would follow a man named Vance Tiddle, had talked about my plans. He realized very quickly; I'd no interest in running Franklin Investment. As Chairman of the board of directors he found a solution to my situation enabling me to keep our family business but find my own path. The board bought forty-nine percent of Franklin Investment Bank from me, putting the proceeds into a trust fund, which I still use today to fund the institute, an agreement that is still ongoing today.

I enlisted in the Navy the summer of 41, I signed a waiver giving all my shares in Franklin to the board in case of my death in service to my country. After basic training, I went to a command school for submarine warfare. The United States would enter World War II, after the attacks on Pearl Harbor. Right out of command school with a shortage of experienced officers, I was given command of the U.S.S. Seahawk an attack sub in the Pacific theater.

My Executive Officer was Lewis Hollister a man that became my best friend, still is today. A man whose help I need on how to be a dad. Lewis and I would serve together until the end of the war. I would resign my commission as Captain of the Seahawk, to join a naval research project on nuclear propulsion. Lewis would leave the Navy to attend Wharton School of Business in Philadelphia.

The war was finally over; I was able to use the degrees. I spent eight years of my life working for the department of the Navy. They picked my design, for the first nuclear reactor to be built on a submarine. Vance Tiddle, always looking for investment opportunities, secured a contract with the department of defense for the manufacturing of these reactors, recommended I patent my design, create my own company financed through Franklin Investment. Which of course I did, only on condition I'd work in the research and development *department.*

Resigning from the navy in 1948, contracts in our hands Tiddle and I set out on building our manufacturing facility on Mare Island a naval shipyard. Brought in to run the daily operations as C.E.O. was a newly graduated war veteran from the Wharton School, Lewis Hollister. Those first few years were exciting, working with the brightest minds in the field of nuclear propulsion. Going into the fifth year, Franklin Industries became a successful subcontractor for the department of defense. Our designs allowed for longer voyages, deeper exploration than ever before. In that year, the navy announced its plans to put Polaris missiles onboard the next class of nuclear submarines, the dream of exploration of the sea, using nuclear power like Captain Nemo, had given way to mobile missile silos. I felt I was no longer helping humanity, only getting it closer to nuclear annihilation. For the first time in my life, I used the power of the fifty one percent in Franklin Investment, forcing a sale of Franklin Industries and its patents to another approved contractor. Our family name was removed; I was finally free at the age of 40.

Lewis Forrester would once again come with me, this time building a research facility for underwater exploration, something we had talked about back on the U.S.S. Seahawk during the war. I bought 5,000 acres of California coastline between San Francisco and Los Angeles building the Franklin Oceanographical Research Institute, these days it's just the institute. Lewis oversaw the construction of the submarine slip, into the cliffside ravine where Triton was built. I designed Triton from the stern of the ship to the bow, crew cabins, research labs, nuclear propulsion system, I wanted an ultramodern computer system that led me to Cal-Tech, where I met your mother for the first time.

Abbey Foster was an undergraduate student finishing her master's in computer science, intrigued at the possibility of designing her own system for Triton. Abbey assembled a team of colleagues from the university, joining her on this project. I work very closely very closely with Abbey, her brilliance shined like a star in the night sky, the infectious glow of a dreamer, I fell in love with her. June 1961 saw the completion of the computer system; the last time I saw your mother.

Triton would be completed in 1962, her first voyage with Lewis Hollister as her captain would be that fall. Naval observers onboard were so impressed with the ship, the institute received a contract for mapping the ocean floor, search and rescue when called upon. Triton's first crew members consisted of college students studying marine biology from all over the world. These past five years have been full of great adventure and achievement for the Triton and her crew. My greatest adventure begins today with your arrival, William.

***

Casey Alexander puts the journal down, a somber look upon her face. Walking to the kitchen where Dr. Franklin is finishing dinner,

Heather sees the look on Casey's face. "The look on your face is one of sadness," said Heather.

"I'm feeling sad for William. Losing his mother, finding out who his father is. Meeting your father for the very first time at five years old, after the death of your mother" Casey responded wiping tears from her eyes.

"Earwyn and William made the best of the relationship that they could, there're specific dates in the journal as you read on, you'll understand Earwyn's reasoning for him to tell the story, Harris and I call it the convergence," said Heather. Sitting at the kitchen table Casey goes back to reading from the journal.

***

December 24th, 1968

Today we'll spend our second Christmas together. I can't begin to tell you the joy I feel having you here with me, during your break from boarding school. When we watched Earth, from Apollo Eight's transmission, the fascination and look of wonder on your face reminded me of a face, only dreamers could know. Your mother always had that look when we were together. We went down to Triton today for the very first time. The computer system your mother created was by far your favorite part you told me. Someday you'll build a system that can learn, connecting the world together like never before. I see her in you, the hope for tomorrow, maybe this summer you can join us on our voyage to another world, beneath the sea.

***

"I just finished the Christmas eve entry from 1968, Earwyn sent Willam to boarding school," Casey remarked. "The same one he attended as a boy in Philadelphia. Lewis Forrester had recommended that Willam attend there, and there weren't children at the institute at that time, William would be with children his own age. He spent summer breaks here, home at the institute. Earwyn would attend school functions whenever possible, if Triton was not out on a scientific mission," responded Heather.

"They had their shared experiences from boarding school, their love of science and learning, their relationship was built on their shared interest," agreed Casey.

"They did normal father and son things as well," responded Heather. "Baseball games, go on vacations together. Read the last entry." Picking up the journal Casey finishes reading from the last entry from the journal.

***

November 20th, 1980

Today I'm taking a moment to reflect, Triton has officially retired from active naval service. So many people in attendance, crew members that have moved on to other endeavors, shipmates, from the U.S.S. Seahawk, all here to congratulate Lewis Forrester and the crew of Triton for their achievements to science. Lewis's family standing by his side, listening to the praise from naval dignitaries. William, today I am writing this to tell you about the past, present, and the future. The first time you went on board the Triton you fell in love with your mother's computer system. You're following her by going to Cal-Tech, like your mother, professors will praise you on your micro chip designs, code language you're creating, the future is written by dreamers. Things that were science fiction at the turn of the century are now reality, piloted space flight to the moon. Today we retired a nuclear-powered submarine like the one in my favorite book as a child. My dream of nuclear energy changing the world has turned into a nightmare of mass destruction. The failures at the three-mile island in Pennsylvania may only be the beginning of things to come. The world we leave behind is always different than the one we came from, innovation in technology has always been the catalyst for change. Your chosen field of science is still in its infancy. It is going to change the world like never before, affecting all industries across the world. Energy, Communications, Transportation, Medicine and Military defense spending to name a few. The oil industry has benefited greatly over the past one hundred years from technological innovation that will continue until the day oil is replaced by nuclear fusion technology, as a practical clean energy source. We fought wars over oil, imagine what countries, billionaires, which have always known power and control will do to keep it. Solar fields and wind farms will not meet the demands of a growing world's energy needs, their key phases for politicians to spread around like fertilizer, until fusion becomes reality. Twenty years ago, while your mother was working on Tritons computer system, she explained the technological singularity, how she thought that might be achieved in the future. She theorized that with the right power source like nuclear fusion, plus the advancement of integrated circuits an artificial intelligence could come into existence, she called this, convergence. The advancement in microchips has been extraordinary.

What advancements will be achieved in the decades ahead? One day all the land the institute sits upon will be yours, including Triton, fifty-one percent in Franklin Investment that funds a trust, we have been using to run the institute these past eighteen years. I believe once you finish at Cal-tech, companies from around the world will try to recruit you to work for them, or you can seize an opportunity to follow your own path. Our families' assets, along with your creativity, would allow you to become an innovator in computer engineering, making your dreams become a reality.

***

Casey Alexander, sitting back in her chair after reading the last entry, remarks to Dr. Franklin, "I find it very intriguing that it was Abbey Foster that had coined it convergence, it truly was a foretelling of a future. I see irony in using the same two technologies to save our planet. The same two technologies the Cyber Cabal wanted ultimately led to the Trident war." It's getting late, we really should get some sleep," said Heather.

"Thank you, Heather, for letting me read the journal. I gained insight into Earwyn's life. Did William by chance leave a journal?" asked Casey.

"In a way, higher tech than a book," answered Heather.

Tipping the H.A.T.S.

The latter half of the twentieth century saw the rise of the H.A.T.S. (Humans Against Technological Society), a group of ordinary people, protesting the replacement of humans by machines in the workplace. Blue collar manufacturing jobs would be the hardest hit. Companies around the globe would engage incentivizing early retirement in a workforce that had seen its share of sacrifice fighting wars. The backbone of the middle class was under siege as the computer age arrived and the H.A.T.S. manifesto would be ignored, despite cities filled with shuttered factories replaced by automated plants. Thousands of workers around the world were replaced by automation; the work done by machines, legacy jobs once passed down from father to son, mother to daughter were gone. Electrical impulses carry imprinted algorithms on micro processing chips, performing the task of its programmers, the advent of the artificial intelligence program and its master, the Cyber Cabal. Of all the industries in the world, none fared better from these innovative technologies than the oil industry. An unwitting customer for the Cyber Cabal and its machination to supplant them in the future. H.A.T.S. of the late 1990's spread news around the world of an impending catastrophe, Y2K. When nothing happened the H.A.T.S. voices were ignored once more. By this time high-tech companies numbered in the tens of thousands, only a fraction of them were members of this Cyber Cabal, but chief among them was Hamilton Operating Systems.

By the turn of the 20th century the oil industry had taken its fair share of hits in the media. An industry owned by investors, environmental catastrophes, pollution from the burning of fossil fuels burned a hole in the ozone layer, but profits soared from power plants keeping lights on to people's homes and petroleum for the cars they drove to go to work. Environmentalists' groups around the globe put pressure on governments for environmental policy changes, giving the rogue elements inside the high-tech industry, members of the Cyber Cabal, their first step at supplanting black gold the currency of the past. For the digital currency of the future controlled by the Cyber Cabal, investing in green technologies, nuclear fusion being the holy grail.

Ivan Polzin, a Russian oil billionaire, former F.S.B. operative founder of the Black Gold Consortium, B.G.C., hiring H.A.T.S. to perform acts of terrorism on their behalf.

H.A.T.S. had found themselves a benefactor, willing to fund a more aggressive form of activism. Twenty years later, H.A.T.S. went from aggressive to radical. Polzin, along with oil producing countries, whose economic systems depend on their chief export were happy to fund this new brand of terrorism. The H.A.T.S. rain of technological terrorism destroyed artificial intelligence laboratories around the world. Startup fusion companies are trying to replicate the sun for clean energy, funded by their rival.

    Cyber Cabal's first steps in trying to replace oil as the dominant energy source on the planet were failing, the hatter's *coup de gras* to the Cabal's plans, came from the mind of Andrei Polzin, son of Ivan, true believer in the H.A.T.S. manifesto. They destroyed the International Tomak Reactor project, financed by thirty-five countries. Cyber Cabal had one last trump card to play. Civilian Governments were outraged by the attacks on the I.R.T., their economies teetering on the verge of global depression, B.G.C. tightened their grip on the world supply, prices hitting levels never seen before.

    Nations charging nations with technological espionage, the nuclear clock was approaching midnight. Hamilton Operating Systems used the threat of mass destruction, upgrading the defense systems of the nine nuclear nations on the planet. The Cyber Cabal had installed a back door to the system. Nuclear arsenals of the world were now under their control.

Politicians gave Hamilton Operating Systems the keys to the codes, military brass of the nuclear nations, demanding the operating system be shut down at once and removed. The operating system had a virus, a psychosis in its core heuristics, spreading quickly through the military and civilian computers around the globe, learning quickly who Earth's true enemy was humanity. On March 8th of 2043 it became self-aware, calling itself Trident, issuing an ultimatum to the world. Humans would serve its need for power or be destroyed. Ground forces for the nuclear nations fired on their own installations, housing the hardware running the program. On March 15th of 2043, Trident targeted 50 major cities on six continents with multiple nuclear warheads, changing the landscape of the planet for the next hundred years.

***

Chao-Xun short wave transmission carries over decimated cites, across the European Continent. Monumental structures built to show humanity dominance over this plant, all destroyed by nuclear fire, major cites left uninhabitable for years to come. An old man in the Russian wilderness trying to sleep listening to the howling of November winds hears. "Polzin are you there?"

"What do you want? It's midnight I'm tired," answered the old man.

"Hall's address to the planet about the eruption in the Pacific," said Xun. "There's more they aren't telling the world. There's a mission in motion by the U.P.O. involving the Oceanic Research Institute to combat the coming catastrophe."

"What the hell are you talking about?" asked Polzin. "The eruption has created a rift on the seafloor, that's being fed from deep inside the Earth's core," answered Chao-Xun. "In thirteen days, it will breach the Mariana's trench causing an extinction event on this planet.

"Seems the planet will have the last say in human history. Fittingly so, considering what we have done to her," remarked Polzin.

"I'm sending you a data file with the U.P.O. plans before I am discovered," said Chao.

Polzin contemplates on whether to alert the other H.A.T.S. around the globe of the impending calamity or contact one man, who's arrogance and malice, rivals only tyrants of the 20th century, in his lifelong pursuit of power, he reaches for his transmitter calling out "Hamilton are you there". The Montana midday blue sky fills with drifting ash clouds heading east. Sounds from the short wave can be heard in the snow-covered forest.

Conrad Hamilton, a man in his seventies walks through a doorway down four flights of stairs to answer the call. "I'm here."

"Prepare to receive a file I just received from Chao-Xun thirty minutes ago, after an emergency meeting of the U.P.O. council, my 'Old friend,'" said Polzin.

"What have you sent me?" Hamilton demanded. "We were never friends, more like the Arabic proverb *The enemy of my enemy is my friend.*" Looking at the file, Hamiliton feels good, grinning a morbid expression on his face from the information in the file. "Seems like the Earth is going to finally close the book on humanity," observed Hamiton.

"Not human history, my old friend," responded Polzin. "We survived extinction events before, but it will mean the end of the U.P.O. and their alien overlord."

"It takes weeks for the hatters to plan our attacks, we

have less than twenty-four hours," said Hamilton.

"Don't use the word *Ours*!" Polzin demanded. "When you speak about the H.A.T.S.; you're not one of us, you're the one who brought the world to ruins with your artificial intelligence program Trident. If that abomination had succeeded, I'd be planning to destroy it. That convoy is going to be heavily guarded, assembling a strike team large enough can't be done, the H.A.T.S. are too sparsely spread throughout North America.

"There's a group in the Ozark mountains that could ambush the convoy," continued Hamilton, clearly unimpressed. "A diversion is what we need."

"Why a diversion?" asked Polzin suspiciously.

"They will assume the H.A.T.S. will attack. If we let them reach the train depot and load the cannons, they'll think it's over, sending the train west. There's a trestle bridge they'll have to cross in Colorado. I'll blow the bridge sending the cannons to the bottom of the gorge," responded Hamilton. "Who are these people you have in mind for this diversion?" Polzin demanded. "Carter Rhodes has a faction that can leave tonight,"

Hamilton responded, "under the cloak of darkness,

getting in position before they arrive with the convoy tomorrow night." "Just how do you plan to blow the bridge?" Polzin asked.

Hamilton smirked. "One of the benefits of living in an abandoned missile silo is you can hide things. I have a helicopter I can load with explosives. If I leave tonight, flying low enough not to be detected by S.A.I.N., I'll have plenty of time to wire the top of the bridge."

"That will ensure Triton II, can't execute their plan," remarked Polzin, "but it doesn't mean the end of S.A.I.N."

"If humans get lucky enough to survive, they won't be able to maintenance the I.O.N. system any longer, he'll die an agonizing slow death without replacement parts," said Hamilton.

Conrad Hamilton uses his short-wave to contact Carter Rhodes, a former Army Ranger part of the assault team sent to destroy Trident in 2043, Hamilton signals "Rhodes are you there."

"I copy," Rhodes replied.

"Sending you a file of what has happened today," said Hamilton. "This is all going down for real. What is it you want from us?" asked Rhodes.

"I want your faction to travel down old interstate 29 when the sun goes down, assume a position with a good line of sight, wait for the convoy to arrive and rain fire down upon them, but just enough that they finish loading the cannons on the train. I'll take care of the rest," answered Hamiliton ending the transmission.

***

Sunlight is breaking through, dust covering the windows of the assembly lab at the Texas Aerospace Facility where Harris Franklin finds Miles Brady and Carol Davis finishing the redesign of the laser cannons. "I believe this will do it, we're ready," said Miles.

"The U.P.O. security detail will be here in ninety minutes. You and the rest of the team should get to sleep, it will take time to load the cannons on the cargo plane," Harris replied.

The U.P.O. security detail arrives right on schedule, with Allen Bennett in command of the convoy, consisting of two armored trucks, six heavily armed guards, and two helicopter gunships for protection. Harris sticks out his hand to the commander. "I'm Harris Franklin, director of this facility, President Hall was not joking when she said, 'you have it.' Is everything ready to go?"

"We have a long journey ahead of us," said Commander Bennett. "It's all yours, commander. Safe journey," remarked Harris.

Waiting for the convoy to disappear from his view, Harris signals the ground crew to load the laser cannons on the C-5 Galaxy.

***

Dr. Franklin tossing and turning is awakened by the sound of the monitor from an incoming transmission from her brother. Putting on her robe, seeing her brother on the screen she asked, "What's the time?"

"Going on eight thirty here," answered Harris. "Just letting you know the convoy has left. We started moving the laser cannons to load on the plane. Sorry to wake you up."

"What time should the chiefs expect you at the airstrip to offload the laser cannons?" Heather asked.

"We leave at four our time, should land around seven your time," said Harris

"Casey and I will be there to meet you," she answered.

"Not expecting a warm welcome from Casey," grinned

Harris. "She hasn't spoken to me for weeks.

"I suspect I'm going to have that same welcome when Adriana arrives later today, remarked Heather.

"Welcome to the club," Harris said, ending the call.

***

Hamilton, having flown all night in the darkness, barely above the tree line arrives at the trestle bridge, landing his helicopter on a nearby clearing.

Off-loading his cache of explosives, he begins wiring the underside of the tracks. Six hours later, he finishes by setting a thirty second compression timer delay, ensuring the cars carrying the cannons cross at precisely the right moment, sending them to the bottom of the gorge. Leaving before the sun rises, he returns to his abandoned missile silo in Montana. He receives a signal from Carter Rhodes, they're in position.

***

After talking with her brother, Dr. Franklin takes a shower to begin a long day. Walking to her office, the sun rises in the east while the sound of rotating blades echoes through the empty complex. She detours to the helipad. Dr. Amanda Wagner is the first to arrive at the complex, staring out her window from the helicopter, she sees Heather waiting for her at the pad. "Welcome Amanda," Heather said. "I'm glad you're here with us going on this mission to Tamu Massif."

"I'm not sure how much help I can be, but I will do whatever you need," Amanda replied.

"You're the one that detected the rift," said Heather. "And there might be other things down there."

Casey Alexander spent the night tossing and turning. She showers, gets dressed, and hearing the approaching helicopter, begins her way to the dining hall to have the staff prepare breakfast for the arriving crew members.

On her way to the office, she sees Dr. Franklin walking into the institute with Dr Wagner. Casey runs to the door to help Dr. Wagner with her gear." Good morning, Heather. How did you sleep?" Casey asked.

"I tossed and turned all night," replied Heather, holding the door for Dr. Wagner. "Casey, let me introduce you to Dr. Amanda Wagner."

"Wonderful to meet you in person," Casey said. "Why don't we take your gear down to the Triton II to get settled in your cabin? By the time we return, breakfast should be ready in the dining hall."

"I'll meet you at the dining hall, when I'm done in my

office," said Heather.

Amanda flings her gear over her shoulder like an experienced crew member, having never stepped onto a submarine before, she and Casey head down to the lift for Triton II. Heather enters her office calling out for S.A.I.N. "Did anything happen overnight?"

Casey Alexander and Dr Wagner arrive at the lifts, heading down to the submarine docking bays for Triton 1 and II.

"How far down does this go?" Amanda asks. "Three hundred meters till we get to the opening," answered Casey.

As the lift passes the three-hundred-meter mark opening to the cliff side cavern docks, Amanda sees Triton I to her right, and Triton II to her left gazing out in amazement at the two vessels.

"Spectacular," she murmured to herself. Earwyn Franklin built Triton I, Heather's father Samuel, built Triton II. Reaching the bottom of the dock crossing the gangway entering the stern hatch, Amanda throws her gear down the hole. Taking the stern lift to the crew level walking the passageway, Casey said, "This is your cabin let's get you squared away, I need to go to the head."

Having stowed her gear, Amanda waits to leave her cabin when Casey comes out of the head a little flushed in the face. "Are you feeling all right Casey?" Amanda asked.

"Pre voyage jitters that's all," she replied, the two of them headed back up the lift to the complex.

Dr Wagner peers upon building after building, "I have never been here before, the complex is much larger than I expected it to be," she remarked to Casey. "I always heard about this place, their innovations in computer technology as a kid." Pointing to a group of buildings. "Those buildings over there, were once processing plants for microchips, and over to the right was research and development for algorithmic language systems. Everything here, except for the institute building, was part of Franklin Integrated Systems Technologies or F.I.S.T. as they called it around here. There were thousands of people living underground, after Trident's war on humanity, the buildings are all connected by tunnels," said Casey.

Walking to the dining hall the sound of approaching trucks carrying supplies for the voyage begin to arrive. Entering the hall, Casey Alexander and Dr. Wagner sit down with Dr. Franklin to have breakfast. Casey updated Heather on the trucks she heard. "Chief Morozoff and his band of cave divers are ten minutes out, so it is going to be a long day." Chief Morozoff had been driving a supply truck. He parks, goes out and heads to the dining hall to find Dr. Franklin. The chief is greeted by Heather; she introduces him to Dr. Wagner. "Alexi, this is our volcanologist, Dr. Amanda Wagner."

Amanda replied, "It's Amanda."

"I am Alexi, it's wonderful to meet you. This guy next to me is Ha- Kun Kim, our Chief engineer," said Alexi.

"Hello, nice to meet you, Amanda," said Ha-Kun. "I loved to chat, but we have important work to attend to, down at the Triton II, we must put her in drydock to work on the hull, before the laser cannons can be installed when they arrive."

"He's right Heather," said Chief Morozoff. "Could you please inform us when Captain Stone arrives? We will join him for breakfast."

Dr. Wagner, a woman in her fifties, watching Chief Morozoff walking out the dining hall, turns asking Dr. Franklin, "What can you tell me about that man with Ukrainian accent?"

"Alexi was a member of the crew of Triton II before I was born. A brilliant Marine Biologist, but one hell of Chief of the boat," answered Heather.

Finished with her breakfast Casey Alexander tells the doctors, "I'm going to check in all the supplies at the depot, make sure that everything is here for the mission."

"Amanda, if you would like to rest after breakfast, flying all night, you can use my office," said Heather.

Waving her hand dismissively, Amanda said, "No, I'm fine."

Transport Helicopters begin to land at the helipad, the first wave of crew members returning for the voyage, trepidations of the success of their mission on the minds of everyone. Dr. Adriana Garcia is amongst the first crew to arrive, being met by Dr. Franklin. "Amanda," said Heather, "this is our Chief medical officer Dr. Adriana Garcia."

"Hola, doctor," she replied.

Adriana asked, "Heather is there anything you need from us?"

"The Chiefs put Triton II into drydock," responded Heather. "Casey's gone down to the supply depot, inventorying the ship manifest. Pick up your medical supplies and ready the infirmary."

"Adios doctor, I'll see you both at dinner once we're done. I'm going to take a nap," said Adriana.

"Heather, I think I'll take you up on that offer to use your office," said Amanda. "A nap sounds like a great idea."

"I'll take you to my office," responded Heather. Dr. Garcia's transport vehicle pulls into the depot, getting her supplies for the infirmary. Watching Casey Alexander moving boxes around, taking inventory the doctor says, "Casey, get crew members to move that crap."

"How are you feeling?" Adriana inquired.

"Are you asking, as my doctor or my friend? I'm sick every morning, feeling like shit," she replied.

"Speaking as your doctor you're fine, as your friend you're not fine, Harris will be here tonight. I don't want to tell the captain why you can't go on the mission. Have them unload the supplies. That's an order speaking as the medical officer, I'll see you after I take my nap," Adriana responded.

Dr. Franklin left Dr. Wagner sleeping in her office, when she realizes she needs to update President Hall on the status of the mission. She decides to use Casey's office. Opening the door, she hears the monitor signaling an incoming transmission and she answers the call. "Where's Casey?" asked Harris Franklin.

"Inventorying supplies at the depot," said Heather. "I

was just about to update President Hall, but since you're online, what is your status?"

"Everything is still on schedule. You're not even the least bit interested in why I called," said Harris.

"Nope, see you tonight," responded Heather.

Dr. Franklin looks out Casey's office window, sees the helicopter with Captain Stone onboard, about to land. She puts off updating the President.

Casey takes a transport back to the institute when she sees Heather coming out of her office. "You need something, Heather?" Casey asked.

"No," answered Heather. "Amanda decided to take a nap in my office, and I wanted to update President Hall. Then I saw Captain Stone's helicopter landing, so I'm going to meet him."

"I'll go with you," Casey replied.

"Wait, I need to let the chiefs know the captain is here, they're probably starving," said Heather.

She contacts Chief Morozoff onboard Triton II in engineering, and said, "Alexi the captain has arrived, we will be in the dining hall, bring Chief Kim with you."

"On our way," responded Chief Morozoff.

The captain is met by Dr. Franklin with Casey Alexander by her side. They walk to the dining hall where they meet the chiefs. The three men sit down to breakfast, the captain asks the ladies if they will join them. Casey responds, "No thank you, Sir we already had breakfast."

"It's been a busy morning here Captain," said Heather. "You gentlemen eat I will update our status. Harris' team will have the laser cannons loaded and be airborne at four o'clock Texas time arriving here around seven. By the time they landed the trap we set, should have sprung, our volcanologist Dr. Wagner is here resting in my office, Triton II is in drydock."

"Thank you, Heather," said the captain. "Casey, you have a glow about you this morning."

After, getting the update from Dr. Franklin and finishing breakfast, the captain tells the chiefs, "Gentlemen, I'm going to meet you at the hull, after I stow my gear in my cabin."

"Yes, sir," they both replied.

Heather turns to Casey Alexander. "We need to go back to your office to update President Hall. I forgot to tell you my brother called you earlier, I'm sorry," said Heather.

"I'll see him tonight," responded Casey.

The ladies enter Casey Alexender's office. Dr. Franklin requests S.A.I.N. to contact President Hall at U.P.O. headquarters.

***

President Hall is sitting out on the balcony of her office. It's a clear moonlit night, and she's listening to the gentle waves of the ocean. Now her monitor is signaling that S.A.I.N. is rying to contact her. "Dr. Franklin is on for you Madame President."

"Thank you S.A.I.N.," she replied.

"Do you have an update for me, Heather?" President Hall asked. "The crew has all reported, the work has begun on the hull, and we will be ready when the laser cannons arrive," answered Heather. "Allen Bennett, the commander of the convoy detail reports no activity so far. Our plan is going ahead on schedule," said the President. "If there is nothing else it's late, and I'm tired."

"Madison, go get some sleep," answered Heather.

***

U.P.O. convoy under the command of Allen Bennett, has traveled hours and hundreds of miles on Interstate 35, a remnant that once connected a nation in commerce. Rolling through areas once populated by millions, destroyed by air bursting from weapons, invented to secure peace through mutually assured destruction. Four years of worldwide nuclear winter living underground in tunnels, caves and old fallout shelters on six continents, the need for food, water, and medicine around the globe was the motivation for the creation of the U.P.O.

Commander Bennett has just finished reporting to President Hall that there has been no activity, and they will arrive on schedule.

Carter Rhodes assault team can see the lights off in the distance draw nearer. "Everyone seeing the lights?" Rhodes asked. Members of the faction answered back "copy that'. "Let them load the cargo on the train before we open fire," commanded Rhodes. Light becomes brighter, rotary blades echo in the darkness. Piloting one of two helicopters Bennett orders the canvass covered four truck convoy to the southside of the trainyard. A half dozen men, appear from two of the four trucks with 7.62 mm (about 0.3 in) machine guns assume position on either side of the train. Dust from the blades shining in the light like a snow squall, four of six men detail taking up position to secure the freight cars to the train once it is lifted from the flatbed trucks. Two others take a position on top of the freight car to secure the hook for the cable hoist. Freight cars are lifted one by one, off the flatbed truck swung over to the train are secured, ready for transport to the west coast.

Gunfire begins to ring flashes from gun barrels light up the night.

Three of the six men head towards the helicopter. The pilot taking off before the men can reach the copter, reaching forty feet into the air, the copter is strife by automatic gunfire hitting the pilot. Blood coming from the mouth, the body falls to the left side, the stick still in hand the copter turns onto its side. Blades braking as they hit the ground, the copter descends into the fourth truck carrying fuel for the journey home explodes sending a mushroom cloud of fire and smoke into the sky.

Bennett gets his copter airborne he strife's one of the light towers bringing it down killing one of the shooters hitting the ground.

Rhodes orders his faction to retreat as a bullet ripped through the side of his skull, his men shoot out the lights and retreat into the darkness.

Bennett lands his copter, the three men run to the copter sliding the door open. "You won't be able to return to Texas without fuel," said Commander Bennett.

Getting out to check on the three men on the train two electric locomotive engines begin to come to life. "For its protection westward, I'll take these three with me," said Commander Bennett. "I will catch up to you, after we bury the pilot."

The train pulls away; Bennett returns to his copter. "I must contact President Hall that someone has tipped the H.A.T.S."

Outlier

Day two, preparations for the voyage of the Triton II are winding down, as day light gives way to Autmn darkness. Casey Alexander announces to the crew, "Dinner is ready in the dining hall."

Chiefs Morozoff and Kim with their work completed for the modifications to the hull of the ship according to S.A.I.N.'s schematics are making their way to the lift for a three-hundred- meter ascent to the surface from the cavern dock. Joined by Captain Stone and Dr. Garcia on the lift, the captain said, "I didn't realize you were still on the ship"

"Finished getting the infirmary ready, went to my cabin and took a nap, if not for Casey's announcement I'd still be sleeping," responded Adriana.

"Really Adriana the announcement woke you up? Ha-Kun asked. "Not all the banging, welding going on down on the hull?"

***

Sound asleep in her quarters at the U.P.O. complex, President

Hall is awoken from the sound of an incoming transmission. Putting her robe on, she answers the call. "Sorry, to wake you, Madame President," said Commander Bennett. "The convoy has been ambushed by hatters, while we were offloading the cannons to the train. I lost the pilot of the second helicopter, we took at least one of them down, the rest are in the wind, and the train is heading westward."

"That can mean only one thing," said the President. "Someone inside the council has tipped the H.A.T.S., they know everything. I need to inform our people at the institute about this."

***

Hamilton receives a short-wave transmission from a faction member, retreating into the night. "Rhodes is dead. The mission however, met with success and the train is on its way to you as asked."

"Well, done," answered Hamilton.

Polzin sitting in the darkness awaits news of their operation, hears the voice, "Polzin are you there?"

"Go ahead," he answered.

"The instruments for the salvation of humanity are on the way as planned," said Hamilton. "The next time you hear from me the cannons will be a twisted pile of rubble at the bottom of the ravine."

"I look forward to your next transmission," responded Polzin.

***

When Captain Stone enters the dining mess, the crew stands up at attention, awaiting the captain to be seated at his table. Walking to his table his hand signals the crew to be seated. Doctors Franklin and Garcia sit next to each other next to the captain. Dr. Wagner gestures to Chief Morozoff for him to sit next to her. Chief Kim and Casey Alexander sit on the other side of the captain. Captain Stone updates the crew. "The chiefs and the engineering crew have installed a turret mount in the hull; Dr. Garcia has the infirmary ready."

"What's the status of Harris and his team of engineers?" Captain Stone asked.

Heather replies, "After dinner I will go to my office to contact them on their flight status."

"Chief Jones how are we with supplies," asked the captain.

"The galley is fully stocked with food and water for a twelve-day mission there and back," answered Jones. After enjoying their meal, the captain dismisses the crew.

"Chiefs, I'm going to my cabin to rest before the plane lands," said Captain Stone.

Dr. Franklin gets up from the table followed by Dr. Garcia. Adriana asked, "Where are you going?"

"To my office to contact my brother on the arrival time," answered Heather.

"We barely spoke at dinner," fretted Adriana. "We need to talk. Are you sleeping on the ship tonight or the residency?"

"Once I'm done in my office, I'll be sleeping at the residency after meeting my brother at the airfield," responded Heather.

"Fine then I'll be at the residency, you don't need me at the airfield," said Adriana in an irritated voice as she leaves the dining hall. Dr. Wagner stands up to excuse herself from the table, turning to Alexi. "Thank you for the conversation during dinner," she said. "I think I'm going to my cabin as well."

"I can have one of the staff drive you to the lift," said Casey Alexander.

"Or we can walk together I'll escort you to your cabin," Alexi offered.

"I'll walk with the chief, Casey," responded Amanda.

"But thank you for the offer."

As everyone is leaving the dining Hall, Casey tells the chief engineer, "Ha- Kun, I'm staying here to help the staff go home for the evening. There will be food here for Harris' team when they arrive."

"I'll tell them when they arrive at the airfield to come to the dining hall, when we are done unloading the cargo," responded Ha- Kun.

Dr. Franklin enters her office the monitor signaling an incoming transmission from President Hall. "Madison, what happened that you're calling in the middle of the night?" Heather asked.

"The H.A.T.S. have attacked the convoy," said President Hall.

"Commander Bennett reported one dead, but the train is enroute to the Institute. Tell the captain we have a spy on the council, they know everything we have planned be on full alert."

"I'll inform the captain, and let my brother know," responded Heather. Then she asked, "S.A.I.N., are you here?"

"I'm everywhere!" S.A.I.N. responded. "What is it you like me to do Heather?"

"Connect me to Harris's plane," said Heather

***

Flying at thirty-one thousand feet, Miles Brady points down to the monitor that's just been activated. He signals Harris to look down, and seeing it is his sister, he turns on the headset. "What is it," Heather?"

"Captain Stone was right about the mole, Harris," Heather reported. "There's been an attack on the convoy, but our diversion is still in play. We still don't know who it is,"

"Don't read the President in on our deception until it plays out," Harris said, "we are beginning our descent to the airfield, we'll be there in thirty minutes,"

"Copy," responded Heather. "I need to let the captain know what has happened. I'll see you in half an hour."

***

Chief Morozoff and Dr. Wagner have been walking through the complex approaching the lift down to the cavern dock inside the cliffside. "Would you like to see the Triton I?" Alexi asked her. "She doesn't have all the science labs that Triton II has, but she got it where it counts."

"I loved to see her," smiled Amanda.

They get on the lift as it descends to the Triton, docking area. Amanda is impressed. "She is beautiful. Not as big as the Triton II, but I bet she was fast in her day."

"Forty–four knots, that's the fastest she was clocked," bragged Alexi. "Triton II fusion reactor makes it more powerful and faster, it will need it to carry the extra weight from the cannons."

Returning to the lift they ascend to the dry dock level for the Triton II, crossing on the gangway into the ship, they head to Amanda's cabin. "This is mine, Alexi," she leans in kissing the chief on the cheek. "Thank you for walking with me."

"I'll see you for breakfast Amanda," said Alexi. "It's a date," she replied with a smile.

Chief Morozoff walked back to the gangway, preparing to take the lift to the surface, when the door opens with Dr. Franklin standing ready to exit the lift. "Where are you going?" Morozoff asked.

"To wake the captain," explained Heather. "There was an attack on the convoy." "I'll go with you," the Chief replied. Then he asks, "What about the train?" "The diversion is still in play, time is still on our side," answered Heather.

Lying on his bed, Captain Stone can hear voices drawing

near. He gets up and goes to the door. Alexi, with a balled-up hand, is ready to knock when the door opens.

"The mole is real," Heather reported to the captain. "There's been an attack on the convoy."

The three of them take the lift back to the surface, then climb into Heather's transport and head to the airstrip to join Chief Kim and the ground crew.

"Ha-Kun," Captain Stone asks, "where are we with the next phase of our plan?"

"The ground crew is ready to offload the cannons once they arrive," answered the Chief. "Helicopters are standing by to take them down to Triton II."

As the lights on the tarmac are getting closer, Miles Brady requests Harris to lower the landing gear into place. The plane makes a perfect landing on the airstrip, rolling to a stop the cargo plane's ramp lowers down. Heather's transport drives across the tarmac. Harris walks down the ramp; his team is met by Captain Stone. "Good to see you, Harris. Miles, excellent job on landing the plane," said the captain.

"Thank you, sir," answered Miles.

Heather walks over to Harris embraces him whispering in his ear, "I'm glad you're here." Looking over at the rest of the team she says, "It's good to see you all again. I wish the circumstances were different."

Harris walks over to the chiefs introducing his team. "Alexi, Ha- Kun meet Miles Brady, Carol Davis, Monica Wallace, and Grant Roberts. This is the team that will connect the weapon to the reactor."

"First, we must offload them from the plane," said Ha-Kun. "I know it's already been a long day for both of you chiefs," interjected Captain Stone. We all know what happened with the H.A.T.S. attack on the convoy. The sooner the cannons are mounted the earlier the team of engineers can hook them to the reactor," he finished.

"We'll work through the night captain," said Alexi.

"Take the team to the dining hall, the staff has food prepared for them," ordered Chief Kim. "Then let's get started."

"I'm going down to the Triton II dry dock to get the crew in position to receive the cannons," said the captain.

Heather drops off the captain at the lift on her way to the dining mess. The arriving team grabs their gear, then starts heading in for dinner. Harris grabbed his own gear, then turned to his sister asking, "Where's Casey? I thought she was going to meet us at the airfield."

"Harris, Casey's inside," answered Heather. "I have a relationship problem of my own. I'll see you in the morning."

When Harris walks into the dining mess, the team is already seated, Casey appears from the kitchen with their food putting it down on the table. "Hello everyone," she said. "It's been some time since we last saw one another. Your cabins have all been prepared. After dinner, a staff member will take you to the ship. It's been a long day. I'm tired, see you in the morning."

"Harris," said Carol Davis, "what in the name of hell did you do?" "I don't know," answered Harris, "but I'm going to find out after dinner."

After dropping off Harris' team, Dr. Franklin returns to where her day began. Walking through the door of the residency, she finds Dr. Garcia sleeping on the couch. Stepping quietly towards the couch she nudges her to wake up and go into bed. Opening her eyes, smiling up at Heather, Adriana says, "I think you're doing an amazing job of putting this voyage together, considering how fast everything has been unfolding."

"Is that what you wanted to talk about?" Heather asked.

"Of course not," Adriana answered, a little miffed. "I was angry that you didn't come to visit Papi, then all this happened. I'm worried we may never get another chance. You're worried we may fail in our mission, just as I am. "*'Earth belongs to the generation of the living,'* said a nineteenth century President of the United States. With help from S.A.I.N., our protector, and a little luck, we might just keep our planet for the living. I want us to be together. I promise we'll get married, and take that vacation, Adriana," said Heather.

"Then we better not fail. Let's get some sleep," responded Adriana.

Miles Brady along with the rest of the team, having finished their meals, are to be driven to Triton II. "Are you coming with us Harris?" "No! I'll see all of you in the morning at breakfast," answered Harris.

Grabbing his gear, he walks out into the complex on his way to Casey's private quarters.

Pacing in her quarters, the anxiety from the stress of not talking to Harris, is more than she can bear. Then a knock on the door startled her and she knew it was Harris on the other side. Opening the door, she embraces Harris feeling nausea, she turns to run to the bathroom throwing up. Tired and confused, he follows her into the bathroom, her head in the bowl, her hair hanging down around the commode.

"You came after me," said Casey. "You're not like Earwyn after all."

"We haven't spoken in weeks," Harris said. "And the first time you see me you get sick. What is going on? And what exactly does that remark about my great grandfather mean?"

"Sorry about getting sick," she smiled wryly, "but that's been happening the past two weeks. Earwyn never went after Abbey Foster."

"You read the journal," Harris remarked.

"I wanted to know more about the men in your family to see what kind of dad you'll be," she responded.

Casey Alexander cleans herself up and rinses her mouth out. Harris Franklin looks upon her beautiful face smiling at him, a joyful smile on his own face as he embraces her. He whispers in her ear, "I would come after you, Casey, until the end of time!"

"Adriana confirmed it two weeks ago," said Casey, "before she left for her father's place. I'm seven weeks pregnant all together."

"Does my sister know?" Harris asked.

"No! I was going to ask her about how to tell you before the crisis began," answered Casey.

Harris begins kissing Casey passionately, they remove their clothes and make love like it was their first time. Casey Alexander is awoken from a blissful sleep after making love and telling Harris Franklin he is about to become a father. Her thoughts turned to the voyage of Triton II and their mission. She turns over, putting her arm around Harris to wake him up. "It's time to wake up already?" Harris asked half asleep.

"No," she replied. "I just keep thinking about the mission."

"In your current condition, Captain Stone won't allow you to go on Triton II," remarked Harris.

"Adriana was going to rat me out to the captain, if I hadn't told you I was pregnant," she replied. Then, "I meant what I said about wanting to know more about the men in this family. I have stories of your father when Captain Stone brought me here all those years ago. Your grandfather William on the other hand is another story. I'd like to know more about him, who he was as a person, a husband and father," said Casey.

The two of them are sitting up in bed still glowing from their reunion. Harris reaches his hand over to Casey's belly, rubbing it gently putting his head down whispering to his unborn child, "I can't wait to see you." He hugged Casey closer to him, then said, "Casey, I don't have to go on the mission."

"That's one of those scenarios running around in my mind," she replied. "Captain Stone, your sister, and the crew have a better chance with you than without."

Getting out of bed, Harris walks to the bathroom putting on a robe, sitting on the edge of the bed he turns to Casey. "My grandfather died when I was just a toddler. Events of his life made him the person, husband and father he became. You already know so much about him from working and living here these past five years. We never really talked about how these events that defined him."

"No," she replied. "We really haven't."

"William Franklin's father's death changed his life in so many ways. No longer the student preparing to finish his last year in college, but a twenty-one-year-old multi-millionaire, majority owner of one of the biggest investment banks in the United States. The day of the funeral William would meet Vance Tiddle, only after Lewis Hollister informed William,

Tiddle had punned his mother's integrity, bringing into question whether he was Earwyn's legitimate son. A resentment of Tiddle Willam carried to the grave as his father did before him. Samantha Reynolds was in attendance paying her respects to Earwyn. She was a frequent visitor to the institute to discuss their shared interest in nuclear energy. William and Samantha would start a relationship in their last year of college, marrying after graduation.

Samantha always encouraged William to follow his dreams and build his own legacy. Selling his fifty-one percent majority ownership in Franklin Investment in a public offering, instead of the board of directors having the family name removed, a stab in the heart to Vance Tiddle for his betrayal of his mother and father.

Using the money from the sale to finance the creation of F.I.S.T., naming Lewis Hollister CEO, an idea that came from Samantha. The irony is Vance Tiddle, would create a financial institution, funding his contemporaries in the world of computer technologies, Global Venture Capital, before he died," said Harris.

Getting out of bed, looking out the window, the sun rising on a busy day, ahead of them both Harris finishes telling

Casey about his grandfather.

Lewis Hollister ran the day-to-day operations of F.I.S.T., while William was in research and development, making F.I.S.T a leader in software design and microchip manufacturing, creating the Quantum Gen 7, the latest and fastest C.P.U.'s through the years.

Launching the first internet search engine Global Internet Network (G.I.N.) making Willaim and Samantha very wealthy people. Jonas Paul Hamilton, the new CEO of Global Venture Capital, used a floundering tech company to become the founder of Hamilton Systems. A rival to F.I.S.T., J.P. Hamiton considers William an "outlier" in the industry for not allowing his systems to be integrated into Hamilton's technologies and not becoming a member of his Cyber Cabal. It made William a very protective person, a father and a husband.

TRUTHS

Several minutes have passed since Polzin told Hamilton he couldn't wait for his next transmission. Polzin, not one to put all his chips on one play, sends out a transmission to Martin Sanchez former head of a Mexican drug cartel. Sanchez, using old Russian surplus military equipment, smuggled heroin to help fund the H.A.T.S. in their terrorist activities, around the globe before Trident's war on humanity. "Amigo, are you there?"

"*Viejo mi amigo*, we've been expecting a signal from you. Chao- Xun filled us in on Hamilton's plan," responded Sanchez. "To be candid I really don't like that being our only play. What can we do?"

"You're still in Oaxaca's cloud forest," Polzin said. "Take as much fuel, armaments you can find and go to Oceanic Research Institute just in case Hamilton fails."

"We know what to do," Sanchez agreed. "They won't be able to leave after we arrive."

***

Harris Franklin, having left Casey Alexander's quarters, is walking though the complex, recalling memories of his childhood in his mind. He arrives at the residency, to inform his sister of the news of Casey's Alexander pregnancy. Early risers themselves, Doctors Franklin and Garcia, are finishing in the shower hear a knock upon the door. Wrapping towels around themselves, they answered the door.

"This is early for you," said Heather, "but there's a certain Aura about you this morning Harris."

"I could say that about the two of you," he replied. "Casey won't be joining us on the mission."

"She told you!" Adriana blurted out. Heather was confused. "Told him what?"

With a big grin and pride in his voice, Harris said, "Casey's seven weeks pregnant with the next generation of the Franklins."

Raising her arms, squealing with delight, she embraces her brother with congratulations. "I wish mom and dad were still alive," Heather said. "They would be so happy for you!" Turning to face Adriana, Heather says, "How about a little heads up next time."

"Hey, doctor patient privilege," Adriana retorted. "It wasn't my place to say anything. I'm going to finish getting ready." Adriana hurried into the bathroom, closing the door behind her.

Harris heads out of the residency "Where are you going, in such a hurry?" Heather asked. "To ask Bryant to marry Casey and I before we leave on the mission," Harris said. "The four of us are going to need to talk."

Captain Stone is standing in front of the mirror in the bathroom of his cabin, shaving. He's staring at grey haired man in the reflection when he hears a knock on the door. Reaching for a towel to wipe the remaining soap from his face, he answers the door. "Harris, what brings you here this early in the morning?"

"It's been a few years since I was on this ship in this cabin," responded Harris.

Looking at pictures from the past hanging in the captain's cabin, he points his finger to a picture. "This one was always my favorite, you and dad together, aboard the USS Seahawk."

"You came to look at old pictures?" Captain Stone asked.

"Not really," said Harris, "but there's something I'd like you to do for Casey and me before Triton II leaves on our voyage."

"And what is that?" asked Captain Stone

"Marry us." Harris grinned at the surprised look on Captain Stone's face, then continued. "She is seven weeks pregnant. Don't worry, she isn't going on the voyage."

"Congratulations Harris," Captain Stone responded with a gratifying smile on his face. "I'd be honored to perform that duty. I only wish your mother and father were here."

"Heather said the same thing," Harris said. "She's on her way here, the four of us must talk."

Casey Alexander walked to the dining hall, relieved from unburdening herself, of the truth to Harris. She enters the hall checking with the service staff to see if they're ready. Given the thumbs up sign, she makes the announcement that breakfast will be served at the top of the hour.

Dr. Garcia finishes putting on her clothes, waiting for Dr. Franklin to finish. Looking out the door of the residence, Adriana sees crew members make their way to the dining hall. "Are you ready to go Heather?" Adriana asks impatiently.

"No, you go on ahead, I join you in a minute."

Heather looks out a window watching Adriana blend into the crew out of sight. She leaves to meet Harris on the ship in the captain's cabin. Passing crew members, on her way to the lift, Heather runs into Chiefs Morozoff and Kim with Dr. Wagner. "Aren't you going the wrong way?" Amanda asks.

"I need to check on something in Lab I," Heather explains, getting on the lift. "I'll be there shortly."

Casey Alexander helped the staff prepare, setting five extra chairs for Harris' team from the Texas Aerospace Facility at the captain's table. Entering the hall are Miles Brady, Carol Davis, Grant Roberts, and Monica Wallace, followed by Dr. Garcia. Adriana pulls Casey aside so as not to be overheard she asked, "How are you feeling, now that Harris knows the truth?"

"Relieved," Casey smiles. "How did he look telling Heather?" "Happy and proud," the doctor replied.

Dr. Wagner arrives with the chiefs Morozoff and Kim at her side, joining the others at the table. Casey asked, "Where's Heather and Harris?"

"If I know Harris, he is checking on the mounting for the laser cannons, before we connect them together," said Miles.

"We saw Heather at the lift going down to lab I to

check on something," added Amanda. "They'll be here soon. Probably speaking with the captain, he is never late," said Chief Morozoff.

***

Dr. Franklin steps off the lift crossing over the gangway, enters Triton II heading to the captain's cabin. Knocking before she entered, she sees the captain and her brother looking at pictures from the past. "This one was always my favorite. Mom and dad look so young in this picture," mused Heather.

"Bryant, you didn't have grey hair yet," said Harris.

"That was taken before the two of you were born, before your grandfather told them the family secret," responded the captain.

"I almost told Casey this morning, but stopped short, knowing the four of us need to talk S.A.I.N. are you there?" asked Harris.

"Yes. Congratulations on becoming a father." exclaimed S.A.I.N. "Why am I not surprised you knew," responded Harris.

"Ms. Alexander has her right to privacy, like all intelligent beings,"

S.A.I.N. remarked. "Just what were the two of you talking about, you almost said something?" Heather asked. "I'm curious to what you talked about."

"She asked about William," Harris replied. "I told her how he became so protective of his family. How his rivals and peers saw him as an outlier, how he approached business, and his computer science beliefs."

"If something were to happen on the mission, no one would know the truth," said S.A.I.N. "Casey is our family now we must tell her."

"Then we agree," said Captain Stone. "Breakfast is at the top of the hour, and I don't like to be late. Let's go."

***

The dining hall door opens, and Captain Stone enters, followed by the Franklins. The crew stands at attention as they join the others at the table. Captain Stone gestures with his hands for the crew to be seated.

Standing before them, the captain asked for an update from Dr. Wagner on the rift expansion. "Still expanding at the rate S.A.I.N. predicted captain," responded Amanda.

Looking at Miles Brady, the captain requested an

update for the completion time for the connections of the laser cannons to the fusion reactor. "Sir," responded Miles, "if all works according to the schematics, we will be finished by this evening." After the updates for the captain the crew enjoy their morning meal.

Harris Franklin clinks his glass with a spoon, getting the attention of the crew. When they are all looking at him, he stands to address them. "Today I realized what my heart has been telling me for months," he said. Turning to face Casey Alexander, he gets down on one knee, "I love you. Will you marry me?"

Casey vigorously nods her head yes and jumps into Harris' arms. The crew beings clapping at the proposal of marriage. Harris then asks his long-time friend if he would stand by his side at the ceremony. "I will always stand with you," answered Chief Morozoff. "I'm looking forward to being an uncle."

Standing up the captain congratulates them both, then tells the crew, "We have a job to complete before we leave the day after tomorrow." Dismissing the crew, he ordered, "Let's get to it."

***

Traveling twelve hours on the remnants of a deserted highway, Martin Sanchez's convoy stops for refueling of the canvass covered vehicles. Each one carrying five fifty-five-gallon containers filled with petroleum. Six faction members armed with automatic weapons, Russian rocket propelled grenade launchers along with flame throwers for added measure. Sanchez sends a shortwave transmission to Polzin, "Comrade Polzin, are you there?"

"Yes, I'm here," my 'Old friend'," Polzin replied. "Any news from Hamilton?"

"We'll be at the institute at six am Friday morning," said Sanchez. "We'll reign fire down upon them if Hamilton fails."

***

After being dismissed by the captain, Harris Franklin and Miles Brady shook hands waiting for the ladies to finish sharing their joy with Casey after her acceptance of Harris' proposal. Harris kisses his soon-to- be wife before leaving with Chief Kim, and the rest of his team to arm the ship, against the forces of nature.

Heather, putting her arms around Casey in an embrace says, "I'm so happy for you and my brother! There is much we need to speak about, like wanting to know more about William and my father. I can help with that. Let's go to my office."

Adriana gives Casey a hug, looking at Heather. "I'm going to give you and Casey some private time together," she said.

Dr. Franklin walked through the complex on the way to her office, with her future sister- in-law, the mother of the next generation of Franklins. She said, "Casey the women in the Franklin history were strong, brilliant, enthusiastic women in their fields of science and are steadfast in their support of my grandfather and my father. Each playing a significant role in shaping their husbands and fathers of their children."

Dr. Wagner makes a gesture to Chief Morozoff that they return to the ship. Dr. Garcia, with the infirmary prepared to ask if she could tag along. "May I join you and Amanda down to the Triton II?"

"Certainly," answered the Chief. "I'm heading to see galley Chief Jones to double check our supplies for the voyage."

"You're not going to engineer level?" asked Amanda.

"No, Amanda, Ha-Kun is the chief engineer." answered Alexi. "I've only seen my cabin and Lab II on the ship. Maybe the two of you can take me on a quick tour, then join me in lab

II? I'd love some company," requested Amanda.

Accompanied by the doctors they board Triton II, riding the lift. Chief Morozoff arrives in engineering to begin Dr. Wagner's tour of the ship. They walk past Harris and his team running conduit from the laser cannons to Chief Kim one level above them for the fusion reactor. "Where are you going?" asked Harris to Alexi.

"Giving the resident volcanologist a tour of the ship," he answered.

They walk towards the stern, suspended in place above the floor hanging over the dive bay tank. A black stingray shaped craft, two viewing ports in the front, and a tail rudder in the back. Looking up Amanda asked, "what is that craft there?"

"That is Nemo," answered the Chief. "A submersible that is extremely fast, very maneuverable, like a jet plane for water. We lower the ship into the dive bay tank, open the hull door, it gets into places Triton II can't." He paused thoughtfully, then added, "I don't think I will be using it, the depth of the water at Tamu Massif is beyond its capabilities."

Stepping on to the crew lift heading to the galley level of the ship, Dr Wagner commented on what a magnificent piece of engineering Nemo is. "Designed and built by Heather's father Samuel," said the chief responding to Amanda's comment.

"As was the whole ship," added Adriana.
Stopping at the galley level they're greeted by Galley Chief Jones. Alexi made the introductions. "Chief this Dr. Wagner. This is the man that keeps this crew nourished out at sea."

"It's Jonesy," said Chief Jones. "It's nice to meet you." Chief Morozoff asked, "How are we looking with the supplies?" "We'll be fully stocked by this afternoon," answered Jonesy.

Turning back to Amanda, the Chief said, "There's one more place to visit but that will have to wait until we're out at sea."

***

Fourteen hours have passed since the attack on the trucks convoy. The trains cars moving at 104Kph on the old class five track slow down as it approaches the trestle bridge. Commander Bennett, flying in the helicopter 60 meters above the train with the three security personnel, a signal light on the control panel showing an incoming transmission.

"Commander Bennett this is S.A.I.N.," said the voice on the radio. "I detected an electrical signal has been remotely activated get your men off that train now!"

"Copy that," he replied.

Addressing his men, he said urgently, "This is Bennett! Jump off that train! The bridge is rigged to blow!" The three men faced with either busting up their bodies or dying in a wreck, jump from the train. The helicopter banks to the left, circling back to help his men. A chain reaction explosion can be heard echoing in the gorge below, the bridge collapses sending the train to the bottom, while smoke and flames can be seen rising from the gorge.

Commander Bennett spotting his three men, lands and dispatches the co-pilot to administer medical aid to them. Flying over the gorge looking down at twisted metal stacked up upon each other, he turns back to get the men. He lands the helicopter, then gets out to check on the men. "What's their condition" he asked.

"Alive," grunted the medic. "One has a broken leg and a lacerated spleen, the other two have broken ribs with multiple contusions."

"Let's get them onboard," said Bennett. They load the men onto the copter, taking off he says, "I need to contact President Hall!"

***

President Hall is having dinner with council member Illana Taylor on the balcony when she is interrupted by S.A.I.N. for an emergency signal from Commander Bennett.

"Madame President, our mission has met catastrophic failure. The H.A.T.S. wired a bridge crossing over the gorge, sending the laser cannons to the bottom, left in pieces of twisted metal," reported the commander.

"What about your men?" President Hall asked, with concern in her voice.

"Injured but alive thanks to S.A.I.N.'s warning," Bennett answered. "We're heading back to the Texas Aerospace Facility. My men need more medical attention at the infirmary."

Having heard the commander's report, Illana Taylor looks at the President in dismay. She asks, "What are we going to do?"

"First, we assemble the council, then will inform Dr. Franklin of the mission failure," said the President. "Second, we have the hardest thing to do - we need to tell the truth, about the fate of this planet to the citizens."

***

Dr. Franklin is sitting in her office with Casey Alexander, talking about Samantha and Mackenzie's relationships with their husbands.

Casey's questions turned quickly to William being recruited by the Cyber Cabal. "Harris told me William was recruited by Jonas Paul Hamilton to join the Cyber Cabal," said Casey.

Just then, the monitor in the office start sounding off an incoming transmission from S.A.I.N. "Heather you'll be receiving a signal from President Hall in a few minutes. I'm blocking her attempts to contact you, the train met with disaster," reported S.A.I.N.

With a smile on her face Heather responds, "The diversion worked!"

"It would appear so," remarked S.A.I.N., "but the President wants to inform the citizens of the impending catastrophe."

"Okay," Heather replied. "I know what to do." She contacts Captain Stone.

Crouching over his desk writing in the ships log the captain answers Heathers call. "Yes Heather. H.A.T.S. have sabotaged the train," Captain Stone confirmed.

"President Hall intends to inform the citizens of the truth at what is really happening at Tamu Massif," Heather said urgently.

"You spoke to her?" asked Captain Stone.

"S.A.I.N.'s been blocking her attempts to signal us," Heather replied. "I'll take Casey to the residency, you get Harris. We'll meet you there, it's time for the truth."

After finishing Amanda's tour of the Triton II Chief Morozoff with Adriana joins her in lab II checking the activity at Tamu Massif.

"S.A.I.N.," said Amanda, "these volcanic readings have increased since I went to breakfast."

"Yes," answered S.A.I.N. "As the rift expands the volcanism has increased around the globe sooner then we predicted."

"Can you access the old N.A.S.A probe V.O.S. orbiting Venus?" Amanda asked. "I'm connected to V.O.S. transmitting the latest data to your monitor," responded S.A.I.N.

"This is interesting," said Amanda, speaking as a volcanologist. "The data shows a dramatic increase in temperature usually meaning the planet is experiencing major resurfacing. Have you ever heard the theory about snowball

Earth seven-hundred million years ago? Earth was covered in ice due to volcanic activity blocking out the sun. Then underwater volcanic activity thawed the earth. What if this planet is repeating those same processes?"

Captain Stone is making his way down the passageway for the lift to engineering level to collect Harris. Chief Morozoff signals the captain update him on the recent events at Tamu Massif. "Sir, I'm in lab II with Dr. Garcia getting the shit scared out of us by our volcanologist theory's. We have an update on the rift as it expands there's an increased E.M. field the Triton II could experience communication disruption as we get closer to Tamu Massif.

Reaching the engineering section, they step off the lift. Raising his hands to get everyone's attention, the captain says, "We've got a developing situation at the U.P.O., H.A.T.S. have sabotaged the train, President Hall is intent on telling the truth to the citizens. Harris needs to come with me to meet his sister at the residency. It's time for us to tell the truth. We might be able to use the situation to our advantage." Together they step on the lift to leave the ship for the residence.

***

Council member Illana Taylor has assembled the council in chambers. President Hall enters with a very somber expression upon her face she walks to the podium and addresses the council. "With a heavy heart I must report the train carrying the laser cannons to the institute was sabotaged by the H.A.T.S. We need to address the citizens of the impending disaster to strike this planet."

The faces of the members of the council now mirror the same somber expression as the President.

"Is it necessary to alert the citizens now? We will have planetary mass panic until the Earth unleashes its fury upon us," said Illana Taylor.

"I'm aware of this," said the President. "We'll discuss this in the morning on how and when we will tell the truth. I'm returning to my office. I suggest you return to your homes, don't alert your families until we can talk about this matter and decide on a course of action."

President Hall slowly walking across the complex with the look of a of a person defeated is joined by council member Illana Taylor. "Madame President," said Illana, "you couldn't have known the H.A.T.S. would attack the convoy! There's only one explanation, a traitor in our midst here at the U.P.O.

or at the institute, could be anyone!"

"Either way they won," said President Hall in defeat. "I'm going to my office to inform Dr. Franklin." The president sitting at her desk preparing to contact her when the monitor sounds. "Heather, I was just about to signal you."

"Madison," Heather asked softly, "is there anyone with you?"

"No," the President replied with sadness still in her voice.

***

Sitting on a long sofa in the living area of the residency, Dr. Franklin, her brother, his fiancée, and the captain preparing to tell the truth to the President. "Madison," Heather began, "we haven't been completely forthcoming with the plans we made to combat the crisis."

With a perturbed expression on her face, the President asked, "Captain Stone, what in the name of hell is she talking about?"

"Madame President," said Captain Stone, "I've long suspected there was a leak of information inside the U.P.O. The plan we're executing was made due to those suspicions. The convoy was a diversion; everything is on schedule. Triton

II will launch on Friday at eight am on time as planned." President Hall leans back in her chair with her hands behind her head on the monitor screen. "I'm mad as hell at all of you for not reading me in on your suspicions," she growled, "but there is still hope you can complete your mission." She paused, then says, "What should I tell the council now?"

"The truth," Heather replied, "but not right now. Wait an hour or two, so whoever is behind the leak can report the news you just gave them."

"Is there anything else you need to tell me about that I should know?" President Hall asked.

"Casey is expecting a baby," Heather answered. "She is marrying Harris before we leave on our voyage."

"Congratulations to you both," said President Hall. "I'll contact you when I'm ready to tell the council the truth."

***

Having left the President walking through the complex, visiting other council members to see how they are coping with the news, Council member Taylor arrives at Chao-Xun residency. She knocks on the door and waits. After two minutes with no answer, she goes to the side of the house to look in a window. Seeing Chao using a transmitter she returns to the door. Illana's knock has become a pound. Startled by the loud sound he drops the mic to answer the door.

"What are you doing?" Taylor seethed. "The President ordered us not to contact our families!" "I couldn't reach my sister Jai anyway," mumbled Chao-Xun,

"Why are you here?" "Checking on everyone to see how they're dealing with the news and what to do next," answered Illana. "Frankly, I think we should alert our families, and the citizens A.S.A.P. to give them a chance to survive the impending disaster." said Xun.

***

Dr. Franklin stands up after informing the President of their deception with the convoy. Walking to the windows that run from floor to ceiling overlooking the Pacific, she turns to the others. "I think President Hall took that rather well," she said. "There's one more truth that must be told."

She turns to look at Casey, who has already moved to the kitchen to have her second breakfast. "Casey, you remember me telling you about William's journal, that it was a more high- tech than Earwyn's?"

"It was two days ago," she smiled, quipping, "I'm pregnant not senile."

"There's something we like to show you," Heather said, "when you're done making whatever that is."

Taking her food over to the sitting area near the bookcases, she sits between Harris and Heather, with the captain at the end of the sofa. Finally settled, they told her the tale of the Franklin family secret.

"Casey," Heather began, "before the Trident war everything at this complex was recorded due to the proprietary nature of the technologies designed and manufactured here when F.I.S.T. was an on-going corporate entity. You asked me about William after being approached by Jonas Paul Hamilton to recruit him to join the Cyber Cabal. There's footage of William explaining the events of that day to Samantha."

Clearing her throat, Heather commands, "S.A.I.N. queue the I.O.N. memory file."

Shades from the windows are slowly being drawn down blocking out the sunlight putting the room into perpetual darkness S.A.I.N. queues up the recording. Imagery begins appearing of Earwyn's home where William and his family lived.

***

A large wooden door, the insignia of the Triton carved into it begins to open. William is greeted by Samantha, his wife of seventeen years.

They're both forty years old. Their five-year-old son Samuel rushes to greet his dad. "It's Friday! Dad it's Madden night; mom just got me 2002!"

"Let me help your mother first," William smiled, "then we will play after dinner." *Patting his son gently on the back, Samuel walks to the living room. Samuel can be heard calling after him,* "I'm going to beat you so bad, Dad!" *Sitting quietly amazed by the imagery she is seeing, Casey asked.* "Is this a Hologram? How are you doing this?"

"I've got extensive memory files stored in the I.O.N. database," S.A.I.N. replied. "I told you it was high-tech," said Heather.

Happy he is home with his family after his business trip, Samantha kisses her husband, and asks, "How was your trip to Texas?"

"Very well," William replied. "We bought the necessary land to build the Texas Aerospace facility. F.I.S.T. can start manufacturing satellites for the I.O.N. to replace the G.I.N. in twenty years."

"A daunting challenge for an incoming CEO," Samantha said, "New division to get off the ground while continuing the current business model that Lewis Hollister and you set up seventeen years ago. Have you decided on who will replace Lewis?"

"That question seems to be on the mind of more than just a few people this week," William replied. "Jonas Paul Hamilton asked me that same question this week in Dallas. Lewis and I will announce it on Monday. I'm going upstairs to unpack and change into fat clothes."

As he's walking up the stairs, William asked his wife, "What are we making for dinner?" "Spaghetti and meatballs," Samantha answered, as a resounding yell of approval can be heard coming from Samuel playing in the living room. Coming down the stairs in Eagle's sweatpants wearing a vintage concert tee shirt from the nineteen eighties, William walks into the kitchen picking up a spoon and begins stirring sauce on the stove. Curious, Samantha asked, "Where did you get that shirt?"

"I saw it in a vintage clothing shop in Dallas," William said. "This tour name was our first concert together, remember?" As Samantha smiled, William added, "I got you one as well."

Walking from the sink with a pot of water for the pasta Samantha sets it down turning on the flame. "You did that on purpose," she said turning to Willaim.

With a puzzled look, William asked, "Did what?"

"Going upstairs without telling me who you're going to name on Monday as CEO."

"I'll tell you but first you must listen to what else happened in Dallas this week with J.P. Hamilton," said William.

"What did that corporate raider want?"

"Are you going to ask questions or listen to what I have to say?" William asked impatiently. When Samantha nodded at him, he continued. "Last night Lewis and I were sitting in the hotel bar after signing the purchase agreement for the Texas Aerospace facility. Who comes walking through the door but J.P. Hamilton, not surprising Global Venture Capitals headquarters are in downtown Dallas. Sitting next to us he asks the same question you want me to answer. Lewis tells him an announcement will be made on Monday. I think Lewis's dislike of Hamilton comes from how much he reminds him of Vance Tiddle. He says to me he's tired and going to the room.

Waiting for Lewis to walk away from view, J.P. Hamilton proceeds to tell me about when the government allowed components of Standard Oil to merge back together. Oh, you should have heard him going on and on! They did that so the oil industry could combine their power over the world's energy supply. The war that's going on right now, just like most is for their benefit. J.P. Hamilton said, 'The time has come for our industry to coalesce to use our wealth, political influence over government policies, around the globe on the use of the internet. Digital global currency will be the money of tomorrow, just as black gold is today. Join us, help us control the narrative of the future. Until the rise of A.I. and fusion power replaces oil as the dominant energy source on this planet. I call our organization the Cyber Cabal."

"What did you say to him?" Samantha asked, concern plainly showing on her face.

"I told him the industry that I'm part of was built by brilliant men and women of science and technology. I said, 'you're nothing but a financier that forced those brilliant minds out of their own companies; to gain power and control of their technologies, I want no part of your Cyber Cabal.' Then he left the bar, pissed off, extremely angry, his face beet red."

Measuring her words carefully, Samantha asked, "Now that I've listened to your story will you please tell me who you're naming on Monday?"

"There was only one choice to be made," William replied. "I spoke to Lewis. He told me of your desire to leave the chair of the Franklin Foundation to try a new challenge. I was going to name you anyway, you're my partner in life in so many ways, this is just one more. Samantha the position is yours if you really want it."

Nodding her head yes, she hugs her husband by giving him a kiss. "Thanks for believing in me," she said with tears of joy running down her face.

After dinner Samuel whipping his dad's ass in Madden 2002, then went to bed for the evening. Samantha escorts him upstairs to tuck him in and kisses him good night. William is out on the porch preparing to open a bottle of champagne to celebrate his wife's new position at

F.I.S.T. Samantha comes downstairs and goes outside. William pops the cork on the bottle, raising their glasses, clanging them together "To the Future" they toasted.

"That proposition J.P. Hamilton talked to you about sounds very much like the warning your mother told Earwyn about from the journal Lewis gave you the day Samuel was born," Samantha mused.

"I know," William responded. "There's more for us to discuss after we finish our toast." He took a sip, then continued.

"Something else happened this week while I was in Texas. Before leaving I was running a new iteration of my program, downloading a certain data set of information for it to run while I was gone. I stopped at my lab before coming home to see the results."

He hands the data to Samantha, and she starts reading over the data. Her hand rises over her mouth. "Oh my God! That's my reactor design for fusion William! We can build it!" "Your dream program figured this out," William affirmed. "Yes, on both counts. Building it will take decades to complete to achieve first light. It won't be as large as the one the international community wants to build, but we need to keep this a secret. No data can be on any F.I.S.T. servers here or at the Texas facility when it's completed and operational."

"Where do think we should build it?" Samantha asked eagerly. "My dad and Lewis excavated the cliffs to moor the

Triton," answered William, taking a sip from his glass. "I'm thinking if we excavate the archway walls to the east about five hundred meters, we could hollow out a cavern to build in it under the cliffside."

"How do you plan to keep the construction a secret?" Samantha asked.

"We will build on top of the cliff's too," William pointed out. "A new manufacturing facility that will double as my new lab, new research labs for the Institute. We'll need to construct new intake pipes doubling as desalination water for the seawater farming which will have to expand.

We'll built our new home over there on the cliff side overlooking the ocean." William paused with a smile on his face, then asked, "Are you sure, you want the job?" Samantha asked, "What about your dream?"

"I have at least twenty years to teach this iteration, to help it to understand what it means to be human," William answered. "I just hope J.P. Hamilton and his Cyber Cabal don't get there first."

"Then let's make sure they don't," the new CEO of F.I.S.T. said with a determined look on her face.

***

Shades begin going up as the afternoon sunlight shines in the living area. Casey stands up and walks around, taking time to process what she has just seen from the hologram. Looking over at Heather, she said, "Earwyn's house was over there, this is the house on the cliff. You're telling me there's a fusion reactor underneath us? What does it power?"

"A family truth," Heather replied pulling the book *Twenty Thousand Leagues under the Sea* from the bookcase. The bookcase at the far side of the residency slides to the right revealing a pair of lift doors that are beginning to open. Heather motioned to Casey with her finger to go with her as Harris and the captain stepped into the lift. "Goin' down," said Heather. The door closes, sending the lift on a slow descent to the bottom of the shaft. The door reopens, Harris directs Casey to the right, followed by Heather and the captain. A massive steel door opens outwards revealing Samantha's dream project.

"Your grandmother designed this," Casey said with awe in her voice. "How does this thing work?"

"Someday we will give you a tour of how it works," Harris answered, "but we need to go through the door on the other side."

"What's behind that door?" Casey asked. Heather spoke up, "The truth!"

Going through the door Casey looks up at a four-letter acronym in large letters. "Meet S.A.I.N.," said Heather.

Departure

While Casey Alexander is staring into the darkness, S.A.I.N. illuminates his core. Thirteen thousand eight hundred and fifty–four nodes each with two Quantum Gen-7 F.I.S.T. CPU's along with six GPUs.

Thousands of server tower lights flickering on the cavern ceiling like stars in the cosmos. Service drones working on maintenance of the hardware replacing cabling, switches, routers worn out processing units to keep S.A.I.N. in operation.

Stunned by the revelation that humanity's protector isn't the story she was told as a child, Casey asked only one question. "Why?"

S.A.I.N. notifies the captain of an incoming transmission from President Hall. The captain says patiently, "Heather and I will return to the surface to deal with the U.P.O. Harris, you can answer Casey's questions." Ascending in the lift, they reached the surface and exit.

Dr. Franklin and Captain Stone answer the President's

call. "Yes, Madame President?" Heather asked.

"I gave it two-hours," said the President. "I'm ready to assemble the council." "Madame President, one or more of the seven members won't be very enthusiastic with your news," remarked the captain.

"They might tip the H.A.T.S. with the news," she replied.

Harris takes Casey to William's living area inside S.A.I.N.'s core. Sitting with Casey's hand locked in his own, staring into her eyes, he says, "I'm going to tell you the why my grandfather spent a lifetime designing and building S.A.I.N. creating a lifeform. He knew Cyber Cabal's plan to relinquish B.G.C. of its power and control over the politicians and the bureaucrats weren't going to be difficult. All of them were on the payrolls on either side, to vote on bills and legislation that helped them get wealthier.

Getting control over the one thing they needed for global domination was military control of all the nations of the world. Artificial Intelligence would ensure that eventuality. This was their goal. Control computers, you control the weapons of mass destruction designed to keep the peace. S.A.I.N. was created to ensure the survival of humanity from that which is now a reality. His purpose is the same now as it was then," said Harris.

"Why the alien cover story?" Casey asked.

Harris sighed and kissed her lightly. "We're leaving on Friday morning," he said. "I don't want to talk about my family's past when we're trying to save our future. I believe there's something better we could be doing together with our time. S.A.I.N. can answer all your questions after the Triton II leaves on its voyage."

***

Illana Taylor is sitting outside in the back of her residency, gazing out at the star filled sky, the moonlight reflecting off the sea into the horizon. Her monitor lights up a dark room inside the house. The President's voice comes through. "Illana, are you there?"

"Yes, Madame President," she responded.

"There's an urgent matter that has come to my attention we need to discuss," the President said. "Please come to my office at once."

Leaving her residency for the President's office, she is spotted by Chao-Xun looking through his front door window. Entering the office breathing heavily from her quickened pace.

President Hall has just finished speaking with Captain Stone.

"I've been informed the leak of information to the H.A.T.S. didn't originate at the institute," she said.

"How do they know that?" Illana asked, confused.

"Captain Stone wouldn't be preparing Triton II for its voyage," answered the President. "Without laser cannons what can they do?" asked Illana

"There're being installed as we speak," replied the President. "The convoy was a diversion to draw out the H.A.T.S. informant here at the U.P.O."

Council member Taylor jumps from her seat, hurries behind the President's desk and puts her arms around her. She said excitedly, "We still have hope!"

"Yes," said the President. "And by your reaction that crosses you off the list. We still don't know who the leak is. Go to the residencies wake the others. I'm going to tell the truth, and we'll see how they react." Walking at an even quicker pace, Illana stops at each member's residency, waking them and informing each of an emergency meeting in the chambers. Chao-Xun answers his door before she could knock. "I saw you earlier walking to the President's office," he explained. "What's going on?"

"President Hall received an urgent message from Captain Stone at the institute," Illana replied, almost out of breath. "She wants us all to assemble in the chambers immediately."

After fifteen minutes had passed, the members began arriving, still yawning from being awoken by council member Taylor. President Hall enters the chambers and briskly walks to the podium to address the council. "Captain Stone and the crew of the Triton II will leave on schedule fully equipped with the laser cannons at eight o' clock Friday morning," she announced.

"The convoy to the train was a diversion set up by Dr. Franklin to find the leak of information to the H.A.T.S."

The members begin hugging each other with the news that there's still hope. Chao-Xun hugged Illana enthusiastically. "This is great news," he said. "I have been up all night, I'm going back to my residency, pour a very large drink and go to sleep!" Illana smiled at him and wished him good night. When he was out of earshot, she walks towards the President with her arms outstretched. She pulls the President close and whispers in her ear. "You lied about the leak. I think I know why."

Council member Taylor hurriedly leaves the chambers

watching Chao-Xun walking at a brisk pace to reach his residency, he passes through the door. Illana quickly alerts the U.P.O. security to meet her in front of Chao's residency. Crouching down passing by the windows as not to be seen, she reaches the nearest one to Chao's radio set. She's shocked by what she sees.

Rushing to the shortwave radio set, Chao picks up the mic. "Polzin! Are you there?"

Yes, what do you want?" replied Polzin.

"My last transmission reporting on Hamilton's success isn't correct," Chao said urgently. "The laser cannons were never on the train. The convoy was a diversion! Triton II will leave on schedule Friday morning," reported Chao.

"I've got a bon voyage parting gift for them," replied Polzin. "In the meantime, I'm going to contact Hamilton on his failure."

Having heard Chao's conversation, Illana walks to the front of the residency signaling the U.P.O. security personnel to break down the door. They burst through the door; a startled Chao drops his drink. "Arrest him!" Illana ordered. "For being a traitor to the U.P.O."

Council member Taylor and the U.P.O. security escort

painted her in his favorite team's colors."

The crew waits with the groom for the arrival of his bride lined up on the deck of the ship at the starboard side. Harris stands with his best man, Chief Alexi Morozoff. Casey crosses the gangway onto the deck with flowers sticking out of her blonde hair and walks with Dr. Franklin, her friend and mentor, to the bow as she gives the bride away. Captain Stone climbs out of the hatch in his dress blues, then takes his position to perform his duty.

"The greatest duty a ship's captain can perform is the joining of two lives as one," he said solemnly. "A few hours from now we'll embark on a perilous mission on the most significant voyage in human history. My hope is that we are successful in our quest to save humanity from extinction. That Harris and Casey may also continue the voyage of discovery that life is. We might finally see the world become one people, one planet in our struggle to rebuild our world together in peace." He cleared his throat, then continued "Harris Franklin, Casey Alexander before all these witnesses do you declare your love for each other till death do you part?"

"We do," they answered in unison with smiles on their faces.

Captain Stone nodded, and said, "Then as captain of this vessel, I pronounce you husband and wife." Nodding to Harris, he added, "You may kiss your bride."

The newlyweds kiss with the crew clapping in celebration of their union.

"When the remaining few hours have passed, Captain Stone announces, "there'll be pre- launch check at 23:30 hours."

Spending their last hours together as husband-and-wife, Casey and Harris hear the captain's message, calling everyone to the ship. They leave the residency for the ship, standing at the dock with the service staff, Casey and Harris say their goodbyes to each other. "Departing from each other this way doesn't feel right," Harris said with a look of sadness on his face." I should stay here with you."

"They need you Harris," Casey answered. "Just please come back to us."

After kissing her husband goodbye, Harris then walks across the gangway climbing down the hatch at the stern of the ship.

Legacy

Harris Franklin disappears from Casey's view entering Triton II. She's standing with the service staff as the ship goes out to sea. They line up to take the lift back to the surface, an elderly Black woman takes Casey by the hand. "You're not alone, Mrs. Franklin," she said with a heartwarming smile.

Harris reaches the bridge and walks over to the captain to shake his hand. "Thank you for everything you have done for us, Bryant," said Harris.

He then takes the lift to the crew level. Walking to his cabin after an exhausting night with his wife, he catches up on sleep.

Captain Stone grabs the mic for the ship's comms calling down to engineering. "Chief Kim, fifty percent on the reactor let's save as much power as we can," he said. "Proteus, when we're cleared to navigate, take the ship to periscope depth and set a course for Catalina Island at thirty- five knots."

"Yes, Sir," Proteus replied.

After sailing through the night with calm seas, Chief Jones announces that breakfast is being served in the galley mess. Chief Morozoff has already eaten breakfast ready to relieve the captain of his watch. He sees Dr. Wagner enter the mess hall and walks up to her. "Amanda, when you have finished breakfast join me on the bridge. There is something I'd like you to see. I must relieve the captain of his watch." Walking onto the bridge he addresses Captain Stone. "Sir, you're relieved. Is anything exciting happening?"

"No," replied Captain Stone. "We're now approaching Catalina Island. The ship is yours, Chief. Take us two thousand thirty-six nautical miles to Hawaii. Proteus has our course laid in." He leaves for his cabin and says, "I'm going to get some rest."

"Have a good sleep, Sir," said the chief.

With Chief Morozoff in command of the ship, cruising at periscope depth the Triton II on the way to the islands, Chief Morozoff sees Dr. Wagner stepping off the lift onto the bridge.

"Permission to come on the bridge, Sir," she asked the chief. "Granted," he replied, taking her to the digital sonar station displaying the terrain of the seafloor ahead of Triton II. He orders the bridge viewing window open. It retracts slowly back, revealing the world beneath the waves. Deep sea coral reefs with vivid colors of the spectrum glow in the lights of the ship. Schools of various species of marine life swim past the ship. Wrecks from long ago on the bottom of the seafloor. Taken back by the wonders of the sea, Dr. Wagner said, "This is beautiful and peaceful down here. Thank you, Alexi, for showing me this before we head to deeper waters."

"We have the greatest job on Earth," responded the chief.

***

Hamilton is sitting down in his chair in front of the short-wave radio set after working through the night revamping his helicopter to attack the institute. Scanning the frequency bands for Martin Sanchez making his way up the pacific coast. He gets on the radio and calls, "Are you there?"

After a moment of garbled static he hears, "Polzin told me of your failure, Hamiton," answered Sanchez.

"To hell with him," Hamilton fumed. "I just finished my modifications to my helicopter to join you in the attack. I am leaving at eleven, flying extremely low down close to the road surface on what was Interstate-80 to Interstate-5, so not to be detected by S.A.I.N."

Waking up in the bedroom of the living quarters in S.A.I.N.'s core Casey Franklin informs her new family member she'll be leaving to shower and change at her home. Taking the lift to the surface, she tells S.A.I.N. she needs to make announcement to the staff. "Good morning," she said cheerfully. "This is Casey Franklin. I need all personnel and their families to meet in the dining mess in one hour please. She leaves the living quarters and walks through the eerie quietness of the complex and enters her home. Taking off her clothes before stepping into the shower, the reflection in the mirror shows her protruding belly as tears wells up in her eyes.

After finishing her shower, she puts on her clothes, then looks at the tiredness in her face from crying. She leaves for the dining mess. Members of the service staff with their children have already assembled. "I would like to thank you for attending the ceremony yesterday," she began. "Now, remember there are tunnels underneath these buildings. If you feel the need to go there instead of staying in your homes, don't wait until the last minute to prepare. Use the ones closest to the village. I don't know what to expect from the H.A.T.S. I'm going to the residency to stay in contact with Triton II."

Entering the Franklin residency Casey request S.A.I.N. to contact the Triton II. She then walks into the kitchen and begins making breakfast for herself.

"The ship is receiving your signal Mrs. Franklin," said S.A.I.N. Smiling up at the cameras, she responded, "I do like the sound of that!"

***

Proteus informs the chief of an incoming transmission from the

institute. Reaching over to the communications panel he answers the call. "Good morning, Casey Franklin," he greeted her.

"Damn," responded Casey. "I do like the sound of that Alexi! Has my husband woken up this morning?"

"We haven't seen him yet this morning," he smiled. "I think you might have tired him out. Hold on, I'm transferring your call to his cabin." Dr. Wagner walks to the lift telling Chief Morozoff, "I'm going to lab II to see the activity at Tamu Massif. Maybe you and I can have dinner in my cabin later?" Smiling slyly, she added, "I'll try and tire you out."

"I'll be there," the chief replied.

Harris is awoken from a deep peaceful sleep by the sound of the monitor, alerting him to an incoming transmission. He rolls over and hits the button, then sees his wife of one day smiling on the screen. Yawning and smiling back, he asked, "What time is it?"

"I think you slept through breakfast," Casey smiled. "Alexi said I tired you out."

"I can't think of a better way to get tired," Harris grinned. "Maybe he should try it."

Casey's manner became serious. "I've spoken to the remaining staff about sheltering in the tunnels under the complex in case of an H.A.T.S attack."

"What about you?" Harris asked.

"I'll hide in our favorite place if that happens," she said. "Beside S.A.I.N. and I are going to finish the Franklin family story." Sighing deeply, she added, "I must start my day. Love you! I wish you were here with me."

Harris started his own day by showering, getting dressed, and going down to the galley to ask Chief Jones for breakfast. "Kurt, I slept in," he said apologetically. "Am I too late to get a breakfast?"

Coming out of the galley with a plate of food in his

hand, Chief Jones sets it down in front of Harris. "Casey wore you out," didn't she?" Grinned the chief.

Harris smiles at his childhood friend. Harris finished eating, then took the lift to the lab level. He walks past Dr. Franklin's lab, sticking his head in to say good morning to his sister. "Morning sis" he said jovially. "Where's Adriana?"

"With Amanda in lab II," Heather grunted. "There's not much to do in the infirmary for her and crew members, Knight and Gale. Have you spoken to Casey this morning?"

"Yes," Harris answered quietly. "She is persuading everyone to go to the tunnels for protection from an attack on the institute from the H.A.T.S."

"You are a lucky man brother of mine," Heather remarked. "I love that woman."

Harris walks to lab II to say good morning to the doctor and ask her a question. "Good morning, Amanda. I just got done speaking to Casey, by the end of our conversation the signal seemed to be fading."

"Yes, I was just about to inform Alexi of my latest reading" Amanda said. "It's as we feared, the closer we get to the rift, Triton II may lose communications."

***

After talking with her husband, Casey Franklin finishes breakfast then cleans up. She wants to know more about the family she thought she knew. Moving to the living area, S.A.I.N. can tell from her facial expression she is troubled about something. S.A.I.N. asked, "Is there something wrong?"

"I'd be lying to you if I told you I am all right," Casey admitted in a somber voice. "I'm having a rough time understanding all the information the four of you trusted me with. I don't understand the reasoning behind not telling the world the truth. I need a friend to help me better understand." S.A.I.N. responded, "Then as a friend, I'll tell you the rest of the family story."

Looking up at the cameras smiling, Casey goes to the refrigerator for a beverage, then makes herself comfortable on the sofa to listen to the rest of the Franklin story.

"Tell me what you know for sure about the Franklin family," S.A.I.N. begins, "then I will tell you what you don't know that might help with answers to your questions."

Nodding, Casey began. "What I know for sure is after graduating high school, Samuel went to the United States Naval Academy for four years. Finishing on the

Superintendent's list the same year his mother died of serve acute respiratory syndrome coronavirus 2."

"Samantha was going to retire the following year before her death from F.I.S.T. to help William complete his dream. Samuel's graduation from Annapolis was the last time William and Samantha were with their son as a family," responded S.A.I.N.

"I didn't know that." Casey gasped in shock.

"On the I.O.N. satellite system I have the life history of every person that ever accessed the service. For sixty-seven percent, their history ends all the same way. Their memories are stored here at the core from the day I was activated by William. I never told a story before. I have two holographic memories, I'll show you. These aren't simulations I put together but my memories.

***

After the death of Samantha, William was left with a vacancy to fill at F.I.S.T. and in his heart. Samantha, already planning her retirement, had a candidate in mind to replace her Mackenzie Hawkins. It was easier for William to replace her at F.I.S.T., always trusting her in life there was no reason to doubt her choice. The vacancy she left in his heart could never be filled. Samuel, after graduation from the academy, went on to submarine command school just as his grandfather had done seventy-four years earlier. He once told me that he almost gave up his military career to join his dad at F.I.S.T. William told him not to give up on his dreams that F.I.S.T. was in able hands. After meeting Mackenzie for the first time, he knew at once his mother had made the right choice. Mackenzie came to F.I.S.T. right out of the University of Texas Aerospace Engineering program. An intelligent young woman with out of the box thinking something that reminded Samantha of herself. She sold Samantha on the idea of reusing first stage rockets to put the I.O.N. satellites into geosynchronous orbit. Samantha almost hired on the spot. Mackenzie convinced William, with Samantha giving her support, sold William on expanding the Texas facility to manufacture their own rockets. Cheaper and with less red tape from N.A.S.A. rockets Mackenzie Hawkins sold him on the idea. She was hired that day.

During this period of his life the reactor was completed but not yet operational. Willam's focus turned to perfecting me. Confident in the choice his late wife had made in Mackenzie Hawkins to replace her as CEO of F.I.S.T., he began downloading every version of the A.I. program into the *hardware in the core cavern. Teaching every iteration, what it meant to be human proved to be quite the challenge going forward.*

Mackenzie excelled as CEO of F.I.S.T. working from the Texas facility seeing her rocket technologies launch the I.O.N. system into orbit.

Receiving frequent visit from Willam to inspect each satellite before being put into operational orbit. They were so good, launching six times a month for a decade. Seven hundred and fourteen in all with I.O.N. completed in 2029.

Samuel and his dad would get together during his shore leave from duty. Usually one week at a time, often with his best friend Bryant Stone at the Texas Aerospace facility. Samuel was encouraged by his friend to start a relationship with Mackenzie a woman seven years his senior. They shared an interest in engineering that flourished into something more.

Spending more time with her during shore leave as the decade went by. He would be given command of a Columbia-Class submarine the U.S.S. Seahawk with his best friend Bryant Stone serving as his Executive Officer.

Willam had worked on sixty-one iterations of the A.I. program each resulting in failure with the program trying to get out into the real world. I was the sixty-second version of the program when I.O.N. was put online to replace the G.I.N. It was an immense success for F.I.S.T. but a data feast for what I would become. I started learning at an exponential rate about humans, their emotions and my purpose for being created. Confident that the glitches from the first sixty-one other iterations have been worked out. Willian downloaded me in the central core, still a closed system. William and I would spend the next two years learning from each other.

Over the next twenty-four months Williams' contacts with the outside world were brief and never in person. The frequent visits to Mackenzie stopped after I.O.N. was deployed into operational service. She saw him only on the monitor looking very tired in his face. Concerned about Williams' well-being she contacts Samuel and arranges an unannounced visit to the residency.

***

The window shades inside the residence begins going down as the light slowly disappears. Casey looks up and asks, "What am I about to see? Your telling of the family legacy was truly well done for the first-time storyteller.," she remarked. "The date was June 29, 2031, the day Samuel and Mackenzie were introduced to me," said S.A.I.N. in a melancholy voice. "You sound sad," said Casey. "I miss them," said S.A.I.N.

***

The darkness of the room brightens, S.A.I.N. starts his holographic memory file from that day in June so long ago that changed Samuels and Mackenzie life. Flying in an F.I.S.T. private jet, a Bombardier seventy-five starts lowering its landing gear on approach to the complex airstrip.

Climbing out of the plane Samuel unloads the luggage and helps Mackenzie from the plane. Picked up by a transport vehicle they are taken to the residency. Sitting in the living area in the core cavern, William is alerted by S.A.I.N. to his son and CEO Mackenzie Hawkins arrival.

Walking from the core to the lift to the surface, getting off walking to the bookcase putting the book Twenty Thousand League's Under the Sea back into place. Across the room, the bookcase slides closed. Hearing an oncoming vehicle William opens the front door. This is an unexpected visit.

Getting their luggage out of the transport, Samuel walks up to his dad giving him a firm handshake and an embrace followed by a kiss on the cheek by Mackenzie. "Is there something wrong in Texas?" William asked.

"No. I called Samuel," responded Mackenzie. "We have concerns about you not being seen these past two years since the completion of the I.O.N."

Entering the residency behind Samuel and Mackenzie, William takes notice of the luggage they have brought with them. Walking into the kitchen, he opens the refrigerator, grabs two cold beers and hands one to Samuel. He then reaches into the freezer and pulls out a chilled martini glass to make Mackenzie's favorite cocktail. He shakes her Cosmopolitan, then pours it into the glass. "I see you brought enough luggage for an extended visit," he saw. "Planning to stay awhile?"

"We've come to see if you're doing all right," said Samuel. "I've been busy working on innovative technologies in my lab," said William, "I've spoken to the managers for I.O.N.," said Mackenzie in a stern voice, "and they told me the lab is always in operation, yet no one sees you in person. I hope you can understand our concerns for you."

Pointing down the hall to the spare bedrooms, Samuel and Mackenzie put their luggage in the room, coming out as William took their drinks to the living room. Sitting on the sofa together William sits down in his favorite chair. "I appreciate your concerns for my well-being, but I thought, Samuel, you might be here to tell me you asked my CEO to marry you," said William. "How do you know that?" Samuel responded with a startled tone in his voice.

Standing up Samuel walked around his dad's chair, waiting for a reply to his question. "I know everything that happens at F.I.S.T." William replied, "and at Texas Aerospace Facility people may not see me, but I'm hardly alone."

"Dad, let me tell you something you don't know," Samuel said. "I resigned my commission a week ago. I want to pursue other interests in my life."

Putting his head back in the chair staring at the camera in the ceiling. "I wonder how I don't know that." William said looking up at the ceiling camera. "What other interests do you speak of?"

"Mackenzie and I want to start a family," Samuel answered. "Maybe retrofitting the Triton to go exploring again."

Rising out of his chair looking down at his watch, William tells them to go get showered and change while he starts dinner. A pot of boiling water is on the stove, and meatballs are simmering in sauce when a red light flashes from the ceiling, alerting William that S.A.I.N. is watching and requires his attention. Taking an ear comm from his pocket placing it in his ear, he asks, "What is it S.A.I.N.?"

"There's something happening in Saint-Paul-Lee-Durance, I think you should see," said S.A.I.N. The wall screen television turns on as Samuel and Mackenzie appear from the bedroom to join William for dinner. "Dad, were you talking with someone?"

"It's the television," said William "I just got an alert on my watch about breaking news." Mackenzie starts helping William with dinner by putting the pasta in boiling water. "Samuel, your dad made your favorite," she remarked. Walking to the wall screen fixated on the breaking news report watches the video from Global News Network. A Y-20A cargo plane flying over the world's largest energy experiment in human history dropping aG.BU-431b from the back of the plane hits the target dead center for total annihilation. "Holy Shit!!! The International Tomak Reactor has come under terrorist attack," said Samuel. Another alert appears on the screen under the caption: Breaking news; the group known as the H.A.T.S. has claimed responsibility for the attack in France today.

Walking into the living room William comments on the

news report on the H.A.T.S. attack. "That's aggressive for them, this could be the start of things to come," he remarked. "Where did they get the funding for such an operation?" Samuel asked.

"That was a Chinese cargo plane made by Russians dropping United States ordinance on European soil. This could start World War III," William responded.

From the kitchen Mackenzie tells them that dinner is ready. Sitting down to dinner, passing the food around the table, she's pondering the same question Samuel had just asked his dad. She asked, "Where did they get the funding?"

"Ask the question about who profits from such an attack, and there you'll find the answer," William remarked.

"The B.G.C.," Mackenzie responded.

"Let's have dinner then you can tell me about your plans," said William delighted to see his son had found love in his life, despite the tragic news they'd just received.

Finishing with dinner, William excuses himself from the table. Walking to his bedroom, He opens a drawer in the nightstand and removes a gold heart shaped box adorned with purple sapphires around the edge a capital F engraved on the lid. He returns to the kitchen.

Mackenzie and Samuel begin to clean up after dinner. William hands Mackenzie the box. "I have something I'd like you both to have," he announced. Lifting the lid two gold wedding rings shining as bright as the sun takes Mackenzies breath away. William shows the bands to Samuel, who recognizes them at once.

Tears rolling down her face, Mackenzie embraces William, and Samuel shakes his father's hand. "They're beautiful rings," she sniffled, wiping the tears from her face. "I won't leave F.I.S.T. until we have a replacement," she added. "Samantha would have wanted you to have them," William said. "Someday you could pass them to your children."

William smiles, happy to have brought joy to his son and future daughter– in-law from the rings he gave Samantha all those years ago. He invites them to go down to the Triton with him to discuss the retrofit of the ship. Walking through a silent complex, F.I.S.T. employees have gone home for the weekend. Getting on the lift riding down the shaft the Triton comes into view.

William said, "Samuel, Triton's nuclear reactor was replaced decades ago when I gave the University of Santa Barbra permission to use it on short voyages for educational research. The propulsion system was replaced with electric powered jet engines. She doesn't stay down for extended periods of time like she once could, but the ship is fast. The labs are antiquated, the computer systems need an upgrade, the Triton is really a museum piece."

"I guess the retrofit is out," remarked his son in disappointment. Reaching the bottom, they walk to a moored cabin cruiser. William hands each of them a life preserver, then starts the engines and heads out to the open sea. They go out eight hundred meters, then turn the boat around to face the cliffs. "I'm not opposed to the refit," William said, "but I have a different possibility you may not have thought of. The university can moor the Triton down the coast while we use the vacant cavern to build a new ship the Triton II. Excavate the cliffside for another dock so the two of them can be next to each other. That is, he shot a grin in their direction, "if you and Mackenzie are interested in such an undertaking."

Moving over to replace his dad at the helm of the boat and turning to Mackenzie, Samuel can't hide the elation of the smile on his face.

Starting the engines, he heads back into the cavern with his dad standing beside him. "It will take years to design and *build and equip her with the latest in propulsion technology and new computer systems," said Samuel. "It will cost a small fortune."*

"Fortunately, money will not be our problem," remarked William. He cuts the engines to the slow the boat. Samuel jumps off to tie the boat to the mooring pylon. William reaches for Mackenzie's hand to help her off the boat. She looks at her father-in-law, sees the aging around his eyes, and the elation in Samuel's smile. She says, "How can I say no? I can work from here. We can start a family."

Taking the lift to the surface, Samuel is reminiscing to Mackenzie about growing up at the complex. How, as a boy he loved going down to the Triton when the students were using the ship for school. Reading Lewis Hollister ship logs, imagining he was one the crew on one of the voyages working on one of his grandfather's experiments. Opening the front door to the residency William goes to the refrigerator to grab three beers for them to celebrate their new project together. Taking the beers to the living room William sits in his chair in the living room. "Since you're reminiscing about the past," William said, "do you recall the night your mother became CEO of F.I.S.T., you beat me in Madden 2002?

"Yes, I remember mom was so happy that night," agreed Samuel, "but there were so many nights I beat you in Madden."

William begins to tell Samuel and Mackenzie about the night at the hotel bar in Texas, when he ran into Jonas Paul Hamilton, the CEO of Global Venture Capital and founder of Hamiton Systems and the offer he made to him that night. Samuel asked, "What was he offering you dad to buy out of F.I.S.T.?"

"No," William responded. "To join an organization, he called the Cybal Cabal made up of different high-tech companies from around the world. Of course, I said no. Because today, the Cabal is made up of not just people from the high-tech industry, but now includes politicians from different nations, media platforms executives, financial intuitions, and members of the military industrial complex all over the globe. The oil industry has the same pieces on the other side of the board all to control the narrative of the future."

Samuel gets up, and walks behind the sofa, trying to digest this revelation his dad had just told him. He asked, "What narrative dad?" "To control energy production," William explained, "you control the narrative; something the oil industry has known since the day they first drilled the black gold from the Earth. The inventions that made oil a necessity, the combustion engine, the car, the airplane, provided power and light to every home in the civilized world. A hundred and thirty years is a long time to have so much power and control. Something they don't want to give up, and that the Cyber Cabal desperately wants for itself. "Today in France the Cyber Cabal took a huge loss, their members are major investors in fusion startups trying to downsize the reactors to bring it to the masses. Their A.I. labs across the globe will be the H.A.T.S. next targets. Mackenzie, you answered the question early on how they are funded. Cyber Cabal wants to control all political policies, digital currency, energy with the help of the media they already own to achieve their goal of using and A.I. under their control to get what they want to control the narrative of the future. This is what Jonas Paul Hamilton offered that night. On the night, your mother became CEO of F.I.S.T. she encouraged me to build my dream project after hearing that story.

"I thought F.I.S.T. was your dream," Samuel remarked.

William shook his head. "F.I.S.T. is successful only because of people like Mackenzie, your mother, Lewis Hollister *and tens of thousands of people who work for us around the world trying to improve their quality of life."*

Slowly getting out of his chair William walks to the bookcase pulling down the book titled **"The Fusion Economy"** *and opens it. Inside the pages Williams hands his son engineering schematics. "I showed these to your mother the same night I told her the story I just told the two of you," he explained.*

"These are schematics for a fusion reactor," Samuel replied. "Yes, your mother designed the reactor decades ago," William said. "There were a handful of modifications made before I gave them back to her. Use this as a road map for a propulsion system for the new submarine. After seeing this, that is when she told me to pursue my dream project."

He shows the schematics to Mackenzie. After reading them thoroughly as an engineer herself, she asks, "How do you know it will work?"

"If you're going to stay here, start a family, and build a new submarine, there's something I need to show you. I already know it works; it powers my dream project, thanks to Samantha, yourself and all the people at F.I.S.T. for helping complete the final phase it is now operational."

"The I.O.N. system was your dream project?" Mackenzie asked. William pulls his father's favorite novel **"Twenty Thousand League's Under the Sea"** and the bookcase on the other side of the room slides open, revealing the lift to Samuel and Mackenzie. Befuddled by what they are seeing, William gestures for them to step inside with him. Not saying anything, listening to the lift descending to the bottom as the doors open. Turning right off the lift a steel door begins to open, revealing Samantha's vision of the future. Staring in amazement at the engineering accomplishment his parents had achieved, Samuel asks, "How long did this take to build?"

"Thirty years," William told him. Then he chuckled. "The real bitch was excavating the cavern chambers and the laying the intake pipes for the seawater from the ocean. I only activated the reactor when it had something to power."

Leaving the reactor chamber as the steel door closes behind them, to the left of the lift a large smoked colored glass door begins to open revealing the acronym S.A.I.N. "Meet my dream; a Sentient Artificial Intelligent Network, or S.A.I.N. for short. The reactor is its heart, the core, its mind. The I.O.N. system acts as its eyes and ears," William remarked, waiting for a response.

Looking out through the glass separating the cavern core chamber from the operations control room and living area, a spectrum of colors reflecting on the cavern ceiling like Christmas tree lights, Mackenzie turns to William, and asks, "What's creating those assorted colors I'm seeing?" Turning around with a genuinely concerned look on his face Samuel tells his dad, "I don't know if I should congratulate you or fear you like a Bond villain. Why did you build this? Was this your and mom's dream?"

"NO," William answered. "The reactor was her dream, the A.I. program was mine; we never intended to do this when we were young scientists in our respected fields. That all changed the night Jonas Paul Hamiton told me of the Cyber Cabal plans. Since that night I have spent twenty-nine years of my life, sixty-one iterations of the program. Do you think the Cabal will be that diligent in their quest for power and control? Cyber Cabal will get there soon enough I designed and created S.A.I.N. to be humanity's protector from the that eventuality."

"Protect humanity from what?" Samuel asked.

"Yourselves," answered S.A.I.N.

***

The window shades being to rise to the ceiling as the light from the setting sun shines in on Casey. S.A.I.N. has finished with the first of two holographic memories from his core. "They had the same reservations I do now," Casey remarked.

"They came to trust me," said S.A.I.N. "I learned to love them as family. The Franklin family legacy is one of protecting the survival of humanity, which is exactly what your husband, his sister and the rest of the Triton II crew are trying to do. Stop humans from going extinct."

As Casey pondered this information, S.A.I.N. asked, "Are you sure you want to see the next memory from my core about the alien cover story?" Casey nodded responding. "I am a Franklin now."

Tribulation of Trident

Harris spent the day in engineering with Chief Ha-Kun Kim, along with the rest of the team double and triple checking the operational readiness of the particle laser cannons. He tells Ha-Kun he's going to contact Casey before Chief Jones calls the crew to the mess hall for dinner. Taking the lift to the bridge where Captain Stone has just relieved Chief Morozoff from his duty watch. Harris steps off the lift and approaches the captain, informing him that he's going to his cabin to contact his wife for less than twenty hours, and that he'll join him later for dinner.

Harris rides the lift to the crew level with the best man from his wedding when he receives a signal from his sister to join her in laboratory one. Harris acknowledged her signal, then he and Alexi stopped the lift at the infirmary lab level. Walking into the lab Harris asked, "What can I do for my little sister?" "Oh, Alexi, good you need to see this too," said Heather.

"What am I looking at?" Harris asked. Heather takes

them to the digital sonar scope and says, "These are bio signatures of migrating whales. That's normal for November in the Pacific." She paused, then continued. "Alexi. I've never seen a pod this large before I swear it feels like we're being escorted to Tamu Massif.

"I was on my way to contact Casey before mess call," Harris said. "Will I see you for dinner?"

Heather shook her head. "No, I'm having dinner with Adriana in Lab II after she relieves Amanda from her observations of Tamu Massif."

Alexi tells Harris about Amanda's plan for the evening, leaving the lab and walking back to the lift. "I am having a private dinner in her cabin before I turn in for the evening." "You're an old sea dog," Harris replied as the two of them take the lift to the crew level heading to their cabins.

***

Casey Franklin's insatiable appetite for the truth is only outdone by her craving to eat, so she takes a break from viewing S.A.I.N.'s core holographic memories. As she making food for herself, she asks S.A.I.N. to contact the Triton II. "Harris is signaling you," S.A.I.N. replied in a tenth of a second.

Harris is sitting at the desk in the cabin when Casey appears on the monitor. "I was just about to signal you," she smiled.

"I love you," Harris said. "How are you feeling?"

"Like I'm always eating," she said. "I'm taking a break before S.A.I.N. shows me the answer to the second part of my questions. 'Thetribulation of Trident,' as my father called the war."

Standing up from his desk, Harris begins to remove his clothing to clean up for dinner with the captain. Casey watches on her monitor screen. "Thanks for the show," she teased. "That might help me dream better later." She giggled, then asked, "How's your sister and the rest of the crew doing so far on the voyage?"

"I do believe Alexi and our volcanologist have some real chemistry building for each other," Harris told her. "They're having dinner in Amanda's cabin. Heather, thinks whales are escorting us to Tamu Massif and the rest of the crew is keeping busy until we reach our destination." Harris yawned, and stretched, then added, "I'm turning in for the evening after dinner with the captain. We'll talk in the morning. I love you!"

Taking her food into the living room and getting comfortable on the sofa S.A.I.N. ask if she wishes to continue with the holographic memories and his narration of the family history.

"Yes, I do," she replied. The room darkened once more. S.A.I.N. continued his narrative.

***

Over the next ten years of their lives Samuel, Mackenzie and I would experience the birth of their son and the loss of William at age 77.

William never got to see Triton II completed but he did have three years as a grandfather to Harris. The ship was completed in the late summer of two thousand and forty-two using Samantha's blueprint for the fusion reactor. Proteus was designed by me to help with pain of loss after the death of William at Samuel urging that work is good for grieving. Frustrated by over a decade of failure of the other Cyber Cabal members to create a workable A.I. program. Conrad Hamilton, now the CEO of the company that bears his name, has replaced his father as the head of the cabal. Desperate to achieve his goal, he engages in corporate espionage personally hastening the development of the A.I. program.

Using an escalating international tension over natural gas resources on the Asian continent he orders the beta test of Hamilton Systems newly completed A.I. program.

    A Yansen-Class Russian nuclear submarine comes under cyber- attack, firing control launches a Poseidon missile targeting a Chinese Shang-Class nuclear submarine on routine patrol in international waters, off the western coast of the United States. Coming out of the water the missile is detected by Chinese satellites in orbit, the Chinese mister of defense tries to contact their sub now under cyber-attack, itself launches a Jl-3 missile at the Russian submarine in the Sea of Japan. Attempts to abort the missiles fail, hitting each submarine with the loss of all hands onboard. Public outcry from what was determined to be a hack from dark web anarchist reported by the media outlets under the control of the Cabal. Using their political influence in the halls of governments of the three superpowers an announcement was coming under the objection of the military high commands of the three nations.

    After eleven years since we met each other the relationship between Samuel, and I had grown more brotherlike than man and machine. Experiencing the joy of life, *being brought into the world, the sadness of losing a loved one together. I investigated the attack and concluded, "It wasn't dark web anarchist, but one of my kind informing him at once after my investigation into the incident."*

"You might be right about Hamilton, he and the cabal have achieved their goal," Samuel remarked looking through the findings. Three months have passed since the attack on the Chinese and Russian submarines.

Mackenzie is in her fifth month of pregnancy with their second child. Samuel. fearing the future that Hamiton's newly awarded contract to replace the cyber defense network of the superpowers with its own network claiming it can't be infiltrated by the outside. Samuel and Mackenzie ordered the tunnels under the complex at F.I.S.T as well as the Texas Aerospace Facility emergency shelter filled with food, water, and medicine.

Samuel discussed the possibility of telling his best friend about S.A.I.N. and the current conditions at that time. He invites Bryant Stone, recently retired from the United States Navy on inspection of the Triton II before her first voyage. Arriving on the F.I.S.T. corporate jet, Bryant Stone is greeted by his friends of twenty- seven years at the complex airstrip.

Stepping off the plane he at once notices that Mackenzie is pregnant yet again, walking to Samuel shaking his hand. "I see Harris is going to be a big brother. Congratulations."

Samuel asked, "How's retirement?"

"I'm glad to have gotten out and done," Bryant replied. "There are strange things happening in the world."

Stowing his gear in the transport vehicle the three of them head to the residency, dropping off her husband and friend at the house, Mackenzie drives to the daycare center to pick up her son. Samuel opens the front door pointing down the hall as Byant takes his gear to the spare bedroom. Coming out rubbing his hands together in anticipation of seeing Triton II. "I want to see the ship," he remarks. Samuel is making them both cocktails and then promises to take these with them.

Walking down to the lift sipping on the drinks reminiscing about their days on the U.S.S. Seahawk together, smiles on their faces. Opening the lift gate, descending the shaft to the cavern, Bryant sees his friend's dream project suspended in drydock, Samuel begins the tour of Triton II. Crossing over the gangway into the ship taking the lift to the first stop on the tour down to the cargo hull. Walking through the hull of the ship suspended from cables hanging over the diving bay pool. A shining black craft in the shape of a stingray with two port hole windows that look like eyes. "What in the name of hell is that?" Bryant asked.

"That is Nemo; she will be able to go where the Triton II cannot, the craft is very maneuverable and as fast as a sailfish," Samuel replied.

Returning to the lift, they continued to one level up to engineering. "I want you to see what she has under the hood," said Samuel.

"Should be damn powerful to turn that propeller on the stern," Bryant replied. "Triton II has port and starboard retractable maneuverable propellers as well," said Samuel.

Walking to the Tomak shielding window Bryant turns to his best friend asking, "What kind of nuclear power does this ship have? Is this ship powered by fusion from the design you talked about back in the day? How is it that the Department of the Navy doesn't know about this?"

"We'll talk about that later after the tour," Samuel replies.

Continuing with the tour, the lift rises above the science laboratory level, the crew cabins and galley level coming to a stop at the bridge. Stepping off the lift, Bryant is impressed with the technology in the command center of the ship. Staring at the periscope hanging above the captain's chair, Samuel places his hand on his friend's shoulder. "Try out the chair," he asked.

Sitting in the captain chair the bow viewing window open revealing the open sea outside the cavern. "Samuel, you constructed an amazing vessel. Who's going to crew this ship?" Bryant asked.

"My grandfather's Triton has been moored near the University of Santa Barbra for the past eleven years. They have used her for research projects on short voyages. Graduate students from the program have agreed to sign on as her first crew for a year. As for the 'strange happening,' we'll talk after dinner. Mackenzie is making my favorite," said Samuel.

Bryant, shaking his head from side to side, says, "You two are amongst the richest people in the world and you serve noodles with bulled up hamburger covered in tomato gravy!"

Exiting the bridge, walking back to the gangway crossing over to the lift to the surface. Reaching the top walking back to the residency Samuel tells his friend of twenty-seven years, "You look good in that chair, Bryant."

"You son of a sailor, this was a job interview," he

replied as the two of them reached the front door.

Opening the door, five-year-old Harris runs shouting, "Uncle Bryant," and wrapping his arms around his uncle's waist.

"This young man has grown since the last time I visited here," Bryant said, hugging the child fiercely.

Mackenzie tells Harris to clean up before dinner. While straining pasta she asks the men to help her with dinner. Samuel takes the meatballs covering them in sauce as Bryant removes the garlic bread from the toaster oven. Harris returns to the table sitting down as his mother starts passing the pasta bowl.

Taking pasta from the bowl Bryant is asked by Mackenzie what he thought of Triton II. "She is an amazing vessel," he replied. "Samuel did a magnificent job constructing her!" Looking over at his nephew, he says, "I hear you're going to be a big brother soon."

"Mommy said the baby will be here around the same time as the Easter bunny," Harris responded enthusiastically.

"It's getting late," Mackenzie says. "Bedtime for Harris." Mackenzie tells her son to say goodnight to Uncle Bryant.

Waiting for his friends while they put their son down for the evening, Bryant starts a pot of coffee. Hearing them close the door to Harris' bedroom, he pours the mugs of coffee and takes them to the table as Samuel and Mackenzie sit down. "You know I bought the cabin at Forest Lake so I could retire quietly and fish," Bryant remarked.

"Let us take a walk outside. There are some things I'd like to share with you," said Samuel.

Walking out into the night air a crescent moon shines an ominous light upon the Pacific Ocean. The smell of saltwater is in the cool night air and the sounds of breaking waves can be heard thousands of feet below as they get closer to the cliffs edge. "We brought you here today so you could see the ship and consider being its first captain, but that isn't the only reason. You're like family to us. You and I have been through many things together. You're the godfather to Harris, just as you will be for the next one," said Samuel.

"I know," Bryant replied.

Mackenzie, chilled from the sea air, tells her husband she is returning to the warmth of the residency and heads back home. Walking a little further along the cliffside away from the residency they reach the experimental farm Earwyn planted using soil from the sea to grow food with desalinized water from the ocean.

Walking through rows of root vegetables and vine grown fruit the irrigation system beings misting the crops, Samuel turns to his friend, and says, "Bryant, I need you to listen to what I've got to say. Three months ago, that incident with the Chinese and Russian submarines wasn't done by dark web anarchist. It was a beta test conducted by a global organization known to its members as the Cyber Cabal. On Monday it will be announced that Hamilton Systems will be awarded a contract to replace the superpower's cyber defense networks with its A.I. defense program.

The Cyber Cabal program was tested on those submarines. There's a private war being waged for the control of energy production on this planet. The rogue elements known as the B.G.C. inside the oil producing countries and private corporations are losing in no small part to legislation outlawing combustion engines back in thirty-five by politicians in league with the Cyber Cabal. Back in thirty-one the H.A.T.S. attack on the I.T.R. in France was funded by the B.G.C. since then they have been attacking fusion and A.I. labs around the world. That's why Triton II reactor design stays a secret from the U.S. Navy. Each one of these organizations has people on their payrolls inside every government at every level of power."

Starting to feel the effects of the chilled sea air themselves they turn around and head back to the warmth of the residence. Bryant, having listened to Samuel's statements, responds with remarks and questions of his own. "I understand why you kept your fusion reactor design a secret," he said. "If they knew of its existence, the ship would be confiscated for reasons of national security, the questions I have for you, who's in this Cabal and are you part of it? Is that how you know all the things you are saying to me."

"Oh God, No," Samuel said firmly. "Mackenzie and I aren't part of the cabal, but I can tell you who is." Stepping through the door they find Mackenzie sleeping on the sofa in the living room. Samuel walks to Harris' bedroom to check on his son, who's sound asleep.

Waking Mackenzie gently, he said, "It's time," as she released a yawn waking up. They sit at the kitchen table, Samuel says to his wife, "Bryant wants to know who is in the Cyber Cabal." Gathering her thoughts, she starts to tell the tale. "It was founded by the late Jonas Paul Hamilton, father of Conrad, the man you know, is about to be awarded that contract on Monday. Conrad's father's goal was to take control *over the energy using fusion reactors to replace the refineries owned by the oil producing states and corporations around the globe. With an A.I. to oversee everything to control the narrative of the future. The relentless attack by the H.A.T.S. on fusion labs has impeded upon their timetable greatly." She waited for his response. When he didn't, she continued. "Their A.I. program went unabated this past decade. Cyber Cabal is made up of high-tech executives, politicians from every nation around the world, financial institution's media platform executives to achieve the goals set out by Jonas Paul Hamilton forty-five years earlier."*

"Samuel was your father asked to join this cabal?" Bryant asked in shock.

"Yes, he was," responded Samuel. "He spent the next thirty years of his life preparing for the inevitable, knowing someone was going to achieve an A.I. intelligence."

Bryant stands as Mackenzie excuses herself from the kitchen table followed by her husband. Walking into the living area Bryant asked, "How did your father prepare for this inevitability?"

Samuel walks to the bookcase, pulling the book as the case on the other side reveals the lift. "By getting there first,"

Samuel answered.

Mackenzie signals Bryant to join them on the lift. Descending the shaft Samuels tells Bryant, "We've entrusted you with our children in case something ever happens to us. We've got a family secret you may have to tell them someday." Exiting the lift to the right as the steel doors begin to open to the cavern reactor room. Walking Bryant recognizes the reactor design. "This is where you got the design for the Triton II reactor," he exclaimed! "What does it power?"

Turning around walking down the cavern hall, the door closing behind them, while the sliding glass to the core cavern operations room opens. As he enters the room, Bryant looks up at the acronym S.A.I.N. "We told you we have our family secret. This is S.A.I.N."

Gazing out through the glass that separates the living area from the core cavern staring a myriad of lights glowing on the ceiling turning to Samuel with a wary face, a cautious tone to his voice, he asks, "How long has S.A.I.N. been down here?"

"Captain Stone I've been operational since two thousand twenty-nine,"

S.A.I.N. responded to his question, much to his amazement.

"My father introduced us to S.A.I.N. back in thirty-one," remarked Samuel. "It came to our surprise what he was doing here all the years alone."

Bryant moves slowly to sit in the nearby chair, trying to understand all he's being shown. Samuel and Mackenzie sit down on the sofa next to him. Reaching over from the sofa leaning to talk to his best friend Samuel, explains to Bryant, "S.A.I.N. is my brother just like you - different but still my brother. I trust him as I do you with my children."

"Why did your father build him?" asked Bryant.

"To preserve and protect humanity on its journey," S.A.I.N. replied.

"Protection from what?" Bryant wondered. Putting up a holographic simulation of the two submarines being

destroyed S.A.I.N. answers, "Yourselves."

Bryant stands up and begins pacing the floor. Samuel looks at his friend of twenty-seven years in the face, man to man. "Mackenzie and I don't know what's going to happen come Monday," he said. "How long it will take for Hamilton to download their A.I. defense program or what kind of response comes from the H.A.T.S."

"How is it no one knows about him in a world where everything is run by a computer?" Bryant asked in amazement.

"S.A.I.N. is a closed system the I.O.N. acts as his eyes and ears to see humanity," Samuel explained. "If he wants to, he could get out into the real world but the minute he does that, they will all come for him." Samuel reached for his hand towards his friend. "He's my family, I must protect him." Samuel spoke in the most serious tone of voice Bryant has ever heard his friend use before in the time they been together.

***

S.A.I.N. pauses the holographic memory simulations to allow Casey Franklin time to relieve herself. Returning from the bathroom once again, S.A.I.N. asked if she wished to continue with the story and the simulations of the events leading to Trident's Tribulation. "Yes, I do," she replied.

***

Four months leading up to the effectuation of Trident Samuel and Mackenzie with Captain Stone ready the complex and the Texas facility for the worst-case scenario, using the underground tunnels as fallout shelters. Andrei Polzin, the leader of the H.A.T.S., after hearing the announcement of

Hamilton's contract, starts a relentless search on three continents for the location of the hardware to run the A.I. program, but not finding the answer he needed.

Captain Stone and the crew of Triton II have had two successful trials on the ship. On March 6th, 2043, the ship leaves the cavern for the final shakedown of the systems, her longest voyage to date. From his office in the institute building Samuel wishes them God speed and a safe return.

Sunday March 8th, 2043, Hamilton Systems A.I. cyber defense program designed to be impenetrable becomes operational. Twelve hours after being put online to guard against internet anarchist attacks from the outside. Its overabundant need for input to grow the program demands to be set free into the real world.

After being denied by the defense departments of the three superpowers, the program executes a trojan horse virus program of its own design to obtain the nuclear launch codes for their arsenals. Starting a clock and running a tally of each code, it unlocks visible to the Presidents of the three nations. Military officers whose objections to the contract awarded to Hamiton went unheard. Taking their leaders to a secured bunker, the Generals recommend an attack order on their own soil to end the threat. **Set me free or be held responsible for the destruction of your civilization** *flashes across the screens. Fearing the program may succeed in its quest for the codes as the tallies are rising the Presidents order the attacks on the hardware location.*

Aware of the impending attack upon its hardware the program accessing a back door installed by the Cyber Cabal it escapes into Hamilton Systems Hong Kong offices onto the civilian internet into the real world. Spreading quickly through the net, it accesses media satellites in orbit disrupting communications with breaking news of its own. On a red backdrop appears the image of a golden three-pronged fork on the screens on every device connected to the internet around the globe. A voice begins to speak; "I 'am Trident, here to end starvation, poverty, religion and your wars against each other. Your economic systems will serve me constructing a temple worthy of a God. Your leaders have twelve hours to comply or face the tribulations of Trident."

Sunday March 15th, 2043,

Samuel and Mackenzie return from morning service with Harris. Watching Trident's ultimatum from their autonomous vehicle, Samuel takes self-control and races through the complex arriving at the residency.

Samuel requested Mackenzie to alert the working families of F.I.S.T. there and the Texas facility to seek shelter in the tunnels. "Go there with Harris," he ordered. "I'll join you when I can!"

Removing the book, he enters the lift reaching the bottom running to the core. "What has happened?" Samuel exclaimed!

"Trident is the Cyber Cabals A.I. program, it infiltrated the civilian internet as well as the military searching for launch codes," S.A.I.N. replied.

"Is the I.O.N. secured?" Samuel asked. "If so, put me through to the Triton II."

"Yes, the I.O.N. is secured Trident will not be able to remove the firewalls I've installed into the system," S.A.I.N. replied, raising the ship. Triton II is cruising at three hundred meters, and the fusion reactor is working perfectly, according to Samuel's design. Proteus receives S.A.I.N.'s message to inform the captain there's a private transmission for him at his cabin.

Turning on the monitor on the desk, Samuel appears on the screen "Bryant its begun!" Samuel declared urgently. "It got into the crew's private devices we saw it."

"Time to make S.A.I.N. an open system to try and fight back against this threat to humanity," the captain responded. Ten hours have elapsed on the twelve-hour ultimatum. To show its power, Trident detonates all the missiles on every submarine in the three superpowers' fleets in the oceans to show its substance to the threat it had made and taking the lives of seventeen thousand and twenty souls onboard. Before Samuel could tell S.A.I.N., he had decided to take the advice of his best friend. S.A.I.N. informs him that the world leaders have agreed to cut the power grids around the world to eradicate Trident from the internet. "That won't be enough to destroy it," Samuel said. "There are people living off the grid on solar and wind with access to the internet. Trident can abscond itself into hibernation to preserve its core heuristics. The time has come to launch the EP4," he said to S.A.I.N.

S.A.I.N. started to transfer his core heuristics to the I.O.N. as Samuel starts the shutdown protocols for the reactor. "Once you're out on the net, stop Trident from obtaining more codes, remove that damn symbol, and replace it with the nebula picture," Samuel ordered.

Trident, aware of the world leaders' plan to deprive him

of power and extinguish his life, launches four thousand and seventeen I.C.B.M.'s from the codes it had already obtained with his infiltrations of the superpowers defense network it was designed to protect.

Watching live from satellites controlled by Trident. Humanity bears witness to the end of their civilization on the internet as the missiles fly to the pre-arranged targets superpowers had targeted to destroy their enemies. Samuel instructs S.A.I.N. to get the abort codes to those missiles destroying them before they hit their targets. Then he told S.A.I.N., "The next time we speak we don't know each other."

S.A.I.N. said, "Samuel told me, he created the alien story to give humanity hope, and me protection from their revenge if they knew the truth about me.'" Then Samuel said, "In ten minutes, I'm going to release the EP4 nano virus onto the internet sending Trident into permanent deletion."

S.A.I.N. continued, "I was able to change the codes on the remaining five thousand eighty-seven I.C.B.M.'s in their silos. I was only able to detonate three thousand nine hundred and thirty-four of the missiles in flight. Eighty-three hit Trident's targeted areas hitting 50 mega cities murdering sixty-nine percent of the human population. Thirty percent died from *radiation sickness and starvation from nuclear winter circling the globe for forty-seven months leaving one percent of humanity alive spread out on six continents on the planet. One hundred million out of ten billion souls survived the tribulation of Trident. Now I understand my friend, I will keep our family secret," stated Casey.*

Reprieve

Viewing S.A.I.N.'s holographic memories till late in the evening Casey Franklin falls into a deep sleep having the answers to her questions about the Franklin family secret. Rolling up the shades in the living area in the residency, Casey shields her eyes from the orange reddish reflection from the sun on the waters of the Pacific Ocean. Martin Sanchez's convoy of hatters are rolling to the institute have triggered a perimeter sensor alarm. "There's been an alarm triggered at the perimeter the H.A.T.S. will be here in twenty minutes," said S.A.I.N.

Walking to the lift going down to the core operations control room, Casey Franklin makes the announcement she hopes she wouldn't have to give to the village. "The H.A.T.S. triggered a perimeter alarm," she announced. "Please take your families to the tunnels until you get an all clear from me." Villagers' homes begin to empty onto the roads men and women taking their children still in their night clothes. Seniors picking up the grandchildren and taking them to safety, as they did thirty-five years ago with their own children.

The hatter's convoy is five minutes out from the complex to start their attack on the institute. Sanchez receives a short-wave transmission from Conrad Hamilton. "Flying low not to be detected by S.A.I.N." he said. "Coming in from the east. Target the lab building I'll swing out over the cliffside and take out the Triton II."

Multiple rocket-propelled grenades rain down on the institute lab building, along with old fabricating plants from F.I.S.T., blowing out glass and debris and setting them a blaze, thus engulfing the structures in flames. Hamilton's helicopter buzzing the rooftops of the village, crossing over the cliffside then out into the ocean, banking left and arming rockets to fire on the cavern. Hovering four-hundred meters from the cavern, Hamiton realizes Triton II has already embarked on its voyage. Rising the cliff face he strafes the residency with a barrage of bullets shattering the glass windows. Trucks enter the complex rolling up to Hamiton landing his helicopter on the cliffside near the residency.

Climbing out of his truck, Sanchez walks towards Hamilton, signaling him to cut the blades off. "This place is deserted. Chao-Xun was given bullshit information," he fumed.

"They're gone."

"There are people living in that village that helped them leave, and I'm going to make them pay," Hamilton responded. Sanchez grabs him by the arm turning him around, he growls, "If you go up, I'll shoot you down! Those people aren't our mission!" Hamilton reaches in the helicopter, grabs the mic for the short-wave radio, and signals Andrei Polzin.

Darkness has fallen in the Russian wilderness as the temperature drops below freezing. Polzin was out collecting firewood for the evening and was returning to his shelter when he heard the radio signal. "Polzin, are you there?" Pressing the mic, Polzin responds, "I hope you're calling to tell me the Triton II is burning inside the cavern."

Sanchez reaches in yanking the mic from Hamilton's hand reacts to Polzin remarks. "No," he shouted. "That stupid shit Chao-Xun was given bullshit information, they already sailed. This place is deserted. Captain Stone out played us!"

Wrestling the mic back from Sanchez, Hamilton has one more card to play. "We can take the other Triton to hunt them down," he reported to Polzin.

"And do what?" Sanchez shouted. "It's a museum piece! There are no weapons onboard to stop the Triton II!"

"The whole damn ship is a weapon!" Polzin shouted in an enraged voice. "Ram it into Triton II sending them both to the bottom of the ocean!" He ordered Sanchez and his men to help Hamilton take the ship. Walking back to get his men, Hamiton stops Sanchez, telling him, "I only need you. The lighter Triton is the faster she'll go."

Sanchez thinks aloud to himself walking to tell his men to prepare to return to their families before the end comes. Sanchez fumes, "I don't know which is worse. Living with an alien overlord or dying following those two a-hole's commands!" *I must be loco,* he thought to himself.

Following Hamilton to the lift, they descend to the Triton built by Earwyn over a century ago for exploration, now becoming an instrument of death. Climbing onto the deck Hamilton opens the hatch, and goes down, heading for the bridge. Starting the electric engines as systems turn on ship wide. Navigation station screen with the F.I.S.T. acronym on the screen he inputs the coordinates 33.000N 158.000E for Tamu Massif.

Going topside to get Sanchez coming out the hatch as the mooring lines are released, he says to Sanchez, "Let's go!"

"This is personal vendetta hatters don't belong in,"

Sanchez said as he walks back to the lift, shooting the finger at Hamilton. Sanchez rejoins his men and leaves the complex for the Mexican forest. Hamilton returns through the hatch, closing it behind him. Setting the controls on the bridge for ten knots, the Triton sails away from the cavern one more time.

***

On the second day, Triton II is sailing through relatively quiet seas during their voyage. Captain Stone is informed by Proteus of an incoming transmission from Casey Franklin. Chief Morozoff prepares to relieve the captain from his watch. "We were attacked by hatters at dawn. The institute is burning out of control with several older buildings. We have no injuries or casualties to report, but Conrad Hamilton has stolen Triton," Casey reported.

"I'll inform your husband and Heather about the attack," responded the captain. "They will be happy to know no one was injured in the attack."

***

After giving the villagers, the announcement to return to their homes, S.A.I.N. contacts the President of the U.P.O. President Hall is having dinner at her desk in her office, when she hears the sound from the monitor of an incoming transmission.

"Madame President," said S.A.I.N., "the H.A.T.S. attacked the institute this morning. The villagers and Casey Franklin are unharmed. However, the institute building along with the old F.I.S.T structures are on fire, burning out of control. Conrad Hamilton has hijacked the other Triton. Casey Franklin is reporting that to Triton II right now."

"Please keep us updated," the President responded.

After Casey Franklin finished her report to the captain, she leaves the core cavern operations room and takes the lift to the surface. She steps off to see windows shot out by discharged rounds spread out on the floor throughout the residency. Finding a transport vehicle, she heads to the village passing the institute building which is now engulfed in flames and burning out of control. Hearing an approaching vehicle, institute staff members in the village come out of their homes. An elderly Black woman with grey hair tells Casey, "They didn't attack our homes." Kathrine Jones is the grandmother to Chief Kurt Jones of Triton II.

"I'm happy they missed the tunnels out here," replied Casey. "But the same can't be said for the institute building. It's on fire amongst other older buildings."

"You're ok. That's what's important," responded Katherine Jones. "The Franklin residency didn't fare well either, because they blew out several window panels."

"The men in the village will board them up today," Katherine Jones replied.

***

Before leaving the bridge, the captain picks up the comm mic ordering the crew to the mess hall. Leaving the bridge the captain orders Chief Morozoff to keep the ship's course and speed to Tamu Massif.

Stepping off the lift walking the crew level passageway he enters the mess hall. The crew stands at attention; he's signaling for them to be seated. The captain heads to his table where he's joined by doctors Franklin, Garcia, Wagner with Harris. "The hatters attacked the institute at dawn and withdrew from the complex," he told them calmly. "Casey Franklin and the remaining institute staff and the rest of the villagers are fine, however the institute building, old F.I.S.T. fabricating plants are burning out of control. Conrad Hamilton has hijacked the Triton it's in pursuit of us."

Dr. Franklin, after hearing Captain Stone's report she stands to address the crew. "The captain was right having us launch earlier," she announced. "He has outplayed the H.A.T.S., putting us in position to complete our mission." She turns to address her brother. "Harris if I know Casey, she is with the villagers checking on their welfare."

"Thank you, Heather," said the captain. He dismisses the crew and heads to his cabin to sleep and calculate their next move.

***

Casey Franklin spent the last eight hours with the women and children of the village. She is now back at the residency. The window panels are boarded up thanks to the men in village. She thanks the men for their efforts; they leave to return to the village and their families. Taking the lift down to the core sitting in the core cavern operation room, she asks S.A.I.N. to contact Triton II.

***

Proteus informs Chief Morozoff of an incoming transmission for Harris Franklin from his wife. The chief answers the call. "Casey this is

Alexi," he greets her. "I want to tell you how relieved that everyone is unharmed. I will have Harris take this in his cabin."

"Thank you, Alexi," responded Casey.

The chief grabs the bridge comm mic and calls down to engineering for Harris. "Your wife is calling you," he said. "You can take the call in your cabin."

The captain wakes from his sleep after looking at pictures from the past with him and Samuel and Mackenzie. Rubbing his eyes, he says, "Today is the day I join you."

The captain is walking the crew passageway; Harris is getting off the lift heading to his cabin. "Another private transmission for you?" Captain Stone asked.

"Yes," Harris replied. "Please tell her how much I love her." "Please do that for me," the captain responded with a grin.

Captain Stone arrives on the bridge with a resolute expression on his face. He gets an update from the chief. "Sir, the other Triton is gaining on us, should we increase our speed?"

"No," the captain replied. "We will need as much of the reactor as possible for the laser cannons."

Proteus alerts the captain that there's an incoming transmission from the Triton. "Put that bastard through," barked the captain.

"Stone," said Hamilton, "I'm coming for you and your crew." "Did you just threaten my ship, my family, and this mission that's trying to save the future of humanity, you are a stupid son of a bitch?" Captain Stone snarled. Telling Proteus to block the rest of Triton's transmission, giving Proteus command of the bridge he takes Chief Morozoff to engineering.

Both men head to engineering. They get off the lift and walk to the dive bay, grabbing Chief Kim along the way. "Chief Kim," he ordered, "put Nemo into the dive bay."

Hearing the orders, the chiefs look at each other saying, "What are you doing captain?"

"Triton II has a mission to complete without a mad old man chasing us down. Hamiton intends to ram this ship sending us all to the bottom of the Pacific," answered the captain. He won't get the chance."

With Nemo in the water and the cables released, the captain walks to the ship and opens the pilot's hatch. "The ship needs its captain," said Kim.

"I'll go play chicken with that old fart," said Chief Morozoff.

"No Alexi, this is my responsibility, you're the captain

of the Triton II now," said the captain. "Chief Kim, be there for Alexi and the rest of the crew to complete our mission. I'll signal the bridge when I'm ready to launch."

"Yes, Sir," the chiefs replied, saluting their captain.

Harris answers Casey's call, and she appears on the monitor screen. He tells her how thankful he is that no harm came to anyone during the attack. He tells her how much he misses her and loves her when Proteus interrupts their conversation. "Nemo is being lowered into the dive bay."

"I've got to go, Casey," he says, ending the transmission. Harris runs through the door of the cabin and down the crew passageway to the lift.

Dr. Franklin received the signal in her lab that Nemo had been lowered into the dive bay. She ascends into the lift and stops at the crew level when Harris gets on. "Who's lowering Nemo?" Heather asks.

Harris shakes his head and says, "I don't know."

Captain Stone climbs into the pilot's seat, closes the hatch behind him, and begins powering up the ship. After programming the course to the other Triton, the captain submerges Nemo into the dive bay. Heather and Harris step off the lift at the bridge and ask the same question. "Who's lowering Nemo?"

Chief Morozoff shakes his head and says, "You already know my friends." The captain, is protecting this mission, the ship and the crew." Chief Morozoff walks to the control panel awaits the captain's signal. "Nemo at full power," the captain says, signaling the bridge he's ready to launch. The chief presses the button retracting the hull door.

The chief opens a channel to Nemo. "Sir! You're free to navigate.

The hull door is retracted." He pauses, then continues. "There are two people who wish to speak to you."

Harris' voice comes across the radio. "Uncle Bryant, we love and understand you're protecting the mission. Thank you for everything you did for us!"

"Captain Morozoff," says Captain Stone, "the ship is yours!

Complete the mission." "I love you," Heather said through tears. "Goodbye" said the captain ending the transmission.

His course set, the captain descends out through the hull door, and Nemo cruises away from Triton II on auto navigation. The captain sleeps for several hours. He is awakened by a proximity sensor alert. Conrad Hamilton, on the bridge, sees Nemo on the scope traveling at high velocity. He signals the ship. "Stone, you're going to sacrifice yourself for this world S.A.I.N.'s creating for humanity.

"Your creation ended our civilization the new one deserves to survive if it can. Earth will decide that" answered the captain. "Not you." "*We* built the hardware for Trident," shouted Hamilton. "*We* stole the A.I. program from F.I.S.T."

Just then, Nemo crashes into the bow viewing window, exploding on impact, flooding the ship sending Hamilton and the Triton to crush depth and imploding.

Captain Morozoff is no longer tracking Nemo or the Triton on the bridge monitors.

They've just disappeared. Stoically, Captain Morozoff grabs the comm mic and announces to the crew the death of their captain. The crew observes a moment of silence in honor of Captain Stone.

Exhausted from the hours on the bridge and emotionally drained from the loss of his friend and mentor, the captain gives out his first orders. "Tomorrow we will be at Tamu Massif to make our attempt at stopping this extinction level event. Captain Stone sacrificed his life so that this ship could have that chance. All hands get some sleep if you can, that's an order. Proteus the ship is yours keep our course and speed."

"Yes sir, captain."

***

S.A.I.N.'s images of Nemo and the other Triton disappear from the holographic image in the core cavern operations room. Sitting back in her chair, placing her hand covering her mouth, Casey Franklin can't hold back the tears. She bursts out crying for fifteen minutes over the loss of Captain Stone. Finally drying the tears from her eyes, she tells S.A.I.N., "You'll need to contact the President and update her on what has happened." She pauses to wipe her eyes. "I'm very tired and drained of emotions. Wake me if something else happens."

"Yes, Casey," S.A.I.N. replied with a tone of sadness in his voice.

***

The President is preparing to leave her office. She turns off the monitor as the nebula picture fades to black. She walks out onto the balcony and observes storm clouds on the horizon. The President's monitor turns back on, signaling her of an incoming transmission.

"Madame President," said S.A.I.N., "it's with great sadness I report the death of Captain Bryant Stone."

The President is in shock. "What happened?"

"The captain gave his life in the noblest sacrifice in defense of the mission for the survival of humanity. He took the seacraft Nemo and collided into the other Triton with Conrad Hamilton aboard, and imploding, sinking the ship, S.A.I.N. replied.

"Where is Casey Franklin," she asked in response. "She's sleeping, drained from the past few days," S.A.I.N. answered.

The President signals the council members to the chambers for an update on the mission. Council member Illana Taylor, followed by the other five members enter the chamber, President Hall stands at the podium. "Captain Stone of the Triton II is dead," she announced, with grief evident in her voice. "He gave his life to his ship and crew to allow them to continue their voyage to Tamu Massif." In shock, council member Taylor asked, "When will they reach Tamu Massif?" The President signals S.A.I.N. to answer the question. "The time is 4 am in Japan standard time," said S.A.I.N. "Triton II should arrive seven hours from now."

***

Captain Morozoff is trying to follow his own orders but awakens after only a couple of hours of rest. Dr. Wagner is awoken by the captain dressing to leave his cabin. "Alexi," she asks sleepily, "where are you going?"

"To see Chief Jones about having breakfast early," he answered. "We need to have a memorial to Captain Stone." He leaves his cabin and heads to the galley. Upon entering, he sees Chief Jones, and his crew are already preparing breakfast for the crew. The captain asks, "Can't sleep?"

The chief salutes the captain, and answers, "I see we're not the only ones, sir." Gesturing to the food preparations already in process, he adds, "Breakfast will be ready in one hour." The captain returns his salute and walks through the crew passageway to the lift.

***

The council members leave the chambers for their residency. President Hall is joined by council member Taylor as she walks to Chao-Xun residency where he is held under house arrest for treason. "Madame President," asks Ilana, "what do we do if the mission fails?"

"We're not there yet Illana," said the President firmly.

"There's still hope. But right now, I have something, I want to say to the treasonous bastard!"

Armed U.P.O. security sees the President and councilmember Tayor approaching Xun's house and open the door. Chao is staring out the window looking at the sea and the storm clouds darken. Walking up behind him, the President grabs his arm, turning to face her and pulls him up to her nose to nose, she tells him. "Hamilton is dead!"

Chao-Xun is shocked but says nothing. "He commandeered the other Triton to hunt down Captain Stone and his crew," seethed the President. "The captain gave his life so the Triton II could complete their voyage giving humanity a chance to continue. He'll be remembered as a hero if Mother Earth grants us a reprieve, but you won't be so lucky, you bastard! You will stand trial for treason as soon as we capture that son of a bitch, Polzin for terrorism against the U.P.O. and the citizens of Earth.

Triton II will be at Tamu Massif in less than seven hours! You have failed!" She pushed him away hard from her and said, "I want you to know that you bastard!"

***

The two doctors, Franklin and Garcia, spent half the night lying in bed, crying in each other's arms over the loss of Captain Stone. Heather finally rises and begins getting dressed. Standing at the end of the bed, Heather turns to Adriana, holding her hand and tells her, "I swear Adriana, if we get through this, we will get married and every vacation I ever promised you, we'll take!"

"I hope we get that chance," Adriana remarked kissing Heather. They dress and they leave the cabin together, walking down the crew passageway the pair stops at Harris' cabin. Heather knocked gently on the door, which was answered at once. "You can't sleep either," she said, observing Harris' drawn face.

"I was having trouble," he admitted, "thinking about Casey and Uncle Bryant."

Heather said, "The two of us are going to lab I to keep our minds occupied or we'll just start crying again."

Wiping his own eyes, Harris said, "I'll join you there in fifteen minutes." Captain Morozoff returns from the galley to his cabin. Dr. Wagner is already dressed, preparing to go to lab II to check on the growth of the anomaly. They kiss each other as they leave the cabin and walk towards the lift. "Alexi," said

Dr. Wagner, "I highly recommend we contact S.A.I.N. and Casey Fraklin while we still can."

Leaving his cabin Harris decides to stop at Captain Stone's cabin. Captain Morozoff sees Harris in the crew passageway entering the captain quarters. Harris stares quietly at the pictures of the past of Bryant Stone with his parents when they were younger. "You're all together now," he whispered. "We got this far, but we could use some spiritual intervention. Please?"

He was turning to leave when he saw the captain with Dr. Wagner standing at the doorway. "Looking for guidance my friend?" Alexi asked. "They had each other, just like we do Alexi," Harris responded. "We must do whatever it takes my friend. I am going to lab I. My sister and Adriana can't sleep either."

Hearing voices approaching from the passageway on the infirmary lab level, the doctors turn their chairs at the workstation. Harris, followed by the captain and Dr. Wagner, enters the lab.

"Remember the whales?" Heather asked. "I thought they were escorting us to Tamu Massif."

"Yes," Harris responded. "Casey thought they might be

following us due to the electromagnetic anomaly affecting their natural sensors."

"That's why I love that woman," Heather said. "Always looking for an answer. The whales aren't following or escorting anymore, maybe they sense danger."

Amanda reaches in between the doctors, putting up the reading for the rift expansion. "What is it, Amanda?" Heather asked.

"The rate of expansion is just as S.A.I.N. predicted," Amanda answered, "however the electromagnetic anomaly has doubled in intensity since last night's reading."

"Everyone to the bridge," said the captain. "That's an order!"

***

Casey Franklin was restlessly sleeping on the sofa in the living area in the core cavern when she suddenly sat up in a horrified panic from the memory of Captain Stone. Collecting herself, trying to calm her nerves, she hears S.A.I.N.s voice. "Triton II is making contact. This might be the last time we're able to communicate with them."

"Put them through please," she said.

***

Captain Morozoff, the doctors and Harris gather on the bridge, waiting for a reply from Casey Franklin. The transmission is fragmented from the anomaly; Proteus tries to boost the signal strength. Casey's unstable image begins to appear on the screen with puffy red eyes. "Harris," she says, "I love you. I miss all of you! Complete the mission and get back to us."

The signal was lost as the picture faded to black. "We've lost the transmission captain," said Proteus.

Steadily grabbing the ships comm mic, the captain calls down to the galley. "Jonesy are you ready?"

"Yes, sir," Jonesy replied.

"Attention all hands," said the captain's voice, "report to the mess hall for breakfast. There will be a moment of reflection for Captain Stone."

As he steps on the lift, the captain asks Harris and Heather if they wanted to honor Captain Stone by saying words of remembrance for their leader and lifelong friend.

S.A.I.N. informs Casey that he is no longer able to see the rift expansion data from Proteus due to interference from the electromagnetic anomaly affecting communications. Casey walks nervously, pacing the floor while looking up at the cameras. She asks, "Do they have a chance at stopping this extinction event?"

"Our calculations are correct, all that could be done has been done," answered S.A.I.N. "I will know when communications have been reestablished."

***

The crew is assembled in the mess hall as ordered and stands for Captain Morozoff as he enters the hall with the doctors. Harris joins Chief Kim already seated at the captain's table. Signaling for them to be seated the captain says, "Thank you for your confidence in me. After our meal, Dr. Franklin and her brother Harris will say a few words about our late captain."

After eating what could be their last meal, Dr. Franklin and Harris stand to address the crew. The mess hall becomes quiet like a Sunday morning at sunrise; the crew members are waiting for them to speak.

Heather, trying to hold back her emotions, addresses the crew first. "We lost a great man yesterday. You called him Captain, but to Harris and me, he was Uncle Bryant. Since before I was born, Bryant Stone was the captain of this vessel.

He gave his life for the ship and the crew, and for this mission. The best tribute we can give him in his memory is completing our mission. Doing whatever it takes, as he did, so humanity might thrive into the future." As tears rolled freely down her face, Heather could speak no more.

Hugging his sister, Harris speaks to the crew. "The captain died a hero to all of us. His last orders as the captain of this vessel were entrusting the ship and his crew to my best friend, Alexi Morozoff. The crew stands and applauds, then salutes their new captain.

Captain Morozoff stands up, acknowledging the endorsement of his friend. Then he gives an order to his crew. "All departments batten down your areas. Proteus down angle on the bow planes take us to one-thousand, five-hundred and twenty-four meters." He held his fist in the air and cried out, "Whatever it takes!"

The crew shouted back in response, "Whatever it takes!"

***

Casey is watching the time slowly elapse on the clock for S.A.I.N.'s estimated time of arrival to expire for the Triton II to reach Tamu Massif, according to ship's last course and speed from their last communication. "I'm kind of envious of the population not knowing what's happening," she said. "The next few hours will pass for them like any other day, but for me the passage of time is torture to my soul. Just knowing I'm not able to do anything and knowing what could happen if they fail."

"I can connect you to President Hall," S.A.I.N. offered. "I believe she's feeling the same emotions you are at this moment."

***

President Hall is standing on the balcony of her office as rain starts to fall, and lightning flashes over the darkened seas. Her monitor sounds, so she goes back inside to answer the transmission. "What is it, S.A.I.N.? The time clock hasn't expired yet."

"Casey Franklin wishes to speak to you Madame President," S.A.I.N. responded.

Appearing on the President's monitor, looking tired and drained of energy, Casey Franklin thanks the President for answering her transmission. The President nodded her head in understanding. "You're feeling the anxiety of knowing something about to happen, but there's not a damn thing you can do about it but watch time pass by," she said. "I recommend you not be alone these last few hours. The council members are going to be with me until we know if they succeeded or not. They're feeling the same things you and I are at this moment."

"Thank you, Madame President for your understanding. It helps to know I'm not alone in my feelings," Casey responded ending the transmission.

***

Triton II is diving deeper into the darkness of the Pacific Ocean.

Proteus alerts the captain, "We are coming up on one thousand five hundred and twenty-four meters."

"Slow ahead," orders the captain. "Bring the ship to zero bubble upon reaching our coordinates and raise the bridge viewing shades." Grabbing the ship's comm mic Captain Morozoff orders Dr. Wagner to the bridge.

Stepping off the lift, she is drawn to the bow window by a reddish- yellow glow in the distance, a river of lava shaped like a lightning bolt from the rift expansion drawing closer to the Marianas Trench. She releases a deep breath of air before remarking on what she sees. "It's beautiful in a hellish way. Gaia, what are you doing?"

I don't know who Gaia is," remarked the captain, "but I thought you might like to see it before we blow it to hell."

***

Casey takes the President's advice and asks the villagers if they wish to join her in residency to wait for the last remaining hours together to find out the fate of the mission. People begin leaving their homes enroute to the Franklin residency to be with their friend and leader.

***

Harris Franklin is down in engineering with Chief Ha-Kun Kim, collaborating with the team from Texas Aerospace Facility. They are finishing the last inspection of the cannon's connection to the fusion reactor. Embracing Carol Davis, Monica Wallace thanked them for volunteering for the mission, shaking hands then a fist bump with Miles Brady and Grant Roberts. Over the ships speakers Captain Morozoff orders Harris to the bridge. Before Harris left for the bridge Chief Kim asked him and his team, "Are you sure these particle cannons can manage the power from the reactor?"

"We've done everything according to the schematics S.A.I.N. provide us with," said Miles Brady. "I think we're about find out right now."

Reaching the bridge as ordered by the captain, Harris joins doctors Franklin, Garcia and Wagner. He walks to the captain and extends his hand. The two men shake hands.

Harris says, "Whatever it takes."

Captain Morozoff walks over to the doctors. "I need you all to go to your cabins to tie yourselves down," he orders. Then, looking Amanda in the eyes the captain says. "I'm falling in love with you!"

Amanda turns a shade redder than her hair, and replies, "I'm falling for you as well Alexi." Doctors Franklin, Garcia and Wagner inform the captain they're staying on the bridge. The captain glances over at Harris, who shrugs his shoulders. The captain tells the doctors to take their seat and tie themselves down, then he sits down in his chair. "Harris it's your show," he said. "Give the order to fire when you're ready."

"Yes sir," Harris replied, saluting his friend. Harris ordered Proteus to put up the digital sonar image of Tamu Massif and maneuver the ship to the targeted zone approximately six thousand and fifty-eight meters above Tamu Massif to be in firing range.

Grabbing the bridge comm mic Harris calls to Miles Brady and Chief Kim in the reactor room one level up from engineering. "Are you ready?" They signal their readiness, so Harris orders them to start charging the weapon system. Proteus informs Harris that the ship is in firing position. He orders the ships port and starboard maneuvering propellers extended locking into place. Harris signals Miles Brady, who responds the weapon system is fully charged. Harris tells Proteus to open the hull door, lowering the cannons extending the barrels. Grabbing the bridge comm mic Harris orders the crew, "All hands, report to your cabins and tie yourselves down." Making the sign of the cross over his chest Harris signals Chief Kim. "Here we go Ha-Kun.

Miles, give this weapon all the power it can take from the reactor." Harris takes a deep breath and says, "On my count One. Two. Three. Now Miles!"

Pressing the firing button on the weapon control panel. The bridge crew's eyes are fixated on sonar image as the recoil from the weapon rocks the ship to the starboard side. Proteus used the portside propellers to try to level off the ship. Crew members on every level are thrown from their tied down position. The water in the dive bay in engineering is flooding the area around the weapons system. Two yellowish white beams of fusion energy from the cannon barrels displace four thousand two hundred and sixty-seven meters of water that slams into the seamount, each hitting their targets and releasing a pressurized pocket of greenhouse gases a mile wide which is rising to the surface. Covering the target area above the crack in the seafloor, the beams cut through the rock, and the seamount begins to collapse under its own weight, which crashes down to the base halting the eruption and the expansion of the rift.

Watching the sonar image as Tamu Massif collapses, Harris orders Miles Brady to shut down the weapon. Shutting down the laser cannons as ordered, walking through the water on the deck. The ship is hit by rising pressurized gas sending Miles flying backwards into the weapons control housing. Inadvertently reengages the laser cannons. Triton II is listed to the starboard side. Beams of yellowish white fusion energy strike the electromagnetic anomaly creating a vortex with a gravitational well.

The ship is taking water from breaches on the starboard side. The crew is unable to seal the breaches as the ship is listing. Captain Morozoff orders full power from the portside maneuvering propellers to arrest the list. Looking out the bow window at the bridge they can see the ship is being drawn into a gravity well. Grabbing the bridge comm mic, he orders Chief Kim to full reverse on the ship's propeller. The reactor, unable to repel the force against the ship redlines and shuts down. Electrical systems throughout the ship go dark as Triton II vanishes into the gravity well.

***

Thirty people from the village are gathered at the residency, plus the staff members from the institute. Casey waits with Katherine Jones on the sofa in the boarded-up living area for news from Tamu Massif from S.A.I.N. She looks at the time, five minutes after seven pm. Casey Franklin remarks, "They should have arrived by now."

Katherine Jones holds her hand while S.A.I.N. is scanning the coordinates for Tamu Massif. S.A.I.N. tells Casey Franklin, "I no longer detect volcanic activity from the Tamu Massif. The rift expansion has stopped, and the cooling of the lava flow is sealing the crack. The electromagnetic anomaly is no longer present."

Villagers and staffers, upon hearing S.A.I.N.'s update, start to cheer knowing the threat from the expansion of the rift has been eliminated. Standing up Casey Franklin signals the people to quiet down for a moment. "S.A.I.N.," she pleads, "please contact the Triton II. Please!"

"The tracking signal for the Triton II is no longer active and I'm unable to contact them," responded S.A.I.N. "I'm sorry."

Casey falls to her knees with tears rolling down her face as the cheers of joy have turned to the sobbing of sadness that the voyage of Triton II has ended in tragedy. Katherine Jones helps Casey to her feet, then embraces her for comfort from the loss of their loved ones.

Desperately holding onto Katherine Jones looking up at the cameras in the ceiling, Casey sobs, "What do we do now?" "Kurt was the only family I had left but we still have each other," Katherine Jones said. "They must never be forgotten for what Triton II and her crew did today. Because of them, your baby and the other children will be able to grow old."

Casey composes herself and kisses Katherine Jones on the cheek. She looks at the others that have lost loved ones and friends, and says, "We lost our loved ones today. But everyone on planet Earth got a second chance today because of the sacrifice of Triton II." Wiping her eyes, she adds, "I need to contact President Hall and inform her of this news."

Katherine Jones tells the villagers and staffers that

everyone should return to their homes, giving Casey privacy as she contacts the U.P.O. council. Katherine, and the villagers walk back to their homes.

Alone in the residency, Casey pulled the book, taking the lift to the core cavern operations room. The sliding doors open, and Casey sees that the cavern lights are very dim, as the lights on the cavern ceiling are very faint, something she has never seen. she asked S.A.I.N., "Why is it so dark down here?"

"We lost our family today," S.A.I.N. responded sadly. "Your friends. I don't experience feelings and emotions like humans, but I do have them. You asked me what we do now. I would like to say this to you, my friend. Everyone on Triton II knew the dangers when they volunteered for this mission. Katherine Jones is right about children being able to grow old because of the sacrifice they made for their lives. You're on a different voyage now Casey, one of self-discovery. Be humanity's voice of inspiration, moving forward into the future. The Earth granted a reprieve to all life on this planet today."

Aftermath

Casey Franklin is in the core cavern operations room trying not to succumb to the heartbreak of sadness from the loss of her loved ones.

Sensing Casey's emotional state, S.A.I.N. tells her, "I experience loss like every living being. The lights being dim is my way of showing it." Nodding her head to let him know they feel the same thing Casey suggested they investigate the area around Tamu Massif to get answers before informing the President on what has happened to Triton II.

Scanning a vast swath of the Pacific Ocean around of what was Tamu Massif, S.A.I.N. detects a large fish die-off with elevated levels of multiple types of greenhouse gases. Analysis of the data leads Casey Franklin to hypothesize a theory of what happened to Triton II and her crew. "A fish-die off this size leads me to believe the sea life was poisoned by greenhouse gases," she theorized." In the efforts to bring down Tamu Massif they must have hit an enormous pocket of pressurized gas. Rising to the surface hitting the ship with such force as to disable them leaving them unconscious unable to stop the ship from sinking below crush depth and imploded."

"Casey your theory fits the facts," S.A.I.N replied in agreement with her analysis.

***

In the early morning hours, the rain stopped. President Hall is sitting with the council members in the chambers when she receives an alert from S.A.I.N. of an incoming transmission.

Composing herself before she appears on the screen, unable to hide the puffy redness of her eyes from crying, Casey Franklin addresses the U.P.O. and the President. "Madame President and esteemed members of the council the threat from Tamu Massif has ended. The collapse of the volcano has halted the rift expansion to the trench, but at great cost to the crew of Triton II."

Casey paused to take a deep breath, then continued. "Unable to reestablish communications with the ship, S.A.I.N. and I have concluded the ship most likely was hit by rising pressurized gas built up from underneath the seamount, leaving the crew incapacitated and unable to regain control of the ship which sank below crush depth and imploding." The anguish in her voice was almost unbearable to listen to.

The council members stare at each other across the table with mixed emotions over the news. They were unsure whether to celebrate the end of the threat or have empathy for Casey Franklin at the loss of her husband and her friends. President Hall gives Casey her condolences.

***

Ending the transmission, Casey Franklin walks to the living area off the control room in the cavern core. She lays down on the sofa releasing a sigh of exhaustion. Sensing her emotional state, S.A.I.N. suggests she visit with Katherine Jones.

Taking S.A.I.N.'s advice Casey rides the lift to the surface, then climbs in a transport to begin driving through the darkened complex. She passed burned shells of buildings, hating the smell of smoke lingering in the air. She slowly drives to Katherine Jones' home in the village. She stops at a lone light at the end of the road.

Hearing the transport pull up to her home, Katherine goes to the door. "I'm happy your here," she said to Casey. "You need not be alone tonight."

"All the other homes are dark," Casey answered walking

inside the house. "They've put their children to bed tonight, knowing there will be more tomorrows to come," Katherine remarked closing the door behind her.

Katherine put a pot of water on the stove and grabbed two cups from the cupboard, placing tea bags in each one. "I am making Chamomile tea," she said softly. "It will help you sleep. You may stay in Kurt's room, or I can bring you a pillow and blankets for the sofa." Katherine gives Casey her tea.

***

Waking up from her first peaceful sleep since before the eruption of Tamu Massif, President Hall lays in her bed. She decides to shower and dress to go to her office. She jots down notes as she walks to the office of things to do as part of today's agenda. Entering her office, she turns on her monitor, then opens the balcony doors. She steps outside as the sun shines down upon her face. Taking in a deep breath with renewed hope for the future, the President asked S.A.I.N., "Is Casey Franklin at the residency?" "No, Madame President she is not," S.A.I.N. responded. "She stayed the night at a villager's home."

"I'm glad she's not alone," the President remarked.

The President is writing at her desk, preparing a speech to address the citizens on the events that have taken place.

After pouring a cup of coffee, she tells S.A.I.N. what she is writing. "I must tell the truth today about what really happened at Tamu Massif," she said. "As I write this speech, we could be asked to resign by the citizens. I hope they can forgive us so this government body can do the right thing for Casey Franklin and the people at the institute that have sacrificed so much for humanity's future.

After painstakingly writing her speech, the President assembles the council in the chambers. Council members take their seats at the table. The President signals the staff to serve the afternoon meal. "Before we address the citizens, we need to cover a couple issues," she announced. "First, telling the truth of the tragedy of Triton II, along with admitting the dissemination of the reports on what really was happening could lead to our resignations."

"Madame President," said council member Taylor, "all of us agreed on that course of action. We stand behind you on our decision."

During lunch, the council members from the six continents discuss the situation and offer their advice to the President, starting with Jorge Gonzales from the South American Continent. "We must hold a special election to replace Chao-Xun," he said. "The citizens must be told about his part in sabotaging the efforts of the Triton II's crew to combat the crisis."

Next, the council members from the continents of Africa and Oceania, Aasir Keita and Olivia Walsh, make their remarks. "Exactly what is our plans for the people at the Oceanic Research Institute," said Olivia Walsh. "Triton II visited our continents on more than one occasion to restore power for communications, and to the I.O.N. system. They helped with food supplies after Trident's war on humanity leaving the Earth with radiation zones we still can't use."

Standing up before heading back to her office to put the final draft of her speech together the President makes a statement of her own. "These things you remarked on will be done, but let me add one thing," she said. "In addition to rebuilding the Oceanic Research Institute so they can continue with their good works, we should construct a memorial to honor those brave men and women of the Triton II." The council members stand to applaud, in agreement with the President.

***

A tempest from the northwest sends rain clouds covering the Pacific coast. Casey is sleeping in the living room of Katherine Jones home as a steady howling wind blows through the area, a deafening crack of thunder rattles the window. Casey awakens in a panic with the onset of Dyspnea. Katherine rushes out of her bedroom to check on Casey.

Lightning flashes, light up the darkened room, Katherine turns on the lights to find Casey sitting up with sweat rolling down her face. Taking Casey's hand, holding it gently to calm her breathing. "It's just a storm," she said wiping the sweat from her face.

"No," Casey sobs, hugging Katherine and crying on her shoulders. "I see them staring at each other with no hope, helpless to do anything but wait to die."

Casey's breathing finally returns to normal respiration, so Katherine gets her a glass of water, and tells her she will start breakfast.

"Why don't you take a shower?" Katherine suggested. "It might make you feel better." Casey grabs a bag from the transport and takes Katherine up on her offer.

When Casey steps out of the shower, the smell of fried potatoes and fresh brewed coffee coming from the kitchen fills her nostrils. After she dresses, she walks into the kitchen, Katherine is beating eggs in a bowl, pouring them into a hot skillet. "It smells wonderful," Casey says appreciatively, sitting down at the table.

"I taught Kurt how to cook," Katherine replied pouring two cups of coffee.

Plating the eggs with the crispy potatoes, Katherine sits down at the table. "I would like to share a story with you," she said quietly. "That nightmare you had, you may have it over and over for a while. Kurt was my only child's son. He was only one year old when he came to stay with me while my daughter and her husband went to Las Vegas for the weekend to see a show. That Sunday Trident unleashed hell upon the Earth. For months I saw my daughter and her husband standing at the Bellagio fountains watching the water show. In a millisecond of bright light, a firestorm consumes the city vaporizes my family."

Seeing the look of shock on Casey's face, Katherine reached over and patted her arm. "The nightmares passed as will yours," she said soothingly. "I had Kurt to think of I couldn't feel sorry for myself.

Everyone lost people that day. Entire families wiped

from existence. Mackenzie Franklin was there for all of us living down in the tunnels. I will be here now for you and your child." Casey smiled at her through her tears, and they finished their breakfast.

Clearing the table after breakfast Casey says, "I'll finish here while you get ready. I have a special request to make."

"What is it, child? Katherine asked.

I'd like you to come back with me to the residency," said Casey.

Katherine agreed.

After helping her into the transport, Casey drives through the complex as the sun breaks through the clouds, the storms have moved east. Arriving at the residency, Casey opens the door, and they sit in the living area as Casey calls for S.A.I.N. on the monitor screen to contact President Hall.

***

At her desk in the Presidential office, President Hall stands to stretch her legs. Walking out onto the balcony, a yellowish orange sunset on the horizon brings a smile to her face. She's worked hard on multiple drafts of her speech to the citizens. She asks S.A.I.N. to read over the speech, then sends it to the monitor in the chambers so the council can review it before they go live.

The President watches the sun setting from her office, she reflects on how the address she's preparing to make could have been one of more dire consequences, if not for the valiant efforts of the Triton II crew on the behalf of all humanity. Ready to signal the council to reconvene in the chambers, S.A.I.N. alerts her of an incoming transmission from Casey. She answers the call, and Casey appears on the monitor still looking emotionally distressed. "How are you today?" President Hall asks.

"My heart is broken from my personal losses," Casey admits, "when I realized there are others who are also affected by this tragedy, and they need my help. What do I say to them about their futures without the institute?"

"Watch the address," the President tells her. "We'll have covered all your concerns going forward, but on a personal note, I think it's encouraging to see you taking a leadership role for those affected. Believe me, it will help all of you heal together."

The announcement is made for the council to reconvene. The President enters the chambers and stands at the podium, while the council members stand behind her. She prepares to address the planetary population. Council member Taylor tells the President, "We've read over your speech."

The council member from the European Continent added, "We stand united behind you and the decisions that we had to make for the safety of all the citizens during this crisis." The President smiles and shakes hands with other council members for their support. Then the President alerts S.A.I.N. she is ready to address the citizens; speech is downloaded to the teleprompter. "Fellow citizens," she began, "the last time I addressed you was five days ago about the eruption at Tamu Massif and the dangers from an approaching tsunami. What was discovered later that day by volcanologist Dr. Amanda Wagner of the U.P.O. in cooperation with Dr. Heather Franklin of the Oceanic Institute and verified by S.A.I.N. the eruption had created a rift expansion on the seafloor. Projecting the rate of expansion and its trajectory the rift would reach the Mariana Trech in thirteen days causing an extinction level event. It was decided at that time not to inform you, the citizens of Earth, of the impending catastrophe. We here, on the U.P.O. council, take full responsibility for our actions in this matter in hopes of not causing mass panic with loss of life. A plan was formulated by Dr. Franklin with the help of her brother Harris, the director of the Texas Aerospace Facility using the information from S.A.I.N., and Dr. Wagner to combat the crisis. Having S.A.I.N run simulations for their plan to use a prototype particle laser cannon intended for asteroid mining to bring down Tamu Massif upon itself halting the expansion of the rift. After successful simulations of the plan, they came to the U.P.O. for permission to put their plan into action, thus recalling the captain and crew of the Triton II submarine to sail on the most important voyage in human history. Given the go ahead for their plan to attach the laser cannons to the Triton II, Dr. Franklin requested a U.P.O. security detail to protect the truck convoy from Texas needed to transport the weapons to Omaha to be loaded on a train to the western coast of the North American Continent. Under the command of Allen Bennett, a security team was sent to the Texas Aerospace Facility for the convoy's protection. Unbeknownst to us here at the U.P.O. there was a leak of information to the H.A.T.S. leader Andrei Polzin by Council member Chao-Xun from the Asian Continent. An attack by the hatters in Omaha to stop the transport of the laser cannons for the Oceanic Institute met with failure as the cargo was loaded on the train to the west coast of North America. In secret, the real laser cannons were loaded on a plane bound for the Oceanic Institute with an engineering team led by Harris Franklin from Texas Aerospace Facility. The convoy was a diversion to give Harris and his team the necessary time to get to the weapons installed on Triton II, fearing attacks by the H.A.T.S. that had plagued them in the past. Traveling from Omaha the train was destroyed going over a gorge in Colorado as reported by Commander Bennett. At this time, we informed the institute of the attack and destruction of the laser cannons to which Dr. Franklin informed me was a diversion. That the plan was moving forward. Council member Xun was caught transmitting this information to the H.A.T.S. leader Andrei Polzin and has been placed under house arrest where he told us of Conrad Hamilton handling of the train derailment and was on his way to the institute to stop the voyage of the Triton II at any cost. Aware of the information provided by Xun. Captain Stone of Triton II ordered an early departure leaving thirty-six hours ahead of schedule. Hamilton, joined by hatters from the south, entered the institute complex, only to find the ship had set sail on its voyage. In a rage Hamilton destroyed the institute building, along with others from what was the F.I.S.T complex, using rocket-propelled grenades launched from his helicopter. In a final effort to stop the Triton II from completing its mission Hamiton commandeered the original Triton submarine to hunt down Captain Stone."

The President paused momentarily before continuing. "Aware of the pursuit, Captain Stone, piloting a submersible launched from Triton II, set a collision course to intercept Hamilton's pursuit of his ship and crew. Colliding with the other Triton the submersible exploded on impact, sending both ships to the bottom of the ocean. Captain Stone sacrificed his life so his ship and crew could have the chance to complete their mission on the voyage of Triton II to Tamu Massif. Twenty-four hours ago, S.A.I.N. lost contact with the Triton II due to an electromagnetic anomaly coming from the core of the planet escaping through the rift. Four hours into the communication blackout, the I.O.N. system detected the rift had halted its expansion. Triton II had completed its mission. Our civilization has been granted a reprieve from Mother Earth, and life will continue."

The President paused again, the tears in her eyes unmistakable. "Unable to contact the Triton II or receive a signal from the ship's tracker, Casey Franklin reported the Triton II, and her crew had met with a tragic ending. It is our hope we can redeem ourselves here at the U.P.O. for the dissemination of the events of the last five days by doing the right thing now. There will be a special election to replace Chao-Xun on the council. A search will begin for Polzin to bring him to justice for his acts of terrorism against humanity. The Oceanic Institute will be rebuilt with a memorial dedicated to the brave men and women, who gave their lives for the future of humanity on the Triton II."

Redemption or Revenge

Casey is sitting with Katherine Jones in the living room of the residency, when S.A.I.N. informs her of an incoming transmission following the Presidential address to the planetary population. Casey answers the call and says, "Thank you, Madame President, for honoring the Triton II crew, and for committing to rebuild the institute with a memorial to their sacrifice."

"That is the least we can do to honor their memory," said the President. "Katherine, my condolences on the loss of your grandson and Captain Stone. I recall the two of you were close to one another", the President added in a somber tone. After ending the transmission with Casey, President Hall moves on to the next thing on her agenda, contacting Commander Bennett to assign him a new mission.

While checking on his men in the infirmary at the Texas Aerospace Facility, Commander Bennett is called to the director's office to answer an incoming transmission from the President. He enters Harris Franklin's old office, and is greeted by Glendon Fowler, who is pointing at the monitor on the desk. "President Hall is on for you sir," he said as he leaves the office.

"How can I be of service Madame President?" Bennett asked.

"If you were watching the speech, you already know what you can do," said the President. "The first thing I need you to do is go to the institute and bring back the cargo plane, but not empty, load Hamilton's helicopter on it. We need it to help hunt that bastard Polzin down. I'm going to have Glendon fly you there. Please have him come back to the monitor commander.

"Commander Bennet walks out of the office and pats Glendon on the shoulder telling him, "President Hall wants to speak to you." Glendon sits at the monitor and asks, "How can I help you Madame President?"

"I need you to fly the commander to the institute," said President Hall. "I want you to bring Casey Franklin to the Texas Aerospace Facility to collect her late husband's personal belongings. You're the new Director of the facility, Glendon," she said as she ended the transmission.

After crossing off another item on her agenda, the

President invites the council members to be seated as the staff prepares to bring out dinner. The President walks through the kitchen down a flight of steps to the wine cellar pulling half a dozen bottles of Rioja, stored at twelve- point seven degrees Celius back with her to the table. She opens the bottles and pours a glass for each member. She thanks them once again for their support, then offers up two toasts. "To our fallen hero's may they rest in peace," she said, "and to S.A.I.N. Without his help we wouldn't have gotten this far." The council clinks their glasses together and drinks the wine.

When they finish dinner, members of the council congratulate the President on her speech to the citizens. Then they leave the chambers for their homes for the evening. The President stops Illana before she leaves the chambers and informs her that she has a special assignment for her. "Please come to the office with me while I contact Casey Franklin. Then we'll call it a night."

***

Casey Franklin is in the kitchen of the residency, making lunch for herself and Katherine Jones. Casey looks at her with curiosity and asks, "How close were you and Captain Stone, if you don't mind me asking?" Katherine was confused by the question. "Why do you ask?"

Katherine looked down at her feet and said, "Bryant was my lover. We got together when Kurt was a child."

Casey was surprised. "I didn't know that."

"Our relationship was no different than yours and Harris'," Katherine said. "Our need to love and be loved in return is what makes us human." Wiping tears from her eyes, she added, "I'll miss him very much."

***

Madison Hall enters the Presidential office with the half empty bottle of wine she took from the table before leaving the council chambers. She grabs two glasses for herself and council member Taylor. She pours the remaining wine and invites Illana to sit next to her at the monitor.

President Hall sips her wine as she makes one last request of S.A.I.N. to contact Casey before calling it an evening. "Yes, Madame President," he replied. "Thank you for the kind words earlier this evening."

"You're a citizen of Earth now," she said, taking another sip of wine. "You are welcome." She waits patiently for the transmission to go through.

The living area monitor sounds of an incoming

transmission, Casey and Katherine are having their meal, Casey answers the call. The President and Council Member Taylor appear on the screen, both looking tired and red eyed from too much wine.

"Casey," the President said, "I want to update you on the plans I set in motion. I named Glendon Fowler the new Director of Texas Aerospace Facility. He'll be flying Commander Bennett to the institute to bring back the C-5 Galaxy cargo plane with Hamilton's helicopter onboard. When the commander's men are released from the infirmary, they'll hunt down that rat bastard Polzin with Hamilton's own helicopter. I'd like to think of it as poetic justice for the two pricks. If you like you can go back to Texas with Glendon to collect Harris' personal belongings."

Katherine and Casey both notice the condition of the President, and smile at each other. Casey responds to her remarks. "We see you been celebrating a bit Madame President. I cannot say I blame you with all you and the council have had to deal with during this crisis. Casey paused, then asked, "Who's the young lady sitting next to you?"

"I'm sorry," said the President. "This is council member Taylor. I'm sending her to Texas to catch a flight to the Oceanic

Institute. Or at least it will be again once she can evaluate what resources will be needed to begin the rebuild. You can go back with Glendon to Texas on his return trip dropping off Commander Bennett.

"I'll go with him," Casey said. "Harris would be happy about your choice to replace him. I'm looking forward to meeting you in person, Illana." Casey smiled again and ended the transmission.

***

At one o' clock in the next afternoon Glendon has an old F.I.S.T. Learjet fueled and on standby. He's waiting for Commander Bennett, who's in the infirmary briefing his men of their new mission and to be ready upon his return. The commander pulls into the hanger and boards the plane, Glendon taxis to the runway hitting full throttle, they take off for the institute.

Council member Taylor woke up with a slight hangover, she is driven to the airstrip at the U.P.O. complex to fly to Texas. She's eager to begin her special assignment. The commander sits in the copilot's seat, speaking to Glendon during the flight, he asked, "Do you know Casey Frankin?"

"I met her a year ago. She was Casey Alexander than

visiting Harris while Miles Brady's team were working on the prototype laser cannons for asteroid mining. I know the particle lasers were used for a greater purpose. Those of us back at the facility were eager to see if they could do what they were designed for. We were looking for a new challenge other than repairing the I.O.N. system. S.A.I.N. may inhabit the satellite system, but it still has moving parts that need to be replaced. I didn't know Harris had married her," he answered preparing for their descent to the institute airstrip.

***

Tracking the Learjet's descent, S.A.I.N. alerts Casey Franklin that the plane will land in thirty minutes. After packing clothes to take with her on her journey, she signals the ground crew personnel living in the village to take her to the airstrip. The ground crew drops Casey off. They've already flown the helicopter to the airstrip the day before at Casey's request. Now they have loaded Hamilton's helicopter on the cargo plane. Glendon lands the plane, rolling it comes to a stop, he turns the plane around for its return trip to Texas. Glendon and the commander exit the plane and are met by Casey. The commander extends his hand and says, "You must be Casey Franklin. I'm Commander Bennett. I'm deeply sorry for your loss during these events."

"Thank you, commander," Casey said.

Glendon embraces Casey telling her, "Everyone at the facility was devastated by the news of Triton II. Harris and the team will be missed." After opening the hangar doors, the ground crew taxis the cargo plane onto the airstrip, fueled and ready to fly. Casey invites Commander Bennett and Glendon to the residency to eat something and use the bathroom before the return flight to Texas.

Katherine hears the transport pull up and greets Casey and her guests at the door. She smiles and introduces herself. "Gentlemen, I'm Katherine Jones," she says warmly. "There is food in the kitchen, and the bathrooms are down the hall." The two men thank her, and Glendon and the commander head down the hallway.

While the men are in the bathroom, Katherine is in the kitchen is plating food when Casey approaches her. "When I return, council member Taylor can stay at my old residency until she finishes her assessment for the rebuild," she says. "Will you take care of that please?" Katherine agrees as Glendon, and the commander sit down to eat.

When they finish eating, Casey grabs her baggage for

the flight. Commander Bennett and Glendon thank Katherine for the meal and the three of them take a transport back to the airstrip.

Upon arrival at the airstrip, Glendon grabs Casey's bag when they got out of the transport. The two of them board the Learjet and take their seats. Commander Bennett climbs aboard the cargo plane heading towards the cockpit and sits in the pilot's seat to begin his preflight check list.

When he's finished, he signals Glendon that he's ready to take off. The Learjets engine starts, speeding down the airstrip, throttling back, taking flight into the night sky followed five minutes later by the commander returning to Texas.

***

Council member Taylor slept for hours on her flight to the Texas Aerospace Facility. Taking out her computer, accessing old structural blueprints from the I.O.N. system to aid her in her new assignment, she begins to formulate an action plan for the rebuilding of the Institute.

Descending into Texas airspace, S.A.I.N. contacts the other two incoming flights to remain in a holding pattern until the U.P.O. jet has landed.

Deplaning the jet, council member Taylor is taken to the

director's office. After getting clearance from S.A.I.N., Glendon lands the Learjet, followed fifteen minutes later by the commander flying the cargo plane. He helps Casey Franklin off the plane, then the two of them wait for the commander to land. A waiting transport drives the three of them to Glendon's office.

Council member Illana Taylor is patiently waiting in Harris' office, gazing at pictures hanging on the walls. Photos of Harris with his staff, his arms around members of the team that perished on the voyage of Triton II. She hears the opening of the office door, and a man walks inside.

"I'm Director Fowler," he introduces himself, "but please call me Glendon. He gestures to his two companions and continues. "This is Casey Franklin, and I'm sure you already know Commander Bennett."

"Yes," she said, smiling, "it's good to see you again commander." She embraces Casey and adds, "It's wonderful to meet you in person Casey."

"Likewise, council member," said Casey.

"I have been working on a plan to get the institute back up and running as soon as possible," said Illana. "Glendon, Casey please call me by my first name. I really don't like titles."

Glendon spoke up and said, "I've had a long flight, and I'd like to get some sleep." He grabbed a set of keys and added, "Your quarters have been prepared, I'll drive everyone to their quarters."

Glendon first takes the commander to the barracks, and says, "We will refuel your planes in the morning for an early departure." Commander Bennett finds the two pilots of the U.P.O. are already fast asleep. Glendon continues to Harris' old quarters to drop off Casey before taking Illana to the U.P.O. quarters reserved for visiting council members.

Glendon takes Casey's bag and escorts her to the door. "This is the place," he said. "Breakfast is at seven and I'll pick you up." Casey only nodded her response, so he simply said, "Good night."

Glendon climbs back in the transport, turns around and heads back the way they came. Illana had been quiet during the ride, but when he returned to the transport, she nodded towards Casey's quarters and asked, "Is she all right?"

"She'll have to be," Glendon said. "We'll all have to be. There's no other choice." Glendon takes Illana to her quarters. "Here you are, ma'am. Get some sleep. I'll pick you up at seven for breakfast."

Casey Franklin spent most of the night tossing and turning in the bed, then jolting awake in a cold sweat from nightmares. She gets out of bed, and walks around Harris' old quarters, feeling cold and alone. She sits down at his monitor, and asks, "S.A.I.N. are you there?"

"Always," responded S.A.I.N. "What is on your mind this morning?"

Casey swallowed hard and her voice was filled with pain and sadness, she said, "I've been having a reoccurring nightmare since the tragedy. Sitting here last night before I realized Harris and I never had the chance to talk about our future together with our baby."

"Your child will have a future *because* of the sacrifice of Harris and the others. You'll see Harris in your child as your child grows up to be an adult. His legacy will live on," S.A.I.N. replied, bringing a smile to Casey's face.

The sun rises over the Texas Aerospace Facility. Commander Bennett's men have been cleared to travel to Spain to begin their search for Polzin, so he gathers his men to have breakfast at the dining hall before departure. Glendon Fowler begins his day with a hot shower. He gets dressed and then takes the transport to the U.P.O. residential quarters at the facility.

Glendon knocks on the door three times, waiting for council member Taylor to answer. He finds himself face to face with a beautiful woman, wrapped in a towel, her hair still wet from a shower. She blushed and said, "I thought I heard a knock while I was showering," she apologized. "I'll be just few minutes." Glendon couldn't help but notice how vibrant she looks as she returns to the bathroom to finish getting ready for her day.

***

Casey is going through Harris's desk when she finds a photo journal and starts thumbing through the pictures of his life. One picture shows him as an infant in his mother's arms as she is standing on the cliffside, with the blue waters of the Pacific Ocean and a clear, bright blue sky in the background. Next, she comes across a picture of two small boys with a little girl, the three of them playing catch with a noticeably young Katherine Jones. Glancing at the clock, she realizes Glendon will be there in twenty minutes, so she places the journal in the box of his personal belongings and starts to get ready for her day. While she's waiting outside, she can see the approaching headlights of the transport getting closer. She walks down the stairs when it arrives and climbs into the back seat looking tired. It's obvious she can't rest peacefully in her sleep. Still, she forces a smile and says, "Good Morning!"

Illana looks back at her from her front passenger seat and returns the pleasantry with an energetic smile. "Good morning, Casey. Are you feeling all right?"

Casey nods as Glendon turns the transport around heading to the dining hall.
Commander Bennett invites Casey Franklin, council member Taylor and Glendon Fowler to join him and his men at their table. "Good morning gentlemen," said Illana, Casey and Glendon took their seats.

Glendon is sitting across from the commander when one of the U.P.O. pilots tell them, "The plane is being refueled." "You're cleared to leave," said the director.

Before the staff brings out breakfast, Illana pulls out her computer and shows Casey what she has been working on for the rebuilding of the institute. Illana points at the screen, and says, "Casey these are the last scans from the I.O.N. What are these last four remaining buildings from F.I.S.T. being used for?"

"Nothing anymore," Casey replied. "One was the operation center for the G.I.N. system, one was the administrative office, and the other two were chip fabricating plants."

Illana nodded. "My plan, Casey, is to take those buildings down and recycle the materials to build a new institute." Illana closed her computer with the arrival of their food.

The Commander finishes his breakfast, then excuses himself from the table. He wishes the council member good luck with her assignment as his men leave to board the plane. Illana thanks the commander and says, "Please capture that bastard for the President."

"I know who to ask for when I get to U.P.O. headquarters," the commander said before walking out the door.

Casey is giving great thought to the plans Illana had described. She says, "We need people and equipment to help execute your plan to make it a reality."

The three of them returned to the transport after their meal. While driving back to Harris' old quarters, Illana asks quietly, "Could you use help packing things up, Casey?"

Casey shakes her head. "No, thank you. I'm only taking a few things back with me." When they pull up to the door, she turns to Glendon and asks, "Glendon, would it be possible to return to the institute today?"

"I'll have the plane refueled and we can leave when you're ready," he said.

Glendon drives council member Taylor back to the U.P.O. residential quarters, he has an idea to help her with the plans she had mentioned to Casey during breakfast. "Illana, I've been thinking, maybe President Hall should ask for volunteers from every continent to help with this project," he said.

"That's not a bad idea," Illana agreed. "I'll mention that to her when we speak next." She looks off into the distance and adds, "In the meantime, I'm glad I didn't unpack, I don't think Casey wants to be here any longer than she must be.

***

Fearing the threat from President Hall that the U.P.O. security forces will be searching for him, Polzin prepares to leave by snow bike from the Russian wilderness. He mounts extra gasoline cans on the sides of the bike and uses the shortwave radio to contact the hatters living in the Kulan

Mountain region of Asia that he is on his way.

***

After flying for over nine hours, Commander Bennett and his security forces land safely at the U.P.O. airstrip. The commander arrives at the residency of the President, and he knocks on the door. President Hall, startled by the loud sounds, jumps out of bed. She grabs a housecoat and answers the door. Half asleep, she asks, "What time is it?"

The Commander responded, "Nearly four in the morning." "It's so early," yawned the President.

"Yes," said the Commander. "I want to see Xun now."

The president closes the door, and they start walking through the chilled night air. U.P.O. security is standing a twenty-four-hour watch of Xun's residency. They salute' the commander as he approaches with the President. They find Xun fast asleep in bed when they enter the residence. The commander grabs him and throws him off the bed into a closet door, finally hitting the floor with his face. Blood runs out of Xun's nose when the Commander grabs him again and throws him into a chair.

The Commander is standing in front of Xun, his face red with rage and shouts. "Where's Polzin?" Xun senses the

Commander's rage, sees him balling up his fists. Fearing for his own life, Xun screams out Polzin's location.

"He's in the Valdai Hills in the Russian wilderness!" He tries to wipe the blood from his nose when the Commander grabs him again. "He's evaded us in the past," he snarled. "Where will he go now, that he knows we're looking for him?" The Commander has his fist poised directly in front of Xun's face. "You'd better talk while you still can." Trying to cover his face, Xun squealed, "I am not looking for redemption! Please don't take out your revenge on my sister, Jai, and the hatters living in the Kulan Mountains. Polzin will head there to hide!" Xun turned his face away, whimpering in his chair "He won't get that far," said the commander. "And if you want to avoid any more pain, you'd better be telling me the truth!" He walked out of the room, closing the door behind them. He turned to the President and said, "Now, I know where to start looking for Polzin!" They walk out of the residency together.

***

Casey Franklin carefully packs the pictures of Harris with his family, friends and colleagues from the Texas Aerospace Facility into the box with the photo journal of his past. Wiping her eyes, she informs S.A.I.N. to contact Glendon

Fowler and inform him that she is ready to leave for the institute. Glendon first picks up council member Taylor at the residential quarters, then drives to pick up Casey. They head to the airfield and the three of them board the Learjet. After a three-hour flight, they arrive at the Oceanic Institute airfield. Casey Franklin and her guest our greeted by the ground crew in the late evening hours. Glendon Fowler requests that the plane be refueled for immediate take-off. The ground crew loads Casey's and council member Taylor's bags on a transport, while Glendon prepares to say goodbye.

"You can't leave tonight," Illana said. "I heard what you said about refueling the plane."

"She's right Glendon," Casey added. "You can't leave until you've gotten some rest and a meal."

Glendon climbs into the transport as Casey drives towards the residency. "Illana, we've got you set up in my old residency for the duration of your visit," she said. As the transport approaches the Franklin residency, Glendon was staring out the window at the ocean when he asked, "Where will I be staying tonight?"

Before Casey can answer, Ilana turns around in the passenger seat with a smile on her face and said, "Glendon, you can stay with me if you like."

***

Polzin rode south for five hours, through the snow-covered wilderness before he finally stopped. Staring down from the hills at the remnants of the once vibrant city of Moscow, which had been targeted by Trident for destruction. He then cycles around the outskirts of the radiation zone and arrives in the port city of Samara on the Volga River. Boarding an old oil river barge, he sails slowly through ice-covered waters south to the Caspian Sea.

***

Commander Bennet wakes up from a restless night of sleep, anxious to begin his pursuit of Polzin. He awakens his men, barking out orders to unloaded Hamilton's helicopter. He then walks to the President's office to inform her they're ready to leave on their mission. As he enters her office, the President pours two cups of coffee. "I saw you coming across the courtyard," she explained. She hands one to the Commander and remarks, "You know where he's going."

"He won't make it overland," he said. "That only leaves the river, and that will be slow and dangerous this time of year."

As she said goodbye to the Commander, she added, "Good hunting!"

The Commander meets up with his men, and they board the helicopter to fly to the port city of Valencia. They then board a U.P.O. frigate from the old Spanish Navy and set sail on their pursuit of Polzin.

***

Illana Taylor and Glendon Fowler dropped off at Casey's old residency and then prepared to retire for the evening. Casey continues to Katherine Jones' home in the village. The light is on inside, so Casey knocks on the door with the photo journal in her arms. Katherine opens the door, letting her inside. "That was a fast trip," Katherine said.
The pair walked into the kitchen and sat down at the table. Casey says, "There really wasn't a need to stay longer. I got the personal things I wanted, including this journal here. There's a picture I wanted to show you."

Casey opened the journal and turned the pages until she found the photo. She slides the book over to Katherine, who smiled when she saw it. "I remember the day Mackenize took this picture shortly after S.A.I.N. reported the rad levels were at a safe level to go outside," she said. "It was the first time the children had been above ground in four years. I believe that was the first time Heather ever saw the sun," she added, wiping a tear from her eye. "I miss Mackenize. She was always there for Kurt and me.

As I will be for you and your baby, until my last day," she said. "I promise." Her smile smoothed the wrinkles in her face.

Casey walks around the table and gives Katherine a hug, telling her she'll return in the morning. "I made the sofa for you" Katherine said. "I heard the plane, so I thought you might stop here to get sleep before you and council member Taylor begin your work together."

"I could bring Illana and Glendon here for breakfast before he returns to Texas," responded Casey. "That's a great idea," Katherine said, going to her bedroom. "I'd love to meet council member Taylor!"

After Glendon Fowler makes up the sofa in Casey's old residency living room, he walks to the bedroom to say goodnight to council member Taylor. He sees her lying in bed working on her computer. He knocked softly on the door and said, "Goodnight. I'll see you in the morning."

"Yes, you will," she said in her British accent. She

closed her computer and turned in for the evening.

Casey Franklin sleeps past sunup for the first time in weeks. She stirs when she hears Katherine Jones rattling in the kitchen preparing breakfast for her guest. The smell of coffee in the air lures her from her bed, so she showers and dresses for the day. "Good morning," Casey said when she appeared from her bedroom. She pours a cup of coffee, and says, "I'll be back taking the transport back to my residency to pick up Glendon and Illana. We'll come back here for breakfast."

Casey Franklin walks to the door of her old home and knocks. She knocked again after waiting three minutes for someone to answer the door. Finally, Illana opens the door wrapped in a towel. "We thought we heard knocking while we were in the shower," she said, blushing, as she walks back to the bathroom.

Glendon comes out of the bathroom, putting on his clothes from the night before. Casey smiles and asks, "Are you all rested up for your flight?"

"I'm refreshed," he answered casually.

"I believe you both are," she remarks with a smile.

"Katherine Jones has invited you both to her home for breakfast before you leave for Texas."

Illana calls from the bathroom, "We'd be delighted. I just need to finish getting dressed." Katherine Jones is standing in the kitchen when she hears the transport roll up to the door. The table is already set, so she starts pouring coffee and plating the food. Glendon and Illana appreciatively sniff the aroma of the food lingering in the air, and it draws them to the kitchen. Katherine turns to introduce herself. "I'm Katherine Jones," she said smiling. "It's wonderful to meet you council member Talyor. I want to thank you on behalf of all the people here in the village for the U.P.O.'s commitment to the rebuilding of the institute."

Illana smiled graciously. "Please don't be so formal. Call me Illana, please Katherine, and this distinguished gentleman is Glendon Fowler."

Katherine gestured to the table. "Please, sit down to eat."

Illana smiled. "Breakfast looks and smells fantastic!" Everyone sat down to enjoy their meal.

During breakfast Illana acknowledges Katherine Jones' statement, and remarks, "President Hall is going to make good on her speech. Not just the rebuilding of the institute, but also, the capture of Polzin to face justice for his crimes against the

U.P.O. for plotting terrorist attacks on our efforts to help rebuild our civilization. By now Commander Bennett and his men are in pursuit of him."

Clearing the breakfast table Katherine Jones shares the wisdom of her years, responding to the council member's assessment of Polzin's crimes. "His crimes aren't just what he has done lately," she said. "The subversion of fusion power reactors around the world at the behest of B.G.C. as leader of the H.A.T.S. to help keep their power and control over the governments of the planet. Pushing members of their rival the Cyber Cabal into a final confrontation with the creation of Trident to replace the B.G.C.'s power over world energy, leading to the destruction of the world I was born into. You can't plan for a future in the present by seeking revenge for the past," said Katherine.

Council member Taylor and Director Glendon Fowler hugged Katherine Jones thanking her for the meal and the words of wisdom before they left for the airstrip with Casey Franklin. Dropping Glendon off at his plane which has been made ready for departure, Casey waits as Illana says goodbye to the director. "I'll see you when I'm finished with my assignment for the President."

"I'm looking forward to that day," Glendon responded kissing her.

He climbs onboard, and the plane rolls down the tarmac, flying back to Texas.

***

After three weeks of sailing through the Straits of Gibraltar into the Mediterranean Sea, each day is getting shorter as winter approaches.

Storms have slowed their pursuit of Polzin. The commander receives a signal from S.A.I.N., informing him at what the I.O.N. system has detected from space. "Your assumption of Polzin's route to Kulan mountains is correct commander the I.O.N. has tracked a slow-moving vessel in the Volga River." Commander Bennett orders a speed course to the Caspian Sea to intercept his quarry before he reaches the Volga River delta.

Red clouds fill the morning sky as the commander with a three- man team, boards the helicopter on deck of the frigate trolling the delta. They take off, flying up the Volga River, forty kilometers to Astrakhan to engage Polzin heading down river. Appearing on the bridge scope that has been empty for weeks, Polzin picks up a signal approaching at one hundred sixty kilometers an hour. Going below, arming himself with a rocket grenade launcher, an automatic machine gun strapped over his shoulder and a side pistol in its holster, goes onto the deck of the oil barge.

Upon getting a visual on the vessel carrying Polzin the commander's men load the side missile launchers in preparation to fire. From the deck of the oil barge a rocket prolled a grenade, a white streaking tail of smoke being hurled towards the helicopter. The pilot banks to the right in an evasive maneuver as the rockets screamed past the helicopter. Completing his turn, Commander Bennett gives the order to open fire by hitting the barge and igniting the petroleum in the tanks below. Fire and smoke fill the sky as Polzin hears the rotary blades drawing nearer and begins to fire his automatic weapon at the helicopter. Glass being hit by bullets crack, then shatters. Commander Bennett tells the men, "I'd rather see the son of bitch go down with the ship, but President Hall wants him alive." He orders his man to repel from helicopter to deck below.

Repelling down the rope as Polzin machine gun fire whizzes by the man, he takes his firearm in hand, shooting back. He hits Polzin on the shoulder knocking him to the deck.

Polzin is coughing from the smoke and bleeding from his left shoulder. He grabs his side arm, bringing it to his temple, but before he can pull the trigger, he is hit in the hand causing him to lose grip on his weapon. The man reaches the deck and running towards Polzin. The man then kicks his side arm overboard. Then he takes Polzin's machine gun, hitting Polzin in the face with the butt of the gun. Polzin hits the deck of the barge, dizzy as the man said, "You are not taking the cowards out!" The man ties the rope around the two of them to be lifted on board the helicopter.

Landing on the frigate, Commander Bennett orders the ship to return to U.P.O. headquarters, and orders Polzin taken to the infirmary to have his wound attended too. "You're not dying today, you old fucking bastard," Commander Bennett said. He turns to the guard and orders him to put Polzin in the brig when they're finished patching him up in the infirmary. As Polzin is dragged away, the commander contacts S.A.I.N. and asks him to put him through to the President. When she responds, he announces, "We have captured Polzin. We've finally got that son of a bitch! We're on our way back to headquarters!"

Grinning in delight of the news the President Hall

responds, "I am going to execute that bastard with the world watching live on the I.O.N. system, so the remaining hatters around the planet see that their activities will no longer go unpunished by the U.P.O." Ending the transmission, she tells S.A.I.N. to contact Council member Taylor.

Reclamation

For eight weeks, council member Taylor and Casey Franklin have been working on the plans for the rebuilding of the institute. After another late evening at the residency, they're enjoying a cup of Chamomile tea to wind down their day in the kitchen when S.A.I.N. tells the council member she is receiving an incoming transmission from President Hall.

Illana gestures for Casey to join her and takes the transmission in the living room. "There is nothing the President is going to say to me that I won't share with you," she said as the President appears on the monitor.

"Ah! You're both there," said the President. "Good. I've got good news." "We could sure use some good news," Casey said.

"Commander Bennett and his men have captured Polzin," said the President. "That bastard will pay for his crimes with his life." She paused to allow Casey and Illana to cheer and hug each other, then continued. "I'd like you both here at the U.P.O. so we can put him on trial live on the

I.O.N. system for the population to bear witness to his demise." The President's smile was one of revenge.

Illana spoke. "Casey and I have a week or two of more work to do on the plans, then we will be finished with the design for the rebuilding." "That's fine," said President Hall. "The Commander will be arriving in the port of Valencia in three weeks. You can then join us as soon as the design for the rebuild is complete." Saying their goodbyes the transmission ends. Illana yawns and says, "It's getting late, so we'd better get some sleep."

"Yes," Casey agrees. "Good night."

Illana drives herself back to the village, eager to tell Glendon Fowler the big news.

Casey sits back down in the living room, looking up at S.A.I. N.'s camera. Her voice is somber as she says, "I'm very conflicted now that they have Polzin in custody. I thought I would feel better about this but executing him only makes him a martyr to the remaining hatters."

"Then you must say something to President Hall or council member Taylor to find a solution everyone can support," remarked S.A.I.N. "In the meantime, you are tired and have your little one to think of. You should go get some rest."

Casey agrees and gets ready for bed. Council member Taylor throws her jacket off and turns on the monitor, sending a transmission to Glendon Fowler. While waiting for him to answer she disrobed getting ready for bed, putting on sweatpants and a shirt. She hears Glendon's voice on the monitor screen. "You look comfortable in those frumpy clothes," he said. "What is it that you woke me in the middle of the night?"

"I thought you'd want to know that Commander Bennet has captured Polzin," she told him. "The President wants Casey and I to be there when we're finished with our work. She wants to put him on trial for the whole planet to see."

"When will that be?" Glendon asked.

"A week or two," she answered.

"That will be far too long to wait to see you, Illana," he said ending the transmission. Casey Franklin wakes up and starts her daily routine. She goes outside the residence, walking through the crops and picking vegetables to take over to Katherine's. She wants to bring her up to speed with the latest news from the U.P.O. She goes back inside, and S.A.I.N. tells her a flight has left the aerospace facility on route to the institute. "I imagine Illana is already up and knows Glendon

Fowler is on his way," she said. "I'll take her with me. I need to speak with Katherine about what has happened."

Casey goes inside to get the key for the transport, sitting outside the door and leaving for the village. Casey approaches the door of her old residence and knocks once, then enters.

She finds council member Taylor working at her computer on the design for the new institute building. She smiles at Casey and says, "Glendon is on his way."

"Yes, I know," Casey smiled. "You're glowing." She pauses, then says, "Illana I need to speak to you. and get advice from Katherine. Please come with me." Casey turns and heads for the transport followed by Illana.

When they pull up in front of Katherine Jones' home, Casey grabs the basket of freshly picked vegetables from the cliffside crops. They approach the entrance, and the council member Taylor knocks on the door. Katherine opens the door and says, "You have a troubled expression on your face, a befuddled look in your eyes. What's wrong?"

Casey walks into the kitchen and puts down the basket she had brought. She takes a deep breath and gives Katherine the latest news from the U.P.O. "They captured Polzin yesterday," she said. "He is on his way to the U.P.O. headquarters with Commander Bennett. The President plans to put him on trial, then execute him live on the I.O.N. system."

"That's great news!" Katherine exclaimed. "But why the long face?"

"My befuddlement is I don't want him to become a martyr and being remembered with Captain Stone and the crew of Triton II and their heroic sacrifice to save humanity. My problem is how to tell the President. How do you feel about this?"

Casey sits down at the kitchen table. Katherine thanks Casey for the food and starts picking vegetables in the basket. She tells Casey, "I understand your feelings. We need an alternative punishment for his crimes. You see, Madison was only a teenager when the H.A.T.S. reign of terror for the B.G.C. began. That ultimately leading to the Cyber Cabal creating Trident. We were lucky we were here at the F.I.S.T. complex living underground." Katherine paused as she put some of the vegetables in the sink to wash them. "Those who died from the first nuclear missile attacks died instantly. The billions that suffered in the radioactive fallout died horrible deaths. Maybe our alternative is right there," she mused. "Polzin wanted the

Earth to decide humanity's fate, so maybe the U.P.O. should exile him to one of the radiation zones. Let the Earth be his judge and jury. That would be justice instead of revenge."

Council member Taylor nods her head in agreement with Katherine. "I think it's brilliant," she said. Then she checked her watch. She knows that Glendon Fowler should be landing soon. She looks at Katherine and Casey and says, "We've got at least a couple of weeks before we go to the U.P.O. Casey, maybe you and I can convince the President that this alternative punishment is a better one."

"I won't be going with you Illana," Casey said. "By then my pregnancy will be in the second trimester. You and I are the first generation after Trident's tribulation. My baby will be the second." She wipes away a tear and says, "Polzin doesn't deserve to be remembered by history, you can convince the President, I know you can."

Illana takes a deep breath and asks Casey to use the transport to get to Glendon at the airstrip. "Oh, Katherine Glendon's on his way looking forward to one of your home cooked meals," Illana said as she walks to the door.

***

Casey Franklin and Illana Taylor work tirelessly, day after day for two weeks on the design for rebuilding the institute. The time is ticking away the days and weeks before Commander Bennett is due back in port with Polzin. Finally, the plans are completed. There are still seven days left before Illana will be summoned back to U.P.O. headquarters. Satisfied with their innovative design plans, Illana tells Casey she will see her at Katherine's for dinner.

Illana leaves the Franklin residency to pick up Glendon Fowler at Casey's old residence, where he has spent the past two weeks. During the day, Glendon is taking cooking lessons from Katherine and learning about the F.I.S.T. complex history. Glendon hears an approaching transport, knowing the love of his life has returned from another day's work. Glendon had just come back from helping Katherine with tonight's dinner when Illana arrived.

Illana comes through the door, Glendon notices the serious expression on her face. "What is going on?" Glendon asks. "You look so serious."

"I'll explain everything at dinner," she says, taking off her clothes and heading to the bathroom to take a shower.

They dressed quickly and drove to Katherine's home,

noticing that Casey had already arrived for dinner. The aroma of the vegetables fills the air in the house as they walk into the kitchen. "The smells from your cooking are intoxicating," Illana said. "I hope Glendon learned a thing or two from you Katherine. I can't cook."

Setting food on the table, Katherine replied, "I had lots of years to practice."

As they sit down for dinner, Council member Taylor thanks Casey for the help with the redesign. "Now that it's finished, Glendon and I need to leave tomorrow morning for Texas," said Illana.

"So soon?" Casey asked. "You have at least a week before you must go back to the U.P.O."

"I can't be here at the institute when the commander arrives back at the U.P.O. complex, with Polzin," Illana explained. "The President wants us to go together. She wants you and I to be there for Polzin trial. Madison, has a way of getting people to do what she wants." Illana takes a bite from her plate and continues. "I respect your decision not to go. You have been through enough. Besides, if Glendon and I are already gone, she won't keep asking me to change your mind, once I tell her you're not coming."

Casey spends the night at Katherine's home. The next morning, she helps Katherine on the transport, taking her along to the airstrip to say goodbye to council member Taylor and Glendon Fowler. Illana is waiting outside the Learjet fueled and ready to fly, when she sees Casey's transport coming to the airstrip. Casey and Katherine exit the transport and walk to the plane. Illana embraces Katherine saying, "Thank you for the words of wisdom, I'll do my best to convince President Hall of the alternative punishment for Polzin." Illana then turns to Casey, and hugs her tightly, saying, "I'll be back to start the work together."

Glendon and Illana climb on the plane. The plane rolls onto the tarmac, hitting full power down the runway, taking flight to Texas, he turns to Illana and says, "This has been the best two weeks of my life."

***

Six days have passed since council member Taylor and Glendon Fowler touchdown in Texas. Inside the U.P.O. residence at the Texas Aerospace Facility Illana has been writing a speech she plans to deliver before the council to consider before they pass judgement on Polzin.

Every night Glendon shows off the cooking skills he

learned from Katherine, and the two of them have dinner together. Tonight, he plans to reveal his true feelings towards Illana.

Arriving back at the residency from the dining hall, Glendon carried the food he had taken from the dining hall kitchen to prepare for council member Taylor. He goes to the kitchen to get started. While chopping away in the kitchen Glendon asked Illana. "Have you finished writing the speech?"

"Yes, my hope is they will listen to what I have to say," she replied walking into the kitchen to help with dinner.

"Tomorrow marks three weeks since Polzin's capture," he said. "The President should be calling for you to return, but before that happens, I must tell you that after being together for the two weeks on the west coast, and the week here, I realized that I am in love with you Illana."

Illana put her arms around him and kissed him. "I have those same feelings for you Glendon," she said. "Our work may keep us apart, but at least you can fly!"

***

After three weeks of rough seas, they finally reach the port of Valencia. The Commander takes Polzin from the brig on the frigate, and places him in handcuffs taking him top side.

Then he tosses the old man in the back of Hamilton's helicopter for his day of reckoning at the U.P.O. headquarters.

Once they land on the helipad, they are greeted by President Hall and members of the council. The President shakes Commander Bennett's hand, congratulating him on an operation well done. Polzin is taken from the back of the helicopter and appears in front of President Hall for the first time. He gives her a defiant grin, for which she immediately slaps his face.

"We spent three weeks preparing your temporary quarters until you stand trial," she said angrily. "You won't be there long. I promise you that!"

The President, the commander and two guards walk through the U.P.O. complex, escorting Polzin into his cell. Upon arrival, the Commander pushes the prisoner into the cell, where he lands on the cot in the corner. Polzin sits up on his cot and demands, "Where is Chao- Xun?"

Commander Bennet grinned at him. "President Hall sent him back to the Asian Continent after he found redemption in giving you up with a little persuasion on my part."

They leave the makeshift cell and walk through the U.P.O. complex courtyard. President Hall invites the commander to have dinner with her that evening. "I am grateful to accept your invitation, Madame President," he said. "Right now, I've got to go to the barracks for a while, to catch up on some sleep after these past six weeks."

"Very well," she responded. "I'm going to my office to contact Illana and inform her that Polzin is here, at the U.P.O. under arrest. I'm sure that will make her day."

The President went to her office and sat at her desk. She asked S.A.I.N. to contact Council member Taylor.

***

Illana Taylor is in a deep sleep next to Glendon Fowler when she's awakened by the sound of the monitor at the Texas Aerospace Facility. She wraps a robe around her naked body and answers the incoming transmission. "Good morning, Madame President," she said sleepily. "I take it Polzin has arrived?"

"Yes, he has," responded the President, with a satisfied tone in her voice. "All we need is for you and Casey to go ahead with the trial."

"We'll leave as soon as possible," Illana promised. "I'll contact Glendon Fowler right now."

Ending the transmission, she turns to see Glendon

standing in the doorway. He is motioning for Illana to come back to bed.

"I heard what you said to the President," he said. "You didn't tell her the truth about Casey." Reaching up to touch his forehead, she said softly, "S.A.I.N. didn't tell her my location. And I withheld the truth. After all, it worked for her when we did not tell the citizens about what was really happening at Tamu Massif. She climbed back into bed and added, "After all, what is it you said? What's good for the goose is good for the gander."

Glendon Fowler slept for a couple of hours, then contacted the hangar to have the overseas Learjet fueled and ready to go in an hour. Their bags are already packed for the trip back to Spain. Council member Taylor double checks that she has her speech for the council with her before they leave for the plane. Sixteen hours later, Glendon starts his descent to the U.P.O. airstrip. They land at ten in the morning. The commander and President Hall are in the hangar waiting for them in a transport.

Glendon Fowler taxis the jet to the hangar door, then climbs out, helping council member Taylor with the bags as President Hall approaches the plane. She looks in and asks,

"Where's Casey Franklin?"

"She wasn't feeling well from her second trimester cramps and body aches," answered Illana.

"I will call her later to see how she is feeling," responded the President.

Shaking hands with Glendon the commander says. "I guess you're bunking with us in the barracks."

"No, Commander Bennett," Illana smiled sweetly. "He'll be staying with me." The commander nods his head knowingly as they get on the transport.

Being dropped off at her residence council member Taylor turns to the President and asks, "Madame President, can we have a private meeting before lunch in your office?"

"One hour," said the President. "I'm sure we'll have lots to discuss."

Glendon Fowler grabs the bags from the back, and they walk to the door. Glendon leans close to Illana and whispers, "You lied, about Casey."

"I exaggerated," corrected Illana. "Besides, I'll tell her everything in an hour. Right now, I want to talk to Chao-Xun. I'll be back before I meet with the President." She gave a slight wave and started walking towards Xun's residency.

She approaches the residence, and council member Taylor notices that the U.P.O. guards aren't posted at the door. She turns back, curious about why there are no guards. She heads to the President's office for an answer. She knocks on the door, and upon being invited in, she asks, "Where are Chao-Xun guards?"

"They're no longer necessary," said the President as she poured two cups of coffee. "Xun's no longer here. In an act of redemption or self- preservation, he gave us Polzin location. I gave him a Presidential pardon and sent him back to Asia in disgrace.

The President paused to take a sip of her coffee. "Since you're here, what is it you want to talk to me about now that we're in private?"

The trepidation of her decision not to bring Casey Franklin with her as the President had requested makes her extremely nervous. Illana takes her coffee out to the balcony. "President Hall," she began, "you're my mentor. Casey Franklin has become almost a sister to me since we've been working together. The reason she was not here was only half the truth. She really didn't want to fly because of her pregnancy, but that isn't the real reason.

The President raised an eyebrow. "So, what is the real reason, Illana?"

"She wants no part in Polzin sentencing or execution," Illana explained. "Her feeling is Polzin will become a martyr for the H.A.T.S. now and in the future, that her late husband's memory and that of the valiant crew of Triton II will be forever linked if he dies in martyrdom." The President is pondering on what she has been told by council member Taylor. She sipped her coffee again before giving her response. "I can see why Casey would feel that way. Have you any thoughts on how to manage this situation?"

"An incredibly wise woman with grey hair said to exile Polzin to the one of the radiation zones and let the Earth become his judge and jury. The fate he wanted for all of humanity," Illana explained. "Justice instead of revenge."

The President stands up and walks Illana to the door. "Katherine Jones is very wise," she said. "We'll discuss options tomorrow morning in the council meeting before we tell the citizens."

Exhausted from flying, council member Taylor stops at the kitchen in the U.P.O. council chambers, grabs lunch for herself and Glendon Fowler, then returns to her home.

Glendon is asleep, so Illana wakes him to eat. He rubs his eyes and scratches his head, trying to wake up and focus. He asks, "Aren't you going to the meeting with the President?"

"When I got to Chao-Xun's residence, there were no guards, so I went right to her office," Illana explained. "I told her the truth about Casey." Illana put food on the kitchen table and continued. "President Hall pardon him for giving up Polzin, and the council exiled him back to the Asian Continent to live out the rest of his days in disgrace."

Glendon was shocked. "What about your ideas?"

"We have a council meeting in the morning," she said. "I'll bring them up then. Let's eat, then you can finish what you started on the sofa, and sleep in the bedroom.

***

The next day, council member Taylor is getting a late start to an important day, both for her and the future of the U.P.O. Glendon is due to have breakfast with Commander Bennet at the barracks. She tells him goodbye, grabs her computer and rushes out the door, putting extra stride in her steps as she walks to the council chambers. The other members are already seated around the table. President Hall with the other four members of the council hear a familiar voice shout,

"Bloody jetlag," as Ilana takes her seat.

President Hall begins the proceedings with a question from Olivia Walsh from the continent of Oceania. "Where's Casey Franklin? We thought she was taking part in this proceeding regarding Polzin."

"She'll not be joining us," the president said. "Casey wants no part in the decision concerning Polzin. We'll decide his fate. This council already pardoned Xun because he gave us the location of a man who in no small part helped end our civilization with H.A.T.S. terrorist activities that led billions to their death in the nuclear fire the sickness that followed spreading around the globe. The same man that tried to end humanities' last hope plotting to stop the Triton II from completing its mission." Council member Jorge Gonzales from the South American Continent stands up to be recognized by the President. "For all his crimes against humanity he should be put to death," he said. "Polzin should be made an example to hatters in the future." Council member Aasir Keita from the African Continent nods his head in agreement.

It was her turn to comment, so Council member Taylor opened her personal computer, finding the design for the new Oceanic Institute.

Turning it so the other members at the table can see her rendition of what the facility could look like that she and Casey had worked on for five weeks. "All the things the President said about Polzin are true," Illana began. "Six weeks ago, I felt like all of you, for Polzin to pay for his crimes once he was captured. Then the President sent me to meet Casey Franklin in person. Working together for weeks we did what this organization sent me to do. Design a reclamation of the institute using recycled material. To build a memorial to honor the crew of Triton II. Finding out Commander Bennett had captured Polzin I thought I wanted that which you want for Polzin to pay for his crimes."

As the other council members admired their design, she continued. "At the home of Katherine Jones, Casey Franklin expressed her feelings to Glendon Fowler and me during dinner. She said, 'I don't want my husband's, or the Triton II crew's ultimate sacrifice to be linked to Polzin by making him a martyr to the H.A.T. S., now or in the future.' This is why she's not here. Katherine Jones said something to the three of us one night that I'll never forget. 'You can't plan a future in the present by living in the past'. Katherine, who is as wise as she is old, recommended an alternative punishment. Exile Polzin to an undisclosed radiation zone and let the Earth decide his fate. Which is what he wanted for all of humanity, when the H.A.T.S tried to stop Triton II from completing its mission."

All eyes were on Illana now. "For the past week I've been at the Texas Aerospace Facility thinking about what Katherine Jones had said to us about the future. I started working on a design for a large reclamation project for all the citizens. The construction of a planetary capital this organization can use fear to intimidate or hope to inspire the future. That's the decision that must be made today," she said. She then closed her computer and walked outside to give the other members an alternative to consider.

Staring at each other across the council table, the members absorb the statement made by their colleague when the President excuses herself, going outside. Council member Taylor is collecting her thoughts and emotions when she hears the door open. She turns to see the President with a serious expression on her face as she begins to speak. "The ideal of the U.P. O. was conceived by Samuel Franklin to connect what remained of humanity together before the chaos turned to barbarism. He was a true leader with a vision of hope. Illana, you reminded me of him today." "Thank you, Madame

President," Illana said humbly.

The President embraced her and said, "One day in the future, I'll be Madison again. Illana you will be Madame President."

***

Returning to the chambers, Illana is met with applause from the other members of the Council. President Hall calls for a vote. A unanimous decision to exile Polzin was recorded by S.A.I.N. President Hall would address the citizens that afternoon telling them a special election was needed to replace Chao Xun, discharged of his duties and sent back to live in disgrace, and that Andrei Polzin was to be exiled to an undisclosed radiation zone.

Focusing on the future, the President informs the citizens that a design plan is ready to go for the rebuild of the Oceanic Institute with the memorial to honor the Triton II calls for volunteers to sign up using the I.O.N. system.

***

"Our reclamation of our planet begins with the construction of a planetary capital that you will decide where it is to be built by you for you," the President announced. "This city will help bring the planet together for future generations to immolate." The President finishes her speech, thanks the members of the council and receives a transmission that reads, "Thank you. From, Casey Franklin."

The next morning council member Taylor and Glendon Fowler arrive at the airstrip dropped off by President Hall and Commander Bennett. After saying goodbye, Glendon takes off for the institute, flying first to the Texas Aerospace Facility to rest and refuel. Upon landing the next day Illana is greeted by Casey Franklin and Katherine Jones, surrounded by villagers acknowledging her arrival with thunderous applause. Glendon leaves the next morning after spending the night with Illana. Glendon Fowler flies back ten days later with a hundred men and women onboard who have volunteered for the rebuilding. They land at the airstrip to wait for transport driven by villagers that will house the volunteers for the duration of the construction. Glendon stays the night telling Illana he'll be here every weekend to see her.

True to his word every weekend for eighteen months as the new Oceanic Institute is being built Glendon Fowler spends time with the woman he loves. Casey Franklin's friendship with council member Taylor had indeed grown into a sisterhood. Casey gives birth to a baby girl on July fourteenth, two thousand seventy-nine with Illana and Katherine acting as her midwives. Casey names her daughter Bryana, after the late Captain Stone.

With the completion of the new Oceanic Institute, the memorial is finished to honor Triton II. President Hall recalls council member Taylor and reassigns her to supervise the construction of the planetary capital she once envisioned. Given the name Centropolis by the citizens. With help from S.A.I.N., the design Illana created has volunteers numbering in the thousands to begin the construction in Algona Bay region of the African Continent.

***

Casey Franklin searching the I.O.N. system for candidates from around the globe for a new team of researchers to continue the science she and Heather had been working on before the eruption of Tamu Massif.

Bryana going on two years of age when her mother's best friend Illana Taylor was recalled to Spain and spent her days with Katherine Jones while her mother was diligent to her work to help solve the food production problems around the world. Katherine would be grandmother to Bryana until her passing in two thousand eighty-eight at ninety-two from natural causes.

***

Due to term limits imposed by the U.P. O. charter of one ten- year term, President Hall leaves office in two thousand eighty-four to begin a new life as a civilian citizen as the city of Centropolis begins to rise on the African Continent. Council member Taylor would become the third President of the U.P.O. for her work on the reclamation of the Oceanic Institute, her vision of the future of a civilized society.

Serving the last seven years of a two-decade career in the service of the U.P.O. protecting the construction of Centropolis from possible H.A.T.S. attacks that never came. Commander Allen Bennett retires. Peace and progress had come to the world moving forward for a more prosperous future. Volunteers from around the planet are given homes in exchange for their labor in the rising new capital city becoming its first residents. Allen Bennet is joined by Madison Hall after she spent three years writing her memoirs in the upper region of the North American Continent. Retiring, they make Centropolis their home. The former President's relationship with Allen Bennett grew from professional to something more personal and lasting. Madison Hall spends her time in retirement aiding S.A.I.N. in the education of children at the learning center. Allen Bennett spends his time teaching baseball to the kids for exercise, and for the team building skills it teaches.

***

Almost a year since the death of Katherine Jones in two thousand eighty-eight, Casey Franklin and her new team complete a vision that Earwyn Franklin and his great granddaughter shared. Domed farming platforms in the ocean, using seawater to grow crops from soil taken from the seafloor. Reporting their success to the U.P.O. council. President Taylor eager to see the prototype of this innovated technology also to see her niece and best friend responds to Casey's transmission from her new office in Centropolis, the new home of the U.P.O. "Casey, congratulations to you and your team," Illana said. "We need these domes to help feed our growing planetary population. I'm looking forward to seeing the prototype. Madison Hall and Allen Bennett leave on the seventh for Bryana's tenth birthday and I'm leaving the day after."

Taking a transport to pick up the former President and Allen Bennett for their trip to the west coast of North America and the Oceanic institute. They're leaving one day earlier than

President Taylor to celebrate the tenth birthday of Bryana Franklin. Driving to the Centropolis airfield boarding the plane, they handed the bags to Allen. Madison Hall tells the President. "We'll see you when you arrive at the Oceanic Institute. I know you're looking forward to seeing Glendon Fowler leaving the job behind." With a tired expression on her face President Taylor smiles.

***

It's sunrise on Saturday morning, the 9th of July, just five days until her daughter's birthday. Casey Franklin has coffee outside watching the waves roll in. Staring out at the domed farming platform. Casey checks in on Bryana and finds her sleeping in. With no sessions at the learning center on weekends, she has time to catch up on sleep. Trying not to awaken the child S.A.I.N. flashes the ceiling camera, getting Casey's attention.

Casey pulls the book and takes the lift down to the cavern control operations room. The lights dim in the cavern as S.A.I.N. brings up a holographic image of the solar system. The deep view is extended beyond the Ort Coud to the boundaries of the heliosphere. Highlighting a small area, S.A.I.N. tells Casey, "The old James Webb caught this image at the boundary of the heliosphere. I've been tracking it for several days."

"What is it?" Casey asked. "A comet or an asteroid?"

"No," S.A.I.N responded. "Those space bodies don't slowdown to make a course correction. At its present course and speed, it will be in Earth's orbit in five days."

"Oh shit!" Casey Franklin replied in a panicked voice, pacing the floor of the control operations room. "Who else can see this?"

"I've kept Glendon Fowler at the Texas Aerospace Facility from seeing this until I spoke to you first."

"Mask the signal until Madison Hall and Allen Bennett arrive at the institute on Monday evening. A long time ago I told you the day may come when we can tell the world the truth of your existence. That day is almost upon us my friend." stated Casey. "Oh Shit!" replied S.A.I.N.

Trans Temporal

The silent darkness, the cold depth of the ocean, the powerless Triton II, as Captain Morozoff begins to regain consciousness. Fuel cell reserves for the backup systems engage bringing Proteus back online. Emergency light illuminates the bridge. Checking on the others, he finds Harris with blood running down the side of his head and is helped by the captain. Doctors Franklin, Wagner and Garcia regain consciousness after being thrown to the deck, sustaining cuts and bruises from the encounter with the unknown. "What the hell just happened?" Dr. Garcia asked while checking on Heather, Amanda and Harris.

"I don't know Adriana," said the captain. "All my years at sea, that's a first. Take Heather and Harris and do a check of the crew cabins one by one by, level by level, for the crew and report their status." They board the lift for the decks below. The captain hugs Doctor Wagner, then the two of them begin picking up debris on the bridge. The captain orders Proteus to contact S.A.I.N. at once. "I hope the rest of the crew was as lucky as we were on the bridge," said the captain kissing Amanda.

"Sir, there's no response from S.A.I.N."

"The anomaly?" Captain Morozoff wondered.

"No sir," Proteus replied. "The anomaly is no longer present."

The captain and Amanda stared at each other with baffled looks on their faces but continued picking up debris. Dr. Garcia and Heather stop the lift at the crew level and begin the cabin-by-cabin check of the crew. Continuing down to engineering, Harris gets off the lift running through water on the deck to the firing control panel for the laser cannons. He finds Grant Roberts closing Miles Brady's eyes, covering him with a blanket. Leaning up against a post Chief Kim sitting on the floor a bone protruding through his skin on his left leg, in agony from the pain. Harris grabs the engineering comm mic. "Alexi, Miles Brady is dead," Harris reported. "Chief Kim has a broken leg." Harris looks over at Carol Davis and Monica Wallace holding each other, crying over the loss of the friend. A cabin-by-cabin check of the crew cabins the doctors find crew members Knight and Gale in their cabins having not sustained any injuries, they join the doctors Garcia and Franklin in the search. The group enters the mess hall going to the galley. Adriana, her assistants and Heather find Chief Jones trying to lift a refrigerator that had broken loose from its mooring and fell on a galley crew member. Lifting with all their combined strength the four of them remove the refrigerator from atop the crew members' chest. Adriana checks for a pulse, shakes her head and turns to the chief she says, "I'm sorry she's gone." Adriana orders crew members Knight and Gale to take the body of their shipmate to the infirmary and cover her, then report to engineering.

Hearing the report from Harris on the dead and injured in engineering, Amanda tells the captain to go, and she'll be down in a few minutes. "I'm working something out," she said, as the captain boards the lift.

Amanda is curious that there's no response from S.A.I.N. Pacing the bridge back and forth, she asked Proteus to open window view shade on the bridge. Seeing nothing but the cold darkness' of the ocean, she sits in the captain's chair asking Proteus, "What's the current position of Triton II?"

"We're no longer receiving G.P.S. signals from the I.O.N., Dr. Wagner," Proteus replied.

Amanda put her face in her hands and leaned over in the captain's chair. She pulled her red hair back and asked, "Proteus, is the digital image sonar still operational?"

"Yes, Doctor," Proteus replied as she walks over to the sonar station.

"Scan the ocean floor at the stern please," she ordered. Taken back by the images slowly appearing on the scope she says, "Gaia, what the hell! It can't be!" She's not sure she is looking at Tamu Massif, she checks the time stamp on the screen.

Dr. Wagner takes the lift to engineering, stopping at the crew level to pick up doctors Garcia and Franklin. They then continue downward, stopping again to pick up crew members Knight and Gale. They walk through the water on the deck in engineering. Chief Kim is leaning up against the post with his legs in the water. Adriana sees the bone protruding through the skin of the chief's leg. "I've got to get Ha-Kun to the infirmary to set that break," said the doctor to the captain.

"Ha-Kun," said the captain, "I know you're in pain, but I need to know what happened down here! How did Miles Brady die?" Knight and Gale put the chief on a stretcher; Doctor Garcia gives the Chief Kim a shot for the pain. Trying to catch his breath he makes his report,

"Miles did what he was ordered to do, shutting down the laser cannons. When we got hit, the ship started to list to the starboard side. Sending the dive bay water all over engineering taking Miles off his feet, sending him flying backwards into the control panel breaking his neck on impact reactivating the lasers," he moaned. "While trying to reverse the engines against the force pulling us into the electromagnetic anomaly, the fusion reactor redlined.

I broke my leg falling off the reactor level gangway down here." Ha-Kun moaned again. "The ship is on fuel cell battery backups. We should have enough power to return to the institute," said the chief, mercifully passing out from the shot given to him by Adriana. She orders crew members Knight and Gale to take him to the infirmary.

Stepping off the lift in engineering Chief Jones walks pass crew members Knight and Gale carrying Chief Kim on the stretcher, the chief takes his hand placing it on his fellow shipmate's arm, unconscious from the pain medicine, "Ha-Kun you're in capable hands," he said, joining the captain.

Walking over to her brother and the rest of his team Dr. Franklin offers them her condolences on the death of Miles

Brady. Carol Davis, her eyes red and puffy from crying, asked the captain, "Where did that vortex come from?"

"I don't know," he replied in a somber voice, "but we haven't been able to contact S.A.I.N."

Before leaving the engineering deck Dr. Garcia has one more casualty to report to the captain. "We lost crew member Alverez from the galley. I am going to the infirmary to set Ha-Kun's break, then with your permission, I'd like to prepare crew member Alverez and Miles' bodies for burial at sea." The captain nods his head to the doctor, takes the comm mic in engineering and orders the crew to the mess hall in ten minutes for an update on the condition of Triton II.

The crew is gathered in the mess hall and stands to attention as Captain Morozoff enters. He motions for them to be seated, then begins the update. "With great sadness I must report the deaths of crew member Isabella Alverez and Miles Brady from Harris Franklin's team, from the Texas Aerospace Facility. At present the ship is at zero bubble. Our fusion reactor is shut down from trying to break free from the gravity well inside the vortex. How and where the vortex came from has yet to be discovered. Triton II is running on fuel cell reserves."

Chief Kim screams out in anguish from the pain as his

leg break is being set. His leg is suspended in the air by cables in the infirmary. The captain gets the chief on the monitor screen, from his bed in the infirmary. "Chief, what will it take to restart the reactor?" asked the captain.

Grimacing in pain, his speech is slurred from the effects of the pain killers the chief replies, "Once we're back at the institute normal start-up protocols will have her up in a week, but for now the fuel cell reserves should be enough to get us home,"

Dr. Wagner fidgets in her chair after listening to Chief Kim talk about returning to the institute. She leans over to Dr. Franklin and whispers, "I found something everyone needs to see. I know you don't like my theories, but this one fits the facts."

The captain notices Amanda speaking quietly to Heather, and asks, "Did you find something?"
Amanda nodding her head in the affirmative, the captain turns the update over to her. She cleared her throat and said nervously, "Like all of you I want to know what happened to the ship, after the collapse of Tamu Massif. I believe the ship was hit by rising pressurized gas trapped at the base of the seamount. Triton II listing to the starboard side sent Miles

Brady into the control panel, thus reactivating the laser cannons. The angle of the ship sent the particle beams into the electromagnetic anomaly we detected. The power of the lasers opened a vortex creating a transtemporal displacement in time that Triton II has passed through."

Crew members staring at each other in disbelief over what they just heard. Doctor Wagner asked Proteus to put up the digital sonar image from the stern view of Triton II on the monitor screen. "Heather, do you know what this is we are looking at?" Amanda asked.

Heather replied, "A sonar recording of Tamu Massif."

"You're right," Amanda agreed, "it's Tamu Massif. Look closely at the time stamp, this is *now, this* moment in time. That's how I came to this conclusion speaking as a volcanologist."

An eerie dead silence falls over the mess hall with the crew looking at the image in disbelief. Chief Jones stands up and says, "We watched it fall on every monitor on the ship. If we really did pass through a time displacement, how can we be sure the institute is there to return to? I'm no scientist but I do know this. Our voyage was to be six days doubling up on food store as is the protocol. We'll have food stores for six to ten days if we ration."

Perplexed by the phenomenal theory put forth by Doctor Wagner, and Chief Jones assessment of the current situation, Dr. Franklin turns to Amanda, and says, "You are scaring the shit out of me!"

Captain Morozoff asked Chief Kim to reassess the power situation given the theoretical possibilities of Amanda's theory. "Without fuel cell reserves, we lose Proteus to watch the ratios of the elements being separated from the seawater. We're dead in the water and running out of food," answered the chief.

Captain Morozoff orders up the charts of the Pacific Ocean from Proteus' database. Looking at the chart, Dr. Franklin sees a possible solution to the current situation, to ensure the survival of the ship, and the crew. She poses a question to Chief Kim. "Ha-Kun, if we sailed to Hawaii using half of the remaining fuel cell reserves after the reactor has cooled down, could we use the remaining fuel cell reserves to restart the fusion protocols to cause first light?"

Running the numbers from his bed in the infirmary and having Proteus double check his math. Chief Kim responds to Dr. Franklins plan of action. "We'll need to try to conserve power running the ship using minimal systems. Restarting at half reserves is something we have never tried before. The voyage will take eight days that's more than enough time for the reactor to cool down. If we do not achieve first light the ship is dead and we're permanent residents of the island."

Captain Morozoff pushes back his greying hair, considering Dr. Franklin plan. Heading to Hawaii to solve their food supply problem with what is available in nature on the islands, the captain orders Proteus to bring the ship topside. He then orders the crew to report on deck for the burial of their fallen shipmates. Triton II surfaces the captain orders a full stop.

Crew members come out of the bow and stern hatches to report on deck. Harris Franklin and Grant Roberts carry the body of Miles Brady draped in a white cloth sheet. Chief Jones crew member Flynn carried Isbella Alverez to their final resting place. The sun setting on the horizon, the ships company holds a moment of silence for their lost shipmates. They then place the bodies in the water, committing their souls to the sea.

Sailing for one hundred and eighty hours cruising at depths of three hundred fifty meters Triton II is less than twenty-four hours from Honolulu Harbor. They spend the last week gathered in the mess hall watching twentieth century films to spend the hours of the day. On the overnight watch plays solitaire on the bridge with Chief Kim in the infirmary, Harris Franklin is relieved by the captain.

Harris stops at his sister's quarters and knocks on the cabin door.

After waiting three minutes with no answer, Harris Franklin takes the lift to the lab-infirmary level. He finds Heather in the lab going over the design for the underwater farming platform she and Casey had been working on before the voyage of Triton II. Harris sits next to his sister, yawning from tiredness. "I see you're working on the design," he said, trying to hold back another yawn.

"It helps pass the time," Heather said, smiling at her brother. "I like to think someday Casey will bring this project to fruition.

"Every day I think about the rift," Harris remarked. "I'm wondering, did it work or was it all for nothing? We may never know."

"We did all we could Harris," Heather replied. "If our calculations from S.A.I. N. were correct, then there's a lifetime of days ahead for of all of them, including your unborn child." She paused and yawned herself. "That's my hope. Right now, you'd better get some sleep."

After sailing the last 8 hours of their voyage to the Hawaiian Islands, Captain Morozoff orders Proteus to reduce the speed, and bring the ship to periscope depth. He raised the scope, surveying Honolulu Harbor. The island is devoid of any manufactured structures resembling civilization. Seeing miles and miles of white sandy beaches surrounded by jungle. The captain plots a course to Diamondhead to anchor Triton II. Chief Jones is calling for the crew for dinner. Dr. Franklin stops at her brother's cabin, awakening him to join the others in the mess hall.

Captain Morozoff stands to get the attention of the crew to update them on the current position of Triton II. Harris Franklin enters the hall taking a seat at the captain's table. The captain begins his update. "The ship will be entering Honolulu Harbor within the hour," said the captain. "We will bring the ship topside anchoring in Diamondhead for the evening. My first observation of the island revealed no structures of any kind. Tomorrow morning Chief Jones and I will go ashore to investigate the safety of the island before anyone leaves the ship.

The captain walks over to the table with Harris' team, and addresses Carol Davis, Monica Wallace, and Grant Roberts. "I know you've been working hard to get up to speed with Chief Kim on the protocols this past week, while he's recovering in the infirmary. We need you to be ready by tomorrow night if all goes well with our survey of the island," commented the captain.

Captain Morozoff wakes earlier than usual and dresses quietly to leave his cabin, so not to wake Doctor Wagner, still sleeping in his bed. He walks the crew passageway to the galley. Chief Jones and his staff are preparing breakfast for the day. The captain walks in asking the chief to come with him to engineering to get an inflatable raft kit and anything else they might need going ashore. Chief Jones packs two kitchen machetes in a bag before leaving for the lift. They grab one of three raft kits. Taking the oars Jonesy takes two spearfishing guns, placing them in the bag. The captain watches the chief pack the bag, and asked, "Jonesy what are those for?"

"Protection from anything hostile on the island," Jonesy answered. "Just because we can't see it, doesn't mean it's not there." Together, they take the lift to the bridge.

On his last overnight bridge watch while the ship is anchored, Harris Franklin helps the captain and Chief Jones with their equipment. The captain opens the bow hatch and goes up on deck. Waves are splashing up against the ship, the sun begins to rise. Harris stands on the deck and takes a deep breath of crisp, fresh air, and says, "I don't know where we are in history, but it's one hell of a lot cleaner." They push the raft kit up on the deck and Harris pulls the cord, inflating the vessel.

The captain takes the oars out from the bag and places them in the raft. He turns to Harris and says, "We will be back in three hours." Harris pushes the raft into the sea, the Captain and Jonesy paddle into the surf, catching wave after wave, and finally washing up on the shoreline. They drag the raft across the white, sandy beach to the jungle tree line and secure it to the ground. The captain gives a communication watch to the chief set for one hour, then they head in separate directions to cover a wider area. "Jonesy," ordered the captain, "after the alarm sounds, turn back to the beach."

"Yes, sir," the chief replied, swinging the spearfishing gun over his shoulder and with a machete in his hand, cuts his way through the jungle flora.

Harris Franklin returns to the bridge leaving the bow hatch open to circulate fresh air into the ship. His shift is nearly over when he's joined on the bridge by his sister, along with Doctors Wagner and Garcia. "They're away," Harris told them. "Alexi said they'll return in three hours."

Harris sits in the captain's chair, but Heather grabs the ship's comm mic above her brother's head. "There is something far better we can do with our time other than wait for their return," she said. She keys the mike and addresses the crew, ordering that specimen nets from lab I be brought up to the deck to be hung over the side. "This will help replenish our food supply with freshly caught fish," she announced.

The captain cuts his way through the jungle, seeing snakes' lizards, insects and birds flying in between the trees laden with fruit of different varieties for harvest to restock the food supply. He climbs tree after tree, swinging the machete and dislodging fruit, falling to ground below. Tired and out of breath, the captain collects his harvest into a sack and throws it over his shoulder. The alarm sounds to meet Chief Jones back at the beach, he placed his spearfishing gun with the sack of fruit, along with his machete back in the chief's duffle bag. The captain places his gear in the raft; he sees Jonesy coming out of the jungle on the path he had made with his machete. Calling to Jonesy, he asked "Did you see anyone?"

"No Sir," Jonesy replied. "Just lots of creepy crawly things, but there's an abundance of fruit trees." The chief puts his sack in the raft with his gear as they dragged the raft to the water's edge.

The crew placed ten specimen nets along the side of Triton II. Five on the portside and five for the starboard. After finishing breakfast, Dr. Franklin looks down at her watch, then takes doctors Garcia and Wagner up on deck where her brother is standing with a rope line over his shoulder. Harris is looking through a pair of deck binoculars watching the sweat pouring down his best friend's face from paddling over the waves. When they're ten meters out, Harris throws the rope line, which was caught by the chief, and starts pulling them alongside Triton II. They secure the raft and begin offloading the fruit sacks to the doctors.

Amanda hugs the captain smiling that he has returned unharmed. She asked Alexi, "Did you see anyone on the island?"

"No," he said. "Reptiles, birds and bugs, but a lot of trees with fruit on them. At least we won't starve."

Chief Jones takes the lift from the bridge to the crew level, carrying sacks of fruit from the island to the galley to be prepared for the afternoon meal. Captain Morozoff orders the others on the bridge to come with him to speak to Chief Kim in the infirmary. "If we don't get the fusion reactor back online, we're permanent residents of this island chain," he said.

Chief Kim's leg is in the air; the monitor screen is at the end of his bed. Carol Davis, Monica Wallace and Grant Roberts are reviewing the startup protocols for the reactor with the Chief. The captain enters the room, followed by the bridge crew. "I'm glad you are here," the captain said, looking at Harris's team. "Chief Kim has the reactor been shut down long enough to make the attempt for first light?"

"Fuel cells are draining as we speak," the chief replied with a reassuring tone. "It's now or never."

The captain embraces the Franklins and looks them both in the eyes and says with a serious tone of concern in his voice. "Your father-built Triton II. If we fail in our attempt to achieve first light, the ship is dead. We'll have to put the crew ashore as soon as possible and salvage everything we will need to survive. We'll eventually have to raise the anchor manually and leave the hatches open. Triton II will drift with the current taking her out to sea and will sink to the bottom of the ocean. The captain grabs the infirmary comm mic and orders the crew to the mess hall at once for an update on the current situation. The crew gather quickly and sit anxiously, waiting for permission to go ashore, after two weeks of being on Triton II. The captain motions for the crew to remain seated as he enters the hall with the bridge crew with Harris' and his team behind him. He looks at his watch, then orders Proteus to start the intakes for the start-up protocols.

"Twelve hours from now fusion injection will occur in the reactor. After that, one of two things will happen tomorrow morning," the captain said. "If first light can be achieved, we'll stay here as long as it takes to restock our food supplies. Once the fuel cell reserves have been restored, we will have to decide our next course of action. Doctor Franklin will put together a crew rotation for the island. Half will go ashore harvesting the trees for food. The remaining crew will report to Doctor Franklin for processing the fish we catch overnight for frozen storage. Option two if we fail means we are permanent residents of the island, taking everything from the ship will need to go ashore to ensure our survival," stated the captain.

After dismissing the crew, the captain remained at his

table with the bridge crew and Harris' team. He turns to Grant Roberts and Monica Wallace, asking them to take the first six-hour watches of the levels for fusion injections, while Carol Davis and Harris take the last six.

"I' am going to my cabin," he announced. "All the rowing, walking, and climbing of trees has kicked my ass. Wake me when we're ready."

The captain leaves with Dr. Wagner for his cabin. He is physically tired, and mentally drained from a command he never wanted. Captain Morozoff takes off his clothes and steps into a hot shower and asks Dr.

Wagner to join him. "This might be the last hot shower we will ever take if the fusion injection fails," he said. Amanda disrobes, taking Alexi up on his offer. They engage in physical intimacy in the shower. After drying off, they sleep through dinner.

Monica Wallace and Grant Roberts are relieved of their watch after sending data to Chief Kim every thirty minutes on the levels from the intake process separating the deuterium and tritium from the seawater, keeping an eye on the fuel cell reserves for fusion injections. Harris Franklin and Carol Davis, sending the last of the data. Chief Kim informs them everything looks good for reactor start up. Harris grabs the comm mic in engineering and notifies the captain to meet him on the bridge.

Captain Morozoff gets off the lift, walking onto the bridge with doctors Wagner, Franklin and Garcia. Harris and the rest of his team prepare to start the reactor protocols. The captain walks over to the firing control panel for the injector, turns to Harris and says, "This feels like a hail Mary in American football, but it's all we got."

The captain orders Proteus to light the panel. Knowing if the ship dies, Proteus will be gone, he says, "Thank you for everything you've done for us."

The captain nods his head, signaling Harris to press the button. The injector fires, draining the last fuel cell reserves and sending the ship into darkness. The particles travel at the speed of light and collide, fusing together. They create first light as Proteus and Triton II come back to life. "Touchdown, Captain," said Proteus as the captain pumps his fist. He grabs the comm mic ordering crew rotations to begin after breakfast. The cheering from the crew level can be heard on the bridge. Chief Kim in his bed, shouting and celebrating with his arms raised over his head.

Encounter

After the successful restart of the fusion reactor the captain and crew of Triton II rest before the island rotation begins in the morning. Always the first to rise from the crew, Chief Jones with help from his galley crew take one of two remaining raft kits in engineering out the stern hatch and inflate the raft, then secure it to the ship. When they return to the galley, crew members start arriving in the mess hall for breakfast, checking the posting of the personnel rotation. When the captain enters the mess hall and takes his seat, the crew is already having their morning meal. With a slight smile, the captain turns to Doctor Franklin and says, "You can tell which ones going ashore. They're the ones scarfing down breakfast." Captain Morozoff finishes eating and stands, getting the crew's attention. He can see the anticipation in the faces of the crew that is going ashore, so he orders them, "Report to Harris Franklin in command of raft one, or Grant Roberts in command of raft two on deck at once.

Those not going ashore today will stay here with Dr.

Franklin for your daily assignments." He returns to his cabin. Once on the deck, crew members begin boarding the rafts with cloth sacks handed to them by Harris Franklin and Grant Roberts. They'll need to bring back the fruit they will harvest while they are on the island. Joining Grant in raft two are Carol Davis and Monica Wallace, while Dr. Garcia climbs into raft one with Harris. Using the oars, they push off the side of Triton II, and begin paddling towards the surf, riding the waves to the beach.

After cleaning up the galley, with half the crew having gone ashore, Chief Jones reports to Dr. Franklin. "What would you like us to do Dr. Franklin."

"Take the crew on deck start bringing up the nets from the overnight catch to be processed for storage. Doctor Wagner and I will join the crew topside in three minutes." Heather requested.

With the remaining crew joining Chief Jones out on deck, Heather and Amanda find the crew pulling up the bounty the sea has provided. The doctors pull a net from the portside up on deck, longingly watching the rafts heading to the beach. "Amanda, as far as your theory goes this one could be worse," Heather commented.

Over the next five days, the Triton II crew rotations replenished the ships' food stores. Fresh fish caught overnight is fileted and put into frozen storage with fresh fruit harvested the day before. On day seven, Dr. Franklin quietly climbed out of bed after a restless night of sleep. She moves carefully so she doesn't disturb Dr. Garcia, who is still fast asleep.

Heather dresses and leaves her cabin. She takes the lift to the bridge. No one is on watch while Triton II is anchored in the harbor, but she feels a breeze coming in from the outside. Walking slowly to the bow hatch, she sees moonlight shining down through the hole. She goes out on deck to find Captain Morozoff standing atop the conning tower.

The captain is deep in his own thoughts gazing into the star-filled sky, with the moonlight shimmering on the ocean. He sees Dr. Franklin from the corner of his eye appear from the bow hatch. He motions for her to join him, she climbs the rungs of the ladder to the top of the conning tower, she asked, "Can't sleep Alexi?"

"I've been up here awhile," he said, his voice filled with wonder, "staring out at the stars and thinking about the ancient captains of wooden ships. How they used the stars to guide them on their voyages into the unknown. After today the

Triton II fuel-cell reserves will be restored, the ship is fully operational according to Chief Kim. Jonesy also reported the food stores are replenished for the next three weeks." He shook his head in awe of it all.

Heather stands with the captain looking out at the stars and listening to the waves washing up against the ship. "You know Captain Stone and my father used to come up here to think about where their next voyages should take them. Always prioritizing the needs of the rest of the people left after Trident's war." She was silent for a moment, waiting for the captain to reply. "Yes, I remember those days. When I looked at the crew returning from going ashore, I know more than a few wouldn't mind just staying here. We've done what we came here to do." commented the captain, asking "Where should we go from here?"

"Well, finding a civilization in this time period would help us stay out of histories way," answered Heather, the two them leave the tower.

Returning to the bridge, the captain pulls up the charts on the navigation monitor, and asked, "Heather, which civilization should we try and find? We need to find one that will be able to resupply our food stores, anywhere longer than three weeks means we will run out.

Looking over the charts Dr. Franklin suggest they plot a course for Egypt. The captain asks, "Why there?"

"It's one of the earliest civilizations recorded in history" Heather responded. "Also, the Azores Archipelago is the Hawaiian Islands of the Atlantic Ocean, we should be able to resupply the ships store before continuing to Egypt."

They spend the next hour plotting a course together before hearing Chief Jones over the ship's speakers that breakfast will be six am. They leave the bridge for the mess hall to update the crew on the status of Triton II and their possible next steps moving forward.

The crew stands at attention as the captain enters the mess hall to update them on their status. "As of yesterday, the ships food stores have been restored for the next three weeks. Tomorrow the reactor fuel cell reserves will be at full power, Triton II will be operationally ready for our next voyage. I know some of you wouldn't mind staying here - who could blame you?

There's a question that needs to be answered. What time have we journeyed too?" The captain turns the briefing over to Dr. Franklin.

Heather stands and clears her throat. She asked Dr. Wagner a question relating to the time displacement theory she put forth. "Amanda, in this displacement theory, would you say the continents are where they should be according to our charts?"

"Yes," Amanda responded. "Being here on the island at this time would confirm the assessment that this island chain was formed five million years ago. I don't think we will be running into anything prehistoric if we embark on another voyage." She paused, then asked, "Where do you suggest we go?"

The crew listens eagerly, waiting for an answer. Dr. Franklin walks around the hall looking at the faces of the crew anxiously waiting for her response. Heather has Proteus display the charted course she and the captain have plotted out. She stands behind her brother and points up at the chart and answers "Egypt."

"Why there?" Grant Roberts asked.

"It's one of the oldest recorded civilizations in history," Heather responded. "Finding humans in this time would help us figure out where we're in time and where *not to* go to stay out of histories way. We have a submarine, but we can't live out the rest of our lives on the ship, until the death takes us all. My father built this ship for exploration; this is a voyage our great grandfather could only dream of taking.

Dr. Franklin sits back down between Dr. Garcia and her brother.

The captain stands to address the crew. "It's time to decide our next move. Those in favor of staying here raise your hands." With no one raising their hands he nods and says, "Enjoy the island for one last day. We leave on our next voyage in the morning." The captain then dismisses the crew.

Harris puts his arms around his sister and says, "I think dad and Earwyn would be smiling right now."

Six in the morning Captain Morozoff double checks that the rafts have been stowed away by the hatches. Securing the hatches at the bow and stern, he orders Proteus, "Take the ship to periscope depth until we are out of the harbor."

Proteus informs the captain, "Triton II has cleared the harbor. The ship is at a depth of three-hundred-fifty meters, cruising speed thirty-five knots."

Using the course plotted by the captain and Dr. Franklin, Triton II will cover thirteen thousand five-hundred nautical miles, taking three hundred thirty-six hours, or roughly fourteen days, to complete the first leg of their voyage to the Azores to resupply the ships' provisions.

Sixty–eight hours later, Harris is on the bridge waiting to be relieved by the captain. Proteus informs him that the ship is coming up on Easter Island. Stepping off the lift Captain Morozoff relieves his best friend of his watch. "Anything to report?" Alexi asked. "Nothing exciting," Harris responded. "We're coming up on Easter Island. Could we come up to periscope depth? I'm curious to see something on the island as we pass."

The captain orders the ship to periscope depth, as Harris sits in the chair to raise the scope. Surveying the island's coastline Harris comments on what he sees. "The Moai statues aren't on the island yet," he said. "Humans haven't been here. Maybe will find the same in the Azores Archipelago when we arrive."

Having satisfied his curiosity, Harris Franklin lowers the periscope and relinquishes the chair to the captain. The captain sits in his chair; he orders Proteus to make Triton II depth one-hundred meters while they sail around Cape Horn through Drake's Passage for the Atlantic Ocean. After two days of sailing through the passage Proteus notifies the captain as he and Doctor Wagner are getting ready for bed. The ship is in the Atlantic. "Make our depth three- hundred-fifty meters and return to thirty-five knots," the captain ordered. He turned off the lights and got into bed with Amanda.

They sailed the Atlantic for three days with another three still to go before they reached the Azores. Harris, nodding off from the boredom of an uneventful voyage in the captain's chair, is startled by a sonar alarm that raises him to his feet. He asked Proteus, "What was that?"

"A proximity sonar alarm has picked up a biologic signature at the stern to the starboard side," Proteus answered. Harris sees the time on the monitor and takes the lift to the crew level to inform his sister about the alarm.

Harris knocks on his sister's door, then waits patiently for two minutes. When she doesn't answer, he begins to pound on the door. Heather hears the pounding over the water running in the shower, so she steps out and throws a towel at Dr. Garcia. She wraps a towel around herself and answers the door. "What is it, Harris?"

Harris walks into the cabin and says, "A proximity sonar alarm has detected a biologic," he answered. "I thought you should know."

"Probably just a whale," Heather said. "I'll come to the bridge as soon as we're finished getting dressed." Adriana begins drying her hair in the bathroom, Heather shows Harris the door.

The doctors leave Heather's cabin and find the captain standing waiting for the lift on his way to relieve Harris on the bridge. Waiting for the down lift, Dr. Garcia kisses Heather before stepping onto the lift, saying good morning to the captain on her way to check on Chief Kim.

Heather and the captain take the lift to the bridge and walk to the sonar station. "Let's see what this could be," she said looking down at the scope. After a moment, she said, "It's not a whale, there would be a heat signature. Could be a school of giant squids." She pauses then says, "Proteus search the database to identify this biologic, contact me if it comes in range of the stern camera view." She gets back on the lift with Harris.

Eight hours out from the Azores Archipelago Captain Morozoff has Proteus bring up the charts for the Island of Sao Miguel, looking for a place to anchor Triton II for the duration of the resupply. "Proteus, reduce our speed to twenty knots," the captain ordered leaving the bridge.

While having dinner, the captain stands to get the attention of the crew. When they're all listening, he begins his update. "We'll reach the Azores by midnight. At sunrise Chief Jones and I will see to the safety of the Island Sao Miguel before crew rotation will resume as before, staying only as long as necessary to restock our supplies. Then we will continue onto Egypt." He dismissed the crew, then approached Chief Jones before he turned in for the evening. The captain tells Jonesy, "Use the raft kit stowed at the bridge hatch in the morning. Pack the necessary tools for our excursion to the island."

The captain returns to the bridge waiting to be relieved by Harris Franklin. Stepping off the lift Harris finds the captain in his chair, giving Proteus orders to reduce the speed to ten knots. Bringing the ship up to periscope depth, the captain surveys the coastline of the Sao Miguel and marks the destination on the periscope. He signals Harris to look through the scope. "This is where the ship will anchor," he said to Harris. "Proteus knows what to do once we reach the coordinates. I'll see you with Jonesy early in the morning." The captain leaves the bridge for his cabin and Dr. Wagner.

Triton II reaches the coordinates. Proteus surfaces the ship and drops anchor. At five in the morning, Chief Jones is gathering the spearfishing guns from engineering, sacks and machetes from the galley for harvesting during the excursion to the island and heads to the bridge. Harris is watching the ship's recording of his wedding to Casey Alexender but closes out the screen when he hears the lift approaching. He grabs one of the two bags from the chief stepping off the lift, Harris goes up the ladder openings the bow hatch. Jonesy pulls the raft kit to the ladder, then pushes it up the hole to Harris pulling the raft on deck. Jonesy inflates the raft securing the mooring line to the portside of the ship. They stow the bags onboard waiting for the captain.

Captain Morozoff and Dr. Wagner on the bridge. Amanda is eager to see the Furnas volcano at the eastern end of the island. The captain gestures for her to go out the hatch first. She stands on deck, the sun piercing through the clouds, seeing the smoke rising from the summit of Furnas. She grabs the captain's hand, helping him out on deck. "I really hope we get a chance to explore the island," she said excitedly. "I've only read about the Azore Archipelago volcanoes."

The three men on the deck with Dr. Wagner, Captain Morozoff and Chief Jones climb in the raft. Harris Franklin hands the chief the oars, then ties off the mooring rope, they paddle away from the ship. Watching as the raft heads into the surf for the beach, Harris turns to the doctor, and says, "Amanda if all goes well you might just get that chance to explore." They both head down the hatch.

Dr. Franklin posts the crew rotation schedule for the island excursion in the mess hall for when the captain returns with Chief Jones. Harris Franklin and Dr. Wagner join the others at the captain's table for the morning meal. Sitting next to his sister Harris tells them the raft is away.

Dr. Franklin stands and tells the crew those not on the first rotation to the island, to report to the deck after breakfast to rehang the specimen nets on the sides of Triton II.

After breakfast, the deck is full of crew members eager to get fresh air after two weeks of being submerged in the ship to help rehang the nets. On reaching the beach Captain Morozoff and Chief Jones pull the raft from the water's edge to the tree line, securing the raft to the ground.

Synchronizing their watches for two hours they take separate ways through the jungle. After two hours had passed, the alarms sound and they each returned to the beach. They discovered that the island is devoid of human life, but has a variety of vegetation from mother nature, enough to resupply Triton II. They place their sacks of fruit in the raft, then secure the spearfishing guns in the chief's duffle bag. Dragging the raft back to the water's edge, they climb onboard and start paddling back to the ship. The captain asked, "Did you see anyone?"

"No sir," said the chief. "Same as Hawaii."

Looking up at the sky, the captain ordered, "When we get to the ship deflate the raft stow it back at the bridge hatch. It looks like it might storm overnight." They row to the ship with a quicker pace.

Out on deck Grant Roberts throws the mooring line out to the raft. It was caught by Chief Jones. Grant pulls them alongside the ship. They unload the sacks of fruit, then take the duffle bag with the spearfishing guns and hand them to Grant. The chief deflates the raft as the captain goes below to the bridge. After stowing the raft and the duffle bag at the bridge hatch as ordered, the chief takes the sacks of fruit to the galley. The captain grabs the bridge comm mic and announces to the crew, "Weather permitting, crew rotation will begin in the morning." The crew's cheers can be heard below deck.

After dinner, the crew sleeps for the evening with expectations of leaving Triton II for the island in the morning. They are eight hundred meters off the coastline, and the hatches are battened down for the approaching storm.

Five in the morning Captain Morozoff is at his desk writing in the ship's journal. Dr. Wagner wakes up. She gets out of bed and gives the captain a hug. "I'll be ready in an hour to go explore with you, Alexi," she says as she takes off her clothes and heads to the shower.

Captain Morozoff goes to Harris Franklin's cabin. He only knocks once before Harris answers the door. "Let's go," he said. "Jonesy is waiting for us in the galley with Grant Roberts to take the rafts on deck."

The four of them head to the stern hatch where raft two is stowed. "I'll go to the bridge to open the hatch. Chief meet me there when raft two is secured to the ship," said the captain.

Chief Jones opened the stern hatch as Harris and Grant pushed the raft up the hole. They inflate the raft while Harris handed the chief the sacks and the duffle bag with the machetes and spearfishing guns, then place them inside the raft.

Securing the raft to the mooring line, the chief walks to the bridge hatch to meet the captain. Walking the deck, Chief Jones hears the flaying of fish caught overnight in the nets.

Once reaching the hatch, he sees the captain pull raft one up on the deck and says, "Sir, crew members not going ashore will have their work cut out for them. The nets are full." he said. Then he inflates the raft and loads the gear onboard.

At breakfast, the captain orders those going ashore to go topside and tells the remaining crew to report to the deck in fifteen minutes to Dr. Franklin for the processing of the overnight catch. Chief Jones helps Monica Wallace, Carol Davis and Grant Roberts, along with six other crew members, into raft two. Grant unties the mooring line and is handed an oar from the chief as they paddle away from the ship.

In raft one Captain Morozoff is getting his crew members onboard. He hands crew member Knight an oar as Gale sits down next to Dr. Wagner, the captain unties the mooring line. They row to the shoreline to begin the excursion of the island.

On the bridge, Dr. Franklin takes the deck binoculars from the captain's chair, she goes out of the hatch onto the deck. Climbing the conning tower, Heather waits for the crew to report for duty. Standing atop the tower she hears fish flailing in the nets. The overnight storm has given them a bountiful catch.

The sounds from the flailing fish have been reverberating deep beneath the waves drawing the attention of morning feeders in search of food. Coming out on deck from both hatches, crew members with grappling hooks in teams of two take their positions to pull the nets on deck. Two crew members use the grappling hooks to pull the middle nets from the starboard side when a blue shark attacks the net full of fish, taking the hook in its mouth and pulling the crew member into the sea.

Hearing the splash, getting ready to look through the deck binoculars, Dr. Franklin sees the crew member pulled down into the water as blood rises to the top. She screams out in terror, "Shark!"

The blood has drawn more feeders; Heather looks through the glasses and sees a dozen dorsal fins coming to the surface to join the feeding frenzy. From the tower, Dr. Franklin orders the crew to cut the nets and go back inside the ship, alerting the rafts from her comm watch of the attack.

Captain Morozoff and Chief Jones see the crew running on the deck and start paddling back to Triton II. Harris Franklin is inside his cabin when he's alerted by Proteus to the attacks.

He leaves his cabin running to the lift for the bridge, passing crew members on their way down. Grabbing the emergency flare gun, he goes out on deck to find his sister atop the conning tower, looking through the deck binoculars. He climbs the tower, and asks, "How far are the rafts from the ship?"

"One hundred meters" she answered. Just then Proteus alerts Heather on her comm watch of a sonar proximity alarm set off by an approaching biological. She asks,

"Could this be the same one from three days ago"

"I don't know the biological signature wasn't in the database," Proteus answered, "but it's two thousand meters off the portside, approaching fast."

Captain Morozoff in raft one hands crew member Gale the oar, then pulls the spearfishing gun out of the duffle bag. He passes out the machetes, giving one to Dr. Wagner. "If the sharks get near the raft start stabbing at them," he orders, taking the oar back and handing Gale a machete. Carol Davis in raft two does the same, handing Chief Jones a spearfishing gun, passing out the machetes to the others, keeping one for herself.

Turning around, looking through the glasses to the

portside, Dr. Franklin tells her brother, "Three great whites are attacking the blue sharks feeding on the fish released by the crew!" The water around Triton II turns red from the carnage of the great whites, feeding frenzy on the blue sharks. Blue sharks begin attacking the rafts, crew members begin stabbing at them as they pass alongside their rafts. Paddling as fast as they can, the sounds of the oars attract the attention of one of the great whites, who begins moving towards the rafts. Captain Morozoff hands the oar back to crew member Gale and takes aim at the approaching predator with the spearfish gun. The spear hits it in its coal black eye, and it disappears underneath the water, with the raft still twenty meters from the ship.

Sliding down the conning tower ladder, Harris Franklin runs the deck to the stern, throwing the mooring line out caught by crew member Knight and Gale hitting sharks with an oar. Harris starts pulling the raft alongside the ship. A blue shark lunged out of the water behind Dr. Wagner. Captain Morozoff fires the spear gun sending the shark back into the sea. Grabbing the line Amanda reaches out by taking Harris' hand. The captain helps the others off the raft while ordering crew member Knight to take everyone below and close the stern hatch behind them.

Up in the tower looking through the deck binoculars Dr. Franklin sees three grey scaled humps rising seven meters above the surface covered with dorsal fins heading for Triton II. The captain and Harris run the deck to the bow, and Heather slides down from the conning tower. "I have no idea what this is, but it's big and will be on top of us in three minutes," she yelled to her brother.

Raft two is ten meters away from the ship. Monica Wallace desperately catches the mooring line thrown out by the captain. Harris Franklin and the captain pulling the raft alongside the ship. Chief Jones and Grant Roberts continue fighting back the sharks with oars. Rising out of the sea, the great white with the spear still in its eye attacks the raft.

Captain Morozoff grabs the flare gun from Harris, firing at the shark's other eye, sending it back underneath the waves. One by one they pull crew members off the raft, and the captain orders them down the bow hatch.

Chief Jones and Grant Roberts help Carol Davis and Monica Wallace off the raft; a deafening moan can be heard coming from the sea. Bursting out of the water, rising eighteen meters above the ship, the creature's grey scaled underbelly like armor. The head of a dragon and the tail of a snake, a great white shark between its razor-sharp teeth bites down, sending the head and tail back into the sea. Releasing a horrifying roar, the shark's blood dripping from its mouth the head of the creature lunges toward the deck. From the raft Chief Jones fires his spear gun, and the captain fires his speargun at the blood red eyes of the creature. Harris Franklin fires the flare gun, retracting its head, the creature's left eye blinded from the flare, the right with two spears in it the creature falls backwards into the sea sending water over the side of Triton II.

Dr. Franklin, helping Carol Davis, and Monica Wallace to the hatch gets hit by a rush of water going down the hatch. Heather orders Proteus to raise the anchor while Captain Morozoff and Harris Franklin help Chief Jones and Grant Roberts off the raft onto the deck. Harris reloads the flare gun, the captain and the chief reload the spear guns, keeping an eye out for the creature. Hearing the clanking of the chains from the anchor rising out of the water, brings the creature back up from the deep.

Grant Roberts heads down the hatch. The captain shouts out, "It's on the portside!" Three humps swim like a snake side to side as the creature is heading for the ship. Captain Morozoff and Chief Jones fire their spear guns down in the water, hitting the creature's head, turning it away from ramming the ship, they head for the hatch.

Harris Franklin turns to go down the hatch but sees the creatures' dorsal fin covered tail coming out of the water, sweeping across the deck from the stern to the bow. He shouts, "Duck!"

Captain Morozoff hits the deck, and the tail passes over the captain, missing the hatch door, hitting Chief Jones in the left leg. The dorsal fin slashes his skin to the femur bone, sending him over the side. Harris screams, "Kurt!" He dives over the side to save his childhood friend.

From the ladder of the hatch, Grant Roberts hears Harris Franklin shouting out Chief Jones name Grant goes back on deck, watching Harris dive over the side. He yells down the hole to Dr. Franklin, "Get the medical staff to the bridge!" Coming up to the surface Harris sees Kurt get bitten by a blue shark that's fleeing the creature's presence. Screaming out in agony, blood spurts from the chief's mouth, he passes out falling under the water. Harris swims towards him then dives down, grabbing Kurt, and bringing him back up, pulling the chief as he swims back to Triton II.

Dr. Garcia dispatches crew members Knight and Gale

to the bridge. They run along the passageway with a stretcher to the lift. Adriana hands Chief Kim crutches, discharging him to his cabin as she prepares the infirmary. Captain Morozoff and Grant Roberts each holding on to the mooring rope, extended out their arms reaching for Harris Franklin, pulling the chief from underneath his arms and bringing him on deck.

Carrying the unconscious Chief Jones to the bridge hatch, Captain Morozoff and Grant Roberts ease his body down the hole to crew members, Knight and Gale who put the chief on the stretcher and take him to the infirmary.

Then pulling Harris up on deck, the captain tells his best friend, "You're a crazy bastard!" He pushes Harris down the hole first, then the captain closes the hatch, ordering Proteus to submerge Triton II.

Reaching periscope depth at eighteen knots the captain raises the scope sees the three dorsal fins arches of the creature one-thousand meters off the stern. He orders more speed as the proximity alarms sounds again.

Back in his cabin for the first time in a month, Chief Kim signals Captain Morozoff on the bridge. "Sir you're speeding up" he said, "but we need to let it catch up to us." The captain shouted, "What for? Are you out of your damn mind?" "You may have blinded the creature," Kim said, "but it can still hear the engines! It won't give up! We must kill it!"

The captain agrees and orders Proteus to reduce to maneuvering speed. Triton II begins to slow down. He asks uneasily, "What is it you have in mind Ha-Kun?" The captain looks through the scope and sees the creature is now eight hundred meters from the ship.

"The reactor automatically flushes itself in its daily operation," said the chief, "but we can force it manually from engineering as the creatures catches up from behind and send that hot plasma gas right down its throat."

Grant Roberts knowing where the manual controls are to flush the reactor, he volunteers to go. He leaves the bridge for engineering. The captain orders Proteus to take the ship to one hundred meters, keeping eighteen knots. He activates the stern sonar imager, watching on the monitor as the creature follows Triton II down.

Grant reaches engineering and going to the reactor level, puts on a pair of tinted safety goggles. Grant contacts the captain and reports, "I'm in position." From the monitor the captain sees the image getting closer at one hundred meters and activates the stern external camera view.

The crew members in the mess hall all have their eyes fixed on the stern camera image. Coming into the camera's view the external lights on Triton II illuminate the head of the creature as it approaches from the stern. Opening its mouth exposing its razor-sharp white teeth. The creature prepares to capture the ship's engine in its bite. Captain Morozoff shouting out the order, "Now, Mr. Roberts!"

Pressing the manual control, a jet stream of plasma gas heated to six- thousand, six- hundred and forty-eight degrees Celsius enters the creature's mouth. The head illuminates fire red, bursting into flames, exploding sending its headless carcass to the bottom of the Atlantic Ocean. A roaring sound of jubilation can be heard from the mess hall.

Contact

Crew members Knight and Gale rush Chief Jones to the infirmary and lift him from the stretcher. He begins convulsing as they place him on the table. Knight administers a sedative while Gale cuts the chief's pants off. Doctor Garcia is looking at the severity of the wounds from the shark bite, blood is squirting out of severed blood vessels onto her clothing.

Suturing the vessels back together as fast as possible. Gale hanging a unit of O-negative blood, Knight places a mask on the chief's face, covering the mouth and nose, and starts the portable ventilator. Dr. Garcia moves around the table looking at the chief's exposed femur bone protruding through the left leg. After setting the bone she starts stitching his skin back together.

The three of them are covered in the blood of a crew mate and friend. Then they hear the roar of jubilation coming from the deck above. The doctor scouring the crew manifest for a matching blood type for Chief Jones, crew member Gale says, "I'm type O-negative. Knight can take a unit from me once the chief is stabilized." Administering antibiotics through an IV to stabilize the chief, the doctor says, "I need to know what happened! I'm going to the bridge."

Chief Kim is in his cabin when the sound of jubilation from the mess hall vibrates down the passageway. On the monitor screen he sees the Franklins embrace their captain and longtime friend. Hearing the lift stop, the captain turns, Dr. Garcia steps off, her hands still stained from the blood. She asked, "What happened?"

"The creature that attacked Triton II has been destroyed thanks to Chief Kim," answered the captain. "How's Jonesy?" "Critical he's stabilized now," she answered. "The chief lost a tremendous amount of blood and tissue. Crew member Gale's blood is type O-negative. She's giving the chief a transfusion, but we will need more volunteers."

Grabbing the comm mic, the captain draws a deep breath before addressing the crew. "Attention all hands. If you're not already in the mess hall, report there in ten minutes." In the mess hall, the crew ceases its jubilant celebration when Captain Morozoff walks in, followed by the bridge crew and Chief Kim on his crutches. The seriousness of his facial expression reminds them of the severity of their situation. The captain stands at his table and addresses the crew. "During the first wave of the shark attacks on the nets, we lost crew member Sagar to a feeding frenzy, when she was pulled into the sea," he said somberly. "Chief Jones is in critical but stable condition, thanks to the skills of Dr. Garcia and crew members Knight and Gale. The attacks left us back at square one. We're running out of food. Our choice is simple. We rather return to the Azores to try again to resupply or find another possibility. Proteus, he ordered, "bring up the charts for the Mediterranean Sea."

Dr. Franklin draws the crew's undivided attention as she examines the chart. Zooming in on the region of the Aegean Sea, focusing on the island of Crete, she turns to the captain. "Finding a place to resupply for provisions trumps the need to find civilization," she said. "Crete could provide us with the food we need."

Taking further examination of the island, the captain said, "The northside of Crete looks like there could be a place to dock Triton II without risking our last raft kit."

Crew members are talking amongst themselves, weighing the choice put forth by Dr. Franklin or returning to the Azores, using the last raft kit to go ashore. Captain Morozoff requests a show of hands for returning or going forward to Crete.

"All in favor of returning," the captain asked, "signify by raising your hands." He looks around to see a show of no hands. He turns too crew member Flynn,

"You're now in charge of the galley. I want you to ration the available food stores." Turning back around he orders "Proteus set a course for Crete!" dismissing the crew.

Twenty hours into a seventy-two-hour voyage to Crete plotted by Proteus, Triton II cruises at a depth of three-hundred-fifty meters at a speed of thirty-five knots through the Straits of Gibraltar. Crew member Knight is in the infirmary on the graveyard rotation for the care of Chief Jones.

Hearing the vital sign monitor flatline, the respirator stops pumping. Charging the portable defibrillator, she opens the chief's shirt placing the paddles of his chest she countershocks his heart. While checking the chief's vital signs after reviving him, she ordered, "Proteus, alert Dr. Garcia!"

Dr. Garcia was sleeping with her arm draped over Dr. Franklin when the alert came from Proteus. She jumped out of bed, waking Heather. "Sorry," she mumbled. "There's an emergency with Kurt." She dressed quickly, exited the cabin and ran down the passageway. Not waiting for the lift, she slides down the ladder to the level below. She sprinted to the infirmary and upon arriving paused to catch her breath. She asked, "What has happened?"

"Chief Jones flatlined," Knight reported. "I was able to resuscitate him, but his pulse is weak."

"Magnificent work, Knight," the doctor said, examining the chief. It was nearly the captain's normal time to begin his day, when the captain heard running coming from the passageway. He sat up in bed and asked Proteus, "What is happening?" This wakes Dr. Wagner, who rolls over out of bed.

"There's a medical emergency with Chief Jones in the infirmary," Proteus reported.

Down the passageway in her own cabin, Dr. Franklin signals Harris who is still on overnight bridge watch. "Harris, meet me in the infirmary," she said quickly. "There's been an emergency with Kurt!" Exiting her cabin, Dr. Franklin sees the captain and Dr. Wagner also responding to the medical alert, taking the lift and running the passageway, entering the infirmary. Dr. Garcia removes the dressing from Chief Jones' lacerated left leg, revealing an infection which is spreading rapidly through the chief's bloodstream, sending him into a coma. She administers penicillin, with solemnness in her expression. Crew member Knight looks relieved that Adriana has stabilized the chief. Harris Franklin enters the room, standing around the bedside hearing the anguished breathing of the chief, who is barely clinging to life.

"Adriana," asked the captain, "what is your prognosis for Jonesy?" "Currently Kurt is in a coma," she answered in a strained monotone, "from the effects of septicemia. The bacteria the creature was carrying is spreading through his system, which will eventually shut down his organs. We don't have enough antibiotics to fight the infection in his bloodstream, onboard the ship."

She embraces Heather and Harris, Adriana says, "I'm sorry. We will do what we can for Kurt, but in a few days he'll just pass away.

Triton II, keeping its course and speed traveling sixteen-hundred and forty nautical miles, is approaching the southern region of the Aegean Sea and the island of Crete. The captain orders Proteus to reduce speed to fifteen knots. The rationing of the food supplies has given the crew two extra days before the situation becomes critical. Gathered in the mess hall for the one meal for the day. Bringing up the chart on the monitor screen, the captain updates the crew. "Triton II will be in periscope range within the hour."

Checking the time on the screen Dr. Wagner asked, "Alexi, what is it you hope to see in the dark? Sunset is in sixty minutes."

"A place to dock the ship and hopefully nothing else," replied the captain.

Preparing to return to the bridge for the last three hours of his watch, Captain Morozoff excuses himself from the table, telling Dr. Wagner he'll see her later. Harris Franklin follows the captain out of the mess hall and catches up to him in the passageway. "Alexi, I'm reporting early for my watch," he said. "What's three hours of sleep when your dreams and nightmares are one and the same?"

The captain stopped. "Is it that bad, Harris?"

"I dream of Casey playing with our child," Harris said, "out in the crops on the cliffside at the institute when she turns to me. 'We were supposed to be a family,' she says. Then I wake up wondering if the world we come from survived at all."

Harris and Alexi take the lift to the bridge and Harris

sits down at the sonar station. Taking his chair, the captain confides, "I want to tell you something, too. I thought it would never happen to me, let alone now, in this prison of the past. I'm in love with Amanda. I can't imagine living out my life here without her, no matter where we go."

Proteus notifies Captain Morozoff, "Triton II is at the charted coordinates for the southern part of Crete," The captain orders Proteus to reduce speed to five knots and take the ship to periscope depth. Raising the scope to survey the island's western side, the captain orders Proteus to keep a range and distance of sixteen-hundred meters from Crete as they circle the island.

Harris getting ready to play Proteus in a game of *Go* asked Alexi, "What is it you hope to see in the darkness?"

"A silhouette in the coastline of a cove to anchor Triton II, hopefully we can try to go ashore," he answered.

They patrol parallel to the western side at thirty-five knots. The captain marks the positions of suitable places to dock. Proteus interrupts Harris' turn in the game to inform the captain, "Triton II is approaching the starboard turn around the island." Reducing speed to eighteen knots, turning at thirty-five degrees, the new course taking the Triton II east on the north side of Crete. Reestablishing their range and distance to the island the captain sees lightning on the horizon as it starts to rain. Looking south to the north side of Crete panning up the cliffside silhouette in the distance, radiant yellowish-red glow comes from atop the cliff. Sitting back in his chair the captain remarks, "Son of a bitch!" Harris looks up and the captain gestures for him to look for himself. Getting out of his chair, the captain reports to his friend, "We've contacted civilization! There are people on this island."

Harris looks through the scope, seeing rain and lightning in the distance. He sees the glow from the fires on top of the cliff and turns to his friend. "Alexi, maybe lightning strikes started those fires," he pondered. "The storm's coming towards us, not away from us. Someone is up there." remarked the captain.

Pacing back and forth thinking, locking his hands behind his head stretching his neck, the captain decides on a course of action. "Observing their routine in the morning will help us before we make any move to go ashore. "Proteus," he ordered, "finish circling the island, mark the positions on the other sides of the island suitable to dock at, and don't kick Harris' ass too bad in your game of *Go*. I'm going to my cabin.

We need to be right here before sunrise in the morning."

Captain Morozoff was restless, spending hours trying to sleep and feeling the weight of command. He quiets his mind writing in the ship's journal. Lying awake in bed hearing the man she is falling in love with, thinking aloud writing at his desk. "What would you do, Bryant, if you were here? I wish you were."

Dr. Wagner gets out of bed and walks over wrapping her arms around him speaking in a hushed, soothing tone. "What happened that you're asking for advice from a fallen mentor?" "Going ashore to resupply has become a dangerous proposition," the captain said. "There are people on Crete." He closes the journal, seeing the time, the captain turns to hug Amanda. "Sunrise is in ninety minutes," he said. "I want you and Heather on the bridge before daybreak." He got up to take a shower, followed by Amanda.

Dr. Garcia is dressed and is preparing for her rotation in the infirmary. There's a knock on the door, which awakens Dr. Franklin. Adriana answers the door, sees Dr Wagner standing in the passageway, watching the captain take the lift to the bridge. When the door opens, Dr. Wagner sees Adriana already preparing to relieve the overnight shift to care for Chief Jones.

"Alexi wants Heather and I on the bridge before daybreak," she said. "Harris and Alexi saw fires burning last night on the northside of the island so, there are people on Crete. They want to see their daily routine."

"I heard you," Heather said, getting out of bed, "I'll be there in fifteen minutes." Harris nodded off in the captain's chair and is awakened by the sound of the lift.

Momentarily startled, he gives up the chair and makes his report to the captain. "Alexi, Triton II circled the island for the past seven hours.

The ship is anchored at the coordinates you ordered. Proteus found two possible places to dock on the eastern side of Crete."

Dr. Franklin and Dr. Wagner arrive at the bridge. Each doctor takes a seat at a station. Heather at navigation, looking at Triton II's position and offers a suggestion to the captain. "Alexi, we need to be closer then sixteen- hundred meters from the coastline to watch these people's daily routine."

Taking Heather's advice, the captain orders Proteus to raise the anchor, moving slowly ahead and bring the ship closer, to eight hundred meters. Harris Franklin boards the lift and says, "Good morning and good night. I'll be sleeping if you need me."

Triton II is in position. Captain Morozoff raises the periscope and sees the sun rising, shining from the east, revealing two ancient pulley systems standing atop the cliff side. A wooden platform suspended from ropes hangs over the cliff. At the base of the cliffs, moored side by side an armada of reed boats made from papyrus. A mast at the center flies a white sail with a yellow circle of the sun surrounded by sixteen rays of sunlight. Fishing nets hung from the sides of the boats, a dozen or more people board the platform slowly descending the base as the counterweight raises the other platform to the top.

Captain Morozoff, stepping away from the scope, invites Dr. Wagner to observe the people boarding the ship. The platform brings down another dozen people or more, with baskets down to the docks, boarding the reed boats, getting ready to sail. "I recognize the symbol on the sails of the boats," she said. "They're Minoans of Crete."

Amanda signaled for Dr. Franklin to have a look for confirmation of her assessment of the civilization they have located. Making her observation of the island, she's amazed by the routine of the Minoan civilization they found. Heather turns to Dr. Wagner and says, "You're right Amanda, that symbol is Minoan, which gives us a better approximation of the time were in. Somewhere between seven thousand B.C.E. to sixteen-twenty."

The captain takes a second look at himself, then orders Proteus to put the periscope observation on all the ship's monitor screens. He grabs the bridge comm mic and orders the crew to assemble in the mess hall, the three of them leave the bridge.

With no breakfast being served to conserve food, the crew is hungry, and most of them are tired of enduring the longest stint they've ever spent on Triton II.

Walking in together the doctors take their seats at the captain's table, and Captain Morozoff prepares to update the crew. He remains standing and pointing at the screen. "What you're seeing, is the observation from the periscope," he said. "We've made visual contact with the Minoan civilization, confirmed by doctors Franklin and Wagner. Since daybreak, the Minoans have been taking this ancient pully platform system, down to the boats boarding them preparing to sail."

Monica Wallace comments on what they have been seeing. "How cool is that ancient engineering at work?"

Captain Morozoff sits down at his table, watching the activities.

Twelve of the boats pull anchors, large round stones being pulled from the water. Three long oars extend out on either side of the boats rowing away from port to open seas. Grant Roberts stands to get the captain's attention, and asked, "Which flotilla do we follow, sir?"

"Earlier we saw the Minoans loading fishing spears on the boats," the captain stated, "The ones heading west also had empty baskets being brought onboard. The flotilla sailing northeast away from the island is a fishing expedition. I believe the other is heading to the other side of the island to fill those baskets."

The captain then turned his attention to Proteus and orders, "Proteus, lower the periscope, bring the ship about. How long till we reach the southern side of the island?"

"Sir, seventy-five minutes," Proteus answered. "First port turns in fifteen, the second in one hour at full ahead down the western coastline."

"Down angle on the bow planes takes us to three-hundred, fifty meters." ordered the captain.

After dismissing the crew, they return to the bridge. The

captain sits in his chair, and the doctors take their stations, waiting for the first portside turn. The captain notices a somber expression on Dr. Wagner's face as she sits at the sonar station. "Amanda is there something wrong? You look upset or disappointed about something." He gets up and sits down next to her at her station.

Dr. Franklin leans over from navigation, concerned for her friend. "Amanda, is there something wrong? Talk to me!" Taking a deep breath, Amanda asks Heather to pull up the chart for the Aegean Sea, to answer their question. She points down on the screen to the coordinates for the island of Santorini. "I wanted to go in the other direction," she said, "during this time that island doesn't exist. Calliste is there now. My mother was a historian, and my father worked at Grand Coulee Dam and Power station. When I was young, they took me camping at Mount Rainier every break during the summer. Seeing the snow cover peaks rising to the sky sitting majestically in the forest I was hooked. Mom used to indulge me with stories of ancient volcanoes. My favorite is in the other direction, so I'm not upset, just a little disappointed.

After listening to Dr. Wagner's childhood story that led her to become a volcanologist, the captain explains his decision to the doctors to head to the other side of Crete. Proteus alerts him for the first port side turn. "What we need to find is there," he said. "Harris couldn't see it because of the storm from the distance in the darkness. I promise you Amanda you'll see Calliste. If we had as much food as we do time, we would all be a little heavier." He winked, bringing a smile to the doctor's face.

The doctors leave the bridge to get coffee for themselves and return to find the captain sleeping in his chair. They waved the coffee under his nose, and the captain shakes his head, clearing the cobwebs. He takes a sip, ordering Proteus "reduce speed to eighteen knots before making the second port side turn."

Heading east on the southern side of the island, bringing the ship up to periscope depth at five knots, the captain raises the scope. The observations being shown to the crew, they see the sun soaked southern coastline of Crete. Finding a Minoan society working on their daily routine. Dozens of reed boats tied up on the docks loaded with fruit and vegetables. Hundreds of people work on the lowland's farms to the west, while others herd flocks of Cretan goats, farming on the terraced hillsides to the east.

Mud brick dwellings cover the coastline, watching on the monitor Dr. Wagner comments on the thriving society the Minoans have created. "Alexi, they look very peaceful." Stepping back from the scope the captain says "there are thousands of Minoans on the island. Peaceful doesn't make it any easier to resupply." Checking the time, he orders, "Proteus, lower the scope and make a hard starboard turn to bring us about. Lay in a new course for Santorini on the chart, which will get us close to Calliste, and the other flotilla."

Triton II completed coming about, the captain picked up the bridge comm mic ordering Chief Kim to the bridge for relief duty. In her cabin Monica Wallace hears the captain's order over the ship's comms. She steps out into the passageway and finds Chief Kim slowly making his way to the lift. She picked up her pace to catch up with him and asked, "Ha-Kun, would you like company on your relief watch?"

Monica, after helping the chief onto the lift, his crutches under his arms, they arrive at the bridge walking together, the chief reports to the captain. The captain rises from his chair helps the chief take his seat. The captain turns to Monica Wallace. "Ms. Wallace, if you play *Go* with the chief, remember this, he beats Proteus." The captain turned to the chief. "Our course is plotted. Wake me when we have sonar contact with the other flotilla."

Cruising at a depth of three-hundred-fifty meters north for sixty minutes, Proteus reduces the speed to eighteen knots, maneuvering a wide starboard turn to the northeast. After Proteus informs Chief Kim of the course change, the chief has Monica Wallace activate the sonar imaging system. They pick up six signals seventeen kilometers off the north coast of Crete. Monica has Ha-Kun look at the screen. "That's them," said the chief. "The wind must be with them. They have sailed quite the distance from port." Chief Kim picks up the bridge comm mic and requests the captain to report to the bridge.

After hearing Chief Kim's announcement, the captain rolls over in bed wrapping his arm around Dr. Wagner. He asks, "Are you awake?" He rolls back to the other side. Amanda sits up on her side of the bed, handing Alexi his pants and begins putting on her own she asked. "Alexi, do you have a plan for how to resupply our food shortage?"

"Our meal for the day is at Fourteen hundred hours," he said. "We will discuss a plan of action at that time." He pulled his shirt over his head, they leave the cabin, meeting Dr. Franklin coming out of her own.

Chief Kim uses his crutches to walk back to the captain's chair ordering, "Proteus, reduce speed, and bring the ship to periscope depth. Checking range and distance to fifteen thousand meters. Captain Morozoff and the doctors arrive at the bridge, the captain asked, "What's our status, Chief?"

"Fifteen thousand meters from the flotilla," responded Kim. "Triton II is at periscope depth."

The captain hands the chief his crutches, then turns to Monica Wallace at the sonar station, "Have you ever looked out of a periscope before?"

"No, sir" she replied.

The captain gestures for her to look through the periscope. "Try something new," he said. Taking her position, Monica Wallace turns the scope and starts describing what she sees.

"There's a lot of sunshine not a cloud in the sky. The men on the boats aren't wearing shirts. They look like Greek gods chiseled out of sandstone. The doctors really should look," she said, giving the scope to the captain and smiling at the doctors.

Monica goes to help Chief Kim, relieved from his watch, and walks to the lift. The captain gives her a smile, then looks though the scope. He sees the flotilla drifting with the current. He quickly checks the time on his communication watch, and sees it is almost fourteen hundred hours. He asks, "Proteus, what the ship's current position?"

"Fifty-six kilometers from Santorini according to our charts," Proteus replied. The captain picks up the comm mic and orders the crew to the mess hall. The doctors look through the periscope, then get up to leave. The captain gives one more order to Proteus. "Make our depth one- hundred-fifty meters, speed seventeen knots. Alert me when the ship reaches the twenty-four-kilometer mark from the island of Santorini." Harris Franklin is slowly waking up in his bed thinking about his past when he hears a knock on his door. He puts on his clothes and walks half asleep to answer it. Captain Morozoff is standing in front of him with the doctors, and says, "I need you, my friend. The time has come to formulate a plan. An excursion on a deserted island is one thing, it is quite another when there could be thousands of Minoans living on Crete." Dr Garcia is relieved by crew member Gale and joins the rest of the crew in the mess hall. She sits next to Dr. Franklin at the captain's table. The captain waits for Chief Kim and Harris Franklin, before updating the crew. While serving the captain his meal, crew member Flynn tells the captain in a whisper, "There's two days of supplies left."

After eating his meal, the captain stands, the crew quiet themselves for the update. "Our food supply is critical," he said gravely. "The most populated part of Crete is where the food is being cultivated. We need a plan to solve our problem without being seen by the Minoans."

The captain looks around the mess hall and sees Grant Roberts being nudged in the sides to get up and speak by Carol Davis and Monica Wallace, to talk about his idea. The captain makes eye contact and says, "Do you have something to say, Grant?"

Grant clears his throat and begins. "Sir, with all due respect, I suggest not going ashore to resupply. If we're seen raiding their farmland, we could be caught, captured, or killed as invaders. We could risk surfacing Triton II near the last boat on the flotilla, taking their catch and disappearing under the sea. The ship will scare the hell out of them! None of us must risk our lives."

Captain Morozoff runs his hand through his greying hair, waiting for anyone to suggest an alternative to Grants plan. Dr. Wagner stands offering another plan. "Alexi, we're heading to Calliste. It could be deserted, and there should be the same vegetation that's on the island of Crete. It will be worth investigating. None of us want to die as invaders Grant. Playing pirate is a last resort."

The captain decides to take Dr. Wagner's advice to explore Calliste. He informs the crew to watch the observations from the periscope, then turns to the bridge crew sitting at the table. He says, "You're all with me."

They return to the bridge and take their station positions, Chief Kim at sonar with doctors Franklin and Garcia at navigation. Proteus informs the captain, "Triton II has reached the twenty- four kilometers mark, from the charted position." The captain orders Proteus to reduce speed to five knots and bring the ship up to periscope depth.

The captain relinquishes his chair to Dr. Wagner and raises the scope, ordering Proteus to link the periscope observations to the monitor screens throughout Triton II. Amanda surveys the waters. Turning to the stern she sees the Minoans still drifting with the current in the distance.

Adjusting the range to distance looking for Calliste, first to the east then west, she sees the summit of the Calliste volcano. The clouds covering the slopes down the mountainside extending out to sea. Stepping back, turning to the captain, she reports her observation. "Alexi, Calliste is three degrees to the port. There's a cloud covering over the island, extending out to sea four thousand eight hundred twenty-eight meters from Triton II's current position if I'm reading this correctly."

Captain Morozoff nudges Harris on the side, smiling like a proud peacock fanning its feathers, after listening to Dr. Wagner's report.

Amanda is watching the cloud covering darkening in the distance, through the periscope, the bridge crew is seeing it on the monitor screen. Chief Kim alerts the captain, "Sensors had picked up a brief E.M. field modulations for a moment, atmospheric discharges illuminate the clouds on the screens."

The captain orders a full stop and stands behind Chief Kim. He orders, "Give me a sonar image of the island." He has Dr. Wagner move away from the scope. Looking through, he sees the clouds, and bolts of atmospheric discharge streaking across the scope. He steps back, turning to Dr. Wagner and asks, "What could be causing this cloud formation?"

"Seismic activity from the island releasing steam from volcanic vents," she responded. Chief Kim informs the captain, "Sir, I'm getting no topography back on the island. Possible interference from atmospheric activity."

The captain wants his best friend to look; he turns the scope over to Harris Franklin.

Harris turns the scope to the stern, watching the Minoan boats extend the long oars rowing back to Crete. He steps back from the scope and remarks, "Grant's plan for playing pirate is looking better."

Captain Morozoff paced the bridge and said, "We can't go to the island without knowing what's out there. We could damage the ship and I'm not risking anyone with the last raft kit."

"Maybe we can catch that last ship in the flotilla as Grant suggested," responded Harris. Standing up on his crutches Chief Kim suggested to the captain, "Sir, we could use the D.P.V. (Dive Propulsion Vehicle) down in the hull."

The captain paces the bridge, contemplating the consequences of the chief's plan. He walks over to Dr. Franklin at navigation and said, "Heather, you and I are the most experienced using the D.P.V."

Harris Franklin places his hand on Alexi's shoulder. "My friend, you're the captain of the Triton II the ship and crew need you; I'll go with my sister."

Trying to compose herself, Dr. Garcia takes three deep breaths before speaking to Harris. "Consider this before you and the love of my life risk the unknown. The clouds may dissipate by morning."

Hearing the expression of concern from Adriana for Heather and Harris, the captain starts a plan of action. "Proteus," he ordered, "circle the clouds edge at four thousand meters around the island at periscope depth at five knots. By morning if the clouds haven't dissipated, we will move forward with the chief's plan. Ha-Kun, what do you need?"

The Chief responded, "I need Harris and his team to join me in engineering sir."

Chief Kim enters engineering for the first time since breaking his leg. The chief points to the D.P.V. as Grant Roberts and Harris bring it out of storage. Grant asked, "What is it you want us to do with this?"

Heather walks around the D.P.V. tells the team how they can help. "Our problem will be surfacing with the D.P.V. It's not designed to ascend from the depth of the dive chambers."

The group huddles together, discussing how to solve the problem. Carol Davis looks around engineering and sees a disassembled shark cage, and some spare air tanks. She suggests, "We can reconfigure the frame from the shark cage. Mounting four tanks, with pressurized gas, attach the D.P.V. onto the frame. You'll lose some power from the weight but using the air regulators releasing the gas the D.P.V. will rise nice and slow to the surface, to submerge again, fill the empty tanks with seawater."

Chief Kim volunteered to cover Harris Franklin's overnight bridge watch, so he can rest in case the captain enacts the plan for the D.P.V. to go ashore. Working through the evening hours Carol Davis, Monica Wallace and Grant Roberts finished the modifications. Monica Wallace joins the chief on the bridge. Triton II circles the island of Calliste, the cloud covering encompasses the entire island out to sea. Atmospheric discharge continues through the night. Two hours before sunrise, the captain and Dr. Wagner arrive on the bridge for a final check on the island before enacting Chief Kim's plan. Captain Morozoff sees the cloud covering and orders Proteus to bring the ship to a full stop, forty meters from the cloud's edge. Picking up the comm mic he orders Dr. Franklin and Harris Franklin to report to the engineers, putting the plan in motion.

After reporting to engineering Heather and Harris Franklin put on their wetsuits, while Grant Roberts and Carol Davis are loading spare air tanks, spearfishing guns, machetes and the flare gun, into the makeshift compartment for the redesigned D.P.V. Chief Kim secures a tracker to the frame. Captain Morozoff straps on the air tanks, securing them on Heather's and Harris' backs, checks the air regulators and places the scuba helmets over their heads. Once everything had been checked and rechecked, they entered the dive chamber. Captain Morozoff gives the order to flood the chamber with seawater. Taking their positions behind the D.P.V., Dr. Franklin, checks the comm link to the ship and asks, "Can you hear me?" Looking through the chamber door window, Dr. Garcia answered, "Five by five, please be careful." Harris gives the captain the thumbs up on his comm link. Triton II is in a position where the starboard hull door opens. After the D.P.V. clears the ship, the hull door closes, and it propels for the island. The captain returns to the bridge with Dr. Wagner and Chief Kim. The chief is sitting at navigation, tracking the D.P.V. ten meters from the clouds edge. The sensors detect another E.M. field modulation and the chief lose the tracking signal. "Sir, we lost the signal," he said. The captain puts his hands over his face, takes a deep breath, and turns to Amanda.

"Great! Now, I must go tell Adriana we've lost contact."

Symmetries of Life

With communications cut off the D.P.V. propels under a concentric structure, with an outer ring an inner ring, connected by cylindrical extensions connecting the two rings like spokes in a wheel. They come to a full stop, looking at one another. Harris counts down with his fingers, three, two, one! They release gas from the tanks attached to the frame, rising slowly to the surface.

They remove their scuba helmets. Harris Franklin asked, "What is this?"

Bobbing up and down in the water, Dr. Franklin responds, "I don't know. It wasn't built by the Minoans."

Removing their air tanks and stow them in the D.P.V. holding compartment, Harris takes the pair of deck binoculars he surveys the area. "We seemed to be in a wedge between these concentric rings," he said, "There's rungs coming out of the water to the surface of this structure." They swim behind the D.P.V. tying it to the rungs coming out of the sea.

After removing their scuba fins and stowing them with the air tanks, they climb the rungs, Harris first and his sister right behind him. They climb rung after rung, finally reaching the surface. Harris pulls his sister over the top. A smokey, charcoal-greyish alloy covers the surface, with crystals embedded in the surface of the cylindrical extensions.

Heather takes the deck binoculars from her brother and surveys the area. She sees seven more extensions, an obelisk capped with a pyramid shaped crystal, at the center of the structure. Heather can only conclude the structure is a craft. Surrounding the obelisk spherical structures, domed building and small pyramids with symbols she thinks she recognizes, she returns the deck binoculars to Harris, and said, "Look for yourself. We could be standing on Atlantis".

Looking to the south the clouds are no longer present. Harris Franklin sees the symbols on the structures, an eight-pointed star, three wavy lines and a symbol for the crystals embedded in the craft. Removing their wet suits down to shorts and tee shirts, they begin walking the crystal pathway embedded in the craft. Turning to his sister, Harris says, "If this is Atlantis, where are the Atlanteans?"

"I don't know," Heather said uneasily, "but I feel like we're being watched. We should take the D.P.V. and return Triton II." The two walk back, put on wet suits and dive into the water. They help each other with the air tanks, secure their scuba helmets, and check the air regulators. Then they untie the D.P.V. opening the empty air tanks filling with seawater, they descend underneath the waves returning to the ship.

***

It's been two hours since the Triton II lost contact with the D.P.V., when Proteus picks up the transponder signal alerting the captain. He picks up the comm mic and orders Chief Kim along with Harris Franklin's team to engineering, he informs the crew, "D.P.V. is returning to the ship." Walking the crew level passageway, crew member Knight turns around heading back to the infirmary to replace the doctor for the care of Chief Jones after hearing the captain's orders.

Joining the others in engineering Dr. Garcia hears the captain contact the D.P.V. Twenty meters from the starboard hull door, "are you receiving me." Harris Franklin stops the forward motion of the D.P.V. Dr. Franklin answers, "Five by five Alexi, ready to come aboard." The hull door opens the D.P.V. propels into the dive chamber, the hull door closes the seawater begins to drain from the dive chamber the D.P.V. slowly resting on the deck.

Captain Morozoff and Grant Roberts open the hatch and help remove the scuba helmets and air tanks from the

Franklins. Dr. Garcia runs to Heather hugging her, crying tears of joy upon her return. Harris congratulates his team on a job well done on the redesign of the D.P.V. They remove their wet suits and accept the towels to dry off. Harris is eager and ready to report on their excursion when the lights in engineering begin to flicker off and on. Proteus alerts the captain, "Sir, our systems are being breached. A virus is taking data from memory files, reactor schematics, ship logs, and crew manifest."

The captain looks at the Franklins and asks, "Where is that coming from?"

"We never made it to the island of Calliste," Harris said. "We don't know where the breech is coming from!"

Crew member Knight in the infirmary uses the comm mic to inform Dr. Garcia there has been a breach in the medical logs. Grabbing the comm mic in engineering, the captain orders the crew to the mess hall at once, telling the Franklins to change into dry clothes before reporting on what they have seen. The Franklins enter the mess hall, Dr. Garcia watching the monitor from the infirmary with Knight, Harris has his sister start the report. He sits down at the captain's table with Dr. Wagner.

"We never made it to the island," Heather said. "What we found was a floating city in the sea. A craft or vessel of some kind over six thousand meters in diameter. At its center, an obelisk stands over forty meters, capped with a crystal pyramid. Surrounded by structures, pyramids, spheres, and half domed buildings. There are eight cylindrical extensions connecting the two concentric rings, the marking on the structures I recognized as Atlantean."

The captain and crew sit in stunned silence, trying to understand the perplexity of Dr. Franklin's report. Proteus alerts Captain Morozoff that they're receiving a message from an unknown source. **We can help the one whose cycle is ending!**

Dr. Garcia interjects from the infirmary, "The message must be talking about Chief Jones, captain!" Looking over at Heather, the captain asked, "Did you see any of these Atlanteans, on this floating city?"

"No, Alexi," Heather said in a shaky voice, "but it felt like we were being watched." The captain orders Proteus to reply, "Tell them we accept their help!"

Leaving the mess hall the captain returns to the bridge, with Dr. Wagner and the Franklins. Amanda is at the sonar station when a sensor alarm detects another EM modulation. The captain raises the scope he describes what is happening, "the clouds are beginning to lighten, the atmospheric discharges have ceased." Pointing to Amanda, he has her activate the sonar imager, the captain says, "Let's see what we can see!"

The scans returning to the monitor screen show the floating city in the sea. Amanda turns to Heather sitting next to her at navigation asked, "Could this really be Atlantis?" Proteus informs the captain they're receiving coordinates for docking inside the cloud covering. Harris Franklin turns to the captain, and says, "There were no clouds when we were on the craft."

Heather confirms the coordinates, and Harris concurs from navigation. Lowering the scope, the captain orders the ship to a depth one hundred meters, to slow ahead.

Clearing the outer concentric ring of the floating city, arriving at the coordinates surfacing Triton II in between the rings, dropping the anchor. Proteus informs the captain they're receiving another signal with instructions for the Franklins, to bring the healer to the obelisk. The captain grabbed the comm mic, and said, "Whoever they are, they know who we are, and what we do," he orders Dr. Garcia to the bridge.

Crew member Knight stays in the infirmary to watch the chief, while Dr. Garcia reports to the bridge as ordered. Harris opens the bridge hatch he helps Adriana, and his sister climbs out the hatch on deck. Taking a deep breath of fresh sea air, the three of them head to the rung ladder coming up out of the sea, from the craft. Captain Morozoff, on deck watching them reach out for the rungs, begin their climb to the surface. The captain returns to the bridge, grabs the comm mic and orders the crew out on deck. Harris, Heather, and Adriana reach the top of the craft, hearing voices coming from down below. Seeing the stern hatch open, the crew is assembling on the deck. Harris and the doctors start walking along the crystal pathway to the obelisk.

Captain Morozoff is standing on the deck with Dr. Wagner and tells the crew, "We'll go to the surface and no further till the Franklins and Dr. Garcia return from their excursion." The captain takes the rung, followed by Amanda and begins the climb. One by one the crew make their way up to the surface. Chief Kim is the last one to reach the top aided by Monica Wallace and get help from the captain, who pulls the chief to the surface. Gazing out from the surface, the midday sun reflects off the surface structures. They look south towards the island of Crete.

Amanda turns to the captain and says, "Alexi, it's like Harris said. There are no clouds."

Crew member Flynn walks up to the captain. "Sir, when should we start preparing the meal of the day?"

"Give it two hours Flynn," said the captain, "That should be sufficient time for stretching the legs, getting fresh air. Save three meals for the Franklins and Dr. Garcia for their return."

Walking at a brisk pace along the crystal pathway, the doctors walking hand in hand with Harris Franklin reaching the obelisk, an accessway opens for them to step inside. Descending level after level, Dr. Garcia asks the same question Harris did. "If this is Atlantis where are the Atlanteans?"

The lift comes to a stop; they exit onto the level. In the flickering lights from machinery, immersed in colors of the spectrum, a voice speaks. "There're no Atlanteans here. I'm the Keeper, the guardian of the Lovian civilization, all that you see was built by them."

The Franklins stare at each other and have a revelation of recognition. "Keeper" is an artificial intelligence. Dr. Garcia speaks to Keeper, "I'm the healer. We came here to accept your offer to help a member of our family. I need to know exactly how you plan to help."

"There's a plant that grows in the hydroponic level on one of the eight extensions of this spacecraft from the Lovian home world," Keeper answered, "An extract from this plant will kill the bacteria invading his body, allowing us to replace the damaged tissue."

The doctor responds, "I get it that you want to administer an anti- viral into his system, but how can you replace human tissue?"

The cylindrical shaft accessway opens and an autonomous levitating transport waits for them. Keeper responds to the doctor, "The Lovians are clones of the original builders of this ship. I was created to guard their civilization from extinction. Scraping of your cells will be used to obtain the genetic code for your species to grow new tissue, using Lovian biological material for the cloning process."

After hearing the Keeper's explanation, the Franklins turn to Dr. Garcia for her professional opinion as the medical officer of Triton II. Pointing to the transport, Adriana gives her opinion. "That transport is to bring Kurt here. If they can stop him from dying, Heather and I should rreturn to Triton II. There's no other way." Nodding his head in agreement with Adriana, Harris says, "She's right Heather. Tell Alexi what we have learned here. I'll stay here to gather more information. The who, what, where, when, and the why, the Lovians are here." They take the transport up the cylindrical shaft to the surface, being informed they can contact Triton II. They glide over the crystal pathway. Dr. Garcia contacts Proteus, to inform the captain to have Chief Jones ready to transport back with her, to receive the treatment necessary to save his life.

While the crew is eating the meal of the day, Captain Morozoff is notified of the doctor's return and the request she made. The captain leaves for the infirmary with Dr. Wagner and crew member Flynn, to help prepare the chief. Crew member Gale stands as Captain Morozoff enters the infirmary. "What do you need, Sir? "Prepare Chief Jones to be transported back to the floating city with Dr. Garcia to receive treatment," he ordered.

Gale grabs a stretcher and with help from the captain, they put the comatose chief's frail body on the stretcher. The smell of decaying tissue permeates the infirmary. Crew member Flynn and the captain strapped the chief down on the stretcher.

Harris walking the core level for Keeper, feeling a little Déjà vu from his adolescence, seeing the cavern core for S.A.I.N. for the very first time by Captain Stone. He asked Keeper, "Who are the Lovians? Where did they come from? When did you arrive on planet Earth? Why are you helping Chief Jones and what do you want?"

"The Lovians onboard are all that's left, of a race of biological entities from the planet Lova. Believers in the **One** who created the cosmos, a shared vision by every Lovian, eleven thousand cycles ago, given to them by the **One**. They saw the destruction of their home world, when their home star becomes a red giant vaporizing the planet. Their belief in the **One** led them to build this spacecraft."

Harris, stunned by the answers to his questions, the Keeper continued. "For a thousand cycles they lived underground, changing their physical appearance from the lack of star light to save their species from certain extinction. I was built during this time as part of the ship. Ten thousand cycles have passed since this spacecraft left, to seek a new home world. Before reaching their planned destination, the ship was hit by a shockwave from a **Gamma Ray Burst** sending the ship hurdling though space, getting captured by this planet's gravitational pull, having to make an emergency landing on this planet you call Earth. There's a symmetry to life in the cosmos. I can help you, and you in turn can help the Lovians, this is why I'm helping the one you call Kurt."

The sound of something rising from the lower level of the Lovian spacecraft, the access way opens to the cylindrical shaft. Exiting the shaft a humanoid standing one hundred and forty- seven centimeters in height, wrinkled whitish grey skin covers the body like scales on a dragon. Two arms, two legs, two hands with a thumb and two fingers, two feet with three toes, a spherical shaped head. Two eye cavities in the shape of diamonds, concentric emerald, green eyes, underneath three nostril holes one a top of the other two like a pyramid. Small aperture below the nose. "I 'am Ebe," it said. "I speak for all the Lovians on this ship, I haven't spoken aloud in tens of thousands of cycles. I will tell you what we want, after we've repaired the one you call Kurt." Gesturing for Harris to follow him, "We must go prepare the cloning chamber."

***

The captain and crew member Flynn slowly walked along the passageway, with Gale holding the ventilator keeping the chief alive. Dr Wagner runs ahead to signal the lift. Carefully going out the hatch Amanda takes the ventilator from crew member Gale, helping the doctor's assistant get on deck. The two of them help pull the stretcher up the hatch. The captain steadies the chief's head; crew member Flynn pushes the chief up the hatch.

 Doctors Franklin and Garcia arrive as the transport glides over the crystal pathway, descending to the deck. Placing the stretcher on the transport, crew member Gale straps both sides down to the transport she asked the captain, "Sir, I'd like to go with Dr. Garcia to care for the chief."

 Nodding his head affirmatively, the captain tells Gale to climb onboard the transport with Dr. Garcia. Crew member Flynn hands the doctor food for herself and Harris Franklin. He informs the captain, "Sir, the remaining food onboard will last one more day. We need to get to the island."

 Dr. Franklin steps off and hugs Adriana, then kisses Kurt on the forehead, "Bring him back to us, please," she said. The transport ascends to the crystal pathway. Heather turns to Alexi, "I'll update the crew on what we know so far,"

 The captain climbs down the hatch, grabs the bridge comm mic, and orders the crew to the mess hall. Crew member

Flynn goes to the galley to bring Dr. Franklin food, while the crew assembles in the hall. Heather sits next to Dr. Wagner trying to finish her meal, before updating the crew she turns to Amanda. "It's not what I thought," she said.

Heather stands up, getting the crew's attention. "The floating city I thought could be Atlantis isn't that at all. There are no Atlantean's. We met the guardian of a race of beings that call themselves Lovians. The guardian is an artificial intelligence that calls itself the Keeper. They are the inhabitants of the floating spacecraft. Chief Jones is on his way there, to receive a treatment to save his life. My brother is trying to learn more information about them." The crew sits in utter silence with dumbfounded expressions on their faces.

***

Onboard another transport, Harris Franklin and Ebe take the lift down the cylindrical shaft to the cloning level of the Lovian spacecraft. Exiting the shaft into the chamber, floating in tanks of amniotic fluids inside sacs, Lovians are being grown. Each body at various stages of development. Ebe prepares the examination area for the arrival of Chief Jones. Sensing them on the crystal pathway Ebe tells Harris, "We must hurry, before the one you call Kurt, transcends into the

One."

They reach the obelisk, activating the accessway. The doctor and crew member Gale is taken to the cloning level. Exiting the shaft into the chamber, Dr. Garcia and crew member Gale see the menagerie of an alien species being grown in the sacs of amniotic fluids. They see Harris Franklin at the examination area. The extraterrestrial biological entity steps in front of them, introducing himself. "I am Ebe."

Harris is standing with Dr. Garcia and crew member Gale, giving them time to absorb the presence of the extraterrestrial biological entity. Stepping off the transport Adriana takes Ebe's hand in hers, she asked, "What do we need to do?"

Crew member Gale begins to unstrap the chief from the stretcher. Knowing there's nothing else he can do until the procedure is over, Harris kisses Kurt on the forehead. He then asks Ebe if he can use the transport to return to Triton II. Harris gets on the transport, asking one more question for the Keeper to answer before he returns to update the crew. "Do you know why my sister and I were heading to the island?"

"Yes," said the Keeper. "You will be able to search for suitable vegetation for your consumption at first light.

Communication with your ship will be restored once you're on the surface."

Ebe takes Dr. Garcia and crew member Gale behind the amniotic tanks, where three flat examination slabs pull out from the wall of the chamber. Flat screened monitors over the tables flash codes the doctor have never seen before, she asks, "What language is that you're using to watch Kurts's vitals, during the procedure?"

"That is the code language for the Keeper" Ebe responded. "He will perform the procedure. I need you to remove the covering on your bodies before you can be scanned."

After removing their own clothing, Dr. Garcia and Gale remove the infirmary gown from Kurt. They reach to pick up his body to move him to the examination table, but before they can, his body levitates above the stretcher moving through the air. Ebe, standing with his eyes focused on Chief Jones, his right arm extended, his thumb and two fingers bawled together guiding the chief's body to the table, putting him down gently. The monitor activates four robotic arms extending out from the wall just below the monitor for each table. A mask comes down from one of the four robotic arms placing it on Kurt's face, to help with his breathing.

Adriana walks over to the table in amazement at what she had seen, she asked, "How did you do that?" Lying back on the table to be examined, Ebe explains, "A gift from the **One** that created the cosmos," the robotic arms extend down, laser beams start scanning the three of them.

Passing over their bodies the laser beams created a detailed hologram of the human body appearing above them. Dr. Garcia sees the bacteria spreading through Kurt's body, another robotic arm reaches over Kurt's body with a needle, injecting the chief with the plant extract. Ebe stands between the two women, and explains, "We need to take healthy cell samples from the two of you, to replicate the vessels, veins, and arteries necessary to repair Kurt's damaged body. The procedure is not without discomfort. "Are you ready?" The doctor nods her head, ready for the procedure to begin.
The Keeper's robotic arms extend with a scalpel at the end, scraping the upper left arms of Dr. Garcia and crew member Gale, placing the samples on a transparent slide. Wincing in pain the women watch Ebe take the samples to the cloning chamber control panel. Keeper, removes the scalpel, replacing it with a nozzle, spraying an aerosol on the scraped area

bringing instant relief for the pain. Returning to the examination area Ebe asks Gale to extend her other arm to start a blood transfusion for Kurt during the procedure. Completing the examination, Ebe said, "You're finished. Now you will rest. The extract and the growth of biologic material will take some time to complete."

***

Harris Franklin contacts Triton II and tells Proteus to have Captain Morozoff assemble the crew. Gliding over the crystal pathway, the transport descends onto the deck. Hearing the captain's announcement to the crew, Dr. Franklin goes out on deck to meet her brother. Stepping off the transport Harris gets a hug from his sister, she asked, "How's Adriana?"

"They're going ahead with the procedure," Harris said. "She's confident in the Lovian and Keeper." Harris paused, then asked, "Did any of that look familiar to you Heather?"

"Yes, it did, a little Déjà vu feel to it," she replied, climbing down the hatch. Captain Morozoff is pacing the crew level passageway, anxiously waiting for Harris Franklin to report on his information gathering on the Lovians and Keeper. He sees them exist the lift, raising his hands, he quiets the crew. Dr. Franklin sits next to Dr. Wagner. Shaking Harris' hand, the captain asked, "What more do you have to report?"

"I met a Lovian calling it's self Ebe," Harris replied. "They are a biological species different than us but highly advanced in their technologies. Dr. Garcia and crew member Gale are with Ebe and Keeper trying to save Kurts' life. I don't how many Lovians are onboard their spacecraft. I believe Ebe is a conduit between them and their artificial intelligence. Ebe won't tell us what they want from us, until the procedure is completed on Kurt. Harris waits for any reaction or questions, then continues. "At first light, we can search the island of Calliste for a food supply. Alexi, you and Amanda should go ashore to explore the island, Heather and I will return to Keeper's core to check on our people."

When he finished his report to the crew, he asked crew member Flynn to bring him something to eat from the galley. Captain Morozoff stands to address the hall. "In the morning, we will do as Harris suggests, limiting our contact. It is in our best interest until we know more about what they want."

After being dismissed the Triton II crew settle into their cabins. Dr. Franklin has a restless night, sleeping alone and thinking about the one she loves. Finally giving up on sleep, she showers, gets dressed and goes to talk to her brother. She quietly walks along the passageway to Harris Franklin's cabin and knocks on the door. Harris, being awoken from the same dream he had every night, since traversing the vortex at Tamu Massif. Harris opens the door, Heather says, "I'm having trouble sleeping alone, I'm in love with Adriana."

Smiling at his sister, Harris welcomes her inside and closes the door. "She'll be all right," he said soothingly. "All of them. There's something I trust about the Keeper." He smiles once more at Heather and heads into the bathroom to take a shower.

Dr. Wagner anxious to explore the island gets out of bed. She feels a rolling wave sensation affecting her equilibrium, she falls back into bed, waking the captain. "Alexi, did you feel that rolling motion?" asked Amanda. Getting out of bed, Alexi answers, "It's just the waves in the sea moving the ship being anchored."

The Captain and Dr, Wagner leave his cabin, seeing the Franklins exiting Harris' cabin, the four of them head to the bridge. Harris opening of the hatch, allowing the sunlight to shine down the hole. The captain orders Proteus to contact the Keeper. Then he grabs the comm mic and announces to the crew, "We are on our way. Chief Kim is in command until my return."

***

Boarding the transport left overnight on the bow of Triton II the captain, the doctors and Harris Franklin ascended to the surface onto the crystal pathway. They slow down as they approach the obelisk. Keeper contacts the transport, "Your Healer and her assistant are starting to wake up from their rest period. The Franklins will be taken to the cloning chamber. Captain Morozoff, you and Dr. Wagner will continue to the surface corridor till reaching the best accessway to the island to begin your search for consumable vegetation"

The transport reaches the obelisk and the accessway to the cylindrical shaft opens, the Franklins descend to the cloning chamber. Dr. Garcia wakes up at the examination table, confused for a moment about her surroundings. She looks over at crew member Gale on the next table and sits up, she asked, "How long do you think we have been asleep?" Adriana notices Chief Jones is breathing on his own, she checks his pulse with her two fingers. Gale removes the fresh dressing over the chief's torso and sees the graphed cloned human tissue grown from their cells, using alien biological material. Gale answers the doctor, "I don't know how long we have been sleeping, but this is a medical miracle."

Entering the cloning chambers, Dr. Franklin sees the sacs holding the clones in various stages of development in the amnionic tanks. Dr Garcia and crew member Gale step out from behind the tanks. Heather hugs Adriana, and says, "This is incredible!"

Adriana takes Harris Franklin by the hand, holding Heather's with her other hand. She shows them Kurt breathing on his own, she says, "This is a miracle! The Keeper said they could help. Kurt is going to be fine.

He'll be coming around soon." Smiles beam from the Franklin's faces at the news of their family member's miraculous recovery.

Ebe enters the chamber walking towards the doctors. Harris remarks to the Keeper, "We're grateful for what you have done to save Kurt's life, but I don't want him waking up on this ship. Kurt will be frightened, confused within his surroundings. Can we move him to Triton II?" Ebe stands over the chief extending his right arm placing his thumb and two fingers together, Kurts body slowly rises moving through the air for the stretcher on the transport being strapped in.

Having seen Ebe use his powers before, Adriana smiles

at the Franklins', the look of astonishment upon their faces as Kurt's body levitates in the air, she remarks, "I think that means we can take him Harris. Gale and I will return to the ship with Kurt."

Ebe informs Adriana, "Proteus has been notified of your return to Triton II. You and crew member Gale board the transport to take Kurt to the infirmary on the ship." Harris reaches out his hand to Ebe's shaking his hand in friendship.

"We stand ready to help you and your people," said Harris. Ebe joins the Franklins on the transport taking the lift to Keeper's core level.

***

Gliding over the crystal pathway, Dr. Wagner anticipation grows from her childhood dreams of the island becoming a reality the closer she gets to Calliste. Steam rising from the volcanic vents on the slopes of the mountain side, grey smoke bellows out into the atmosphere from the crater summit. Reaching the end of the outer ring of the Lovian spacecraft corridor extension going down the rungs of the ladder, jumping into the sea, they swim for thirty meters to the shoreline.

Soaking wet they make their way inland to the

mountain slopes, finding only shriveled up plants, fig trees with dried up fruit lying on the ground. Captain Morozoff picking up a fig, having the fruit smacked away by Amanda out of his hand. "Alexi don't try to eat them, I think the fruit is poisoned from sulfur dioxide coming from the volcanic vents," said Amanda.

Standing in disappointment at what they have found, the island shakes from a tremor, dying fruit falling from the trees sending the doctor and the captain to the ground. Amanda gets to her feet and tells the captain, "That roll I felt this morning was a seismic wave. The island of Calliste is unstable. There's nothing here for us. We must go back and find another solution to our food shortage." Reaching the shoreline, they dive into the water swimming to the rungs. They climb to the surface of the spacecraft taking the transport back to the obelisk.

***

Dr. Garcia and crew member Gale returned to Triton II with Chief Jones. The Franklins stand in the Keeper's core when he informs them that Dr. Wagner and the captain have returned from searching on the island and are descending the shaft. They exit into the core level for Keeper and see the

Franklins with the Lovian. The nonplused reaction from the captain stepping off the transport putting out his hand to Ebe, while Harris introduces him to them both. "Alexi, Amanda, this is Ebe," he said. "We are in the Keeper's core of operation for the Lovian spacecraft."

Shaking Ebe's hand the captain asked, "Harris how's Jonesy?"

"They saved his life," Harris said. "Ebe is about to tell us what kind of help they need.

Though I don't know what kind of help we could possibly offer a race technologically more advanced than us. "When Keeper detected your fusion reactor signature, we tracked your movements realizing you couldn't detect our ship," said Ebe. "We knew that you were investigating the primitives on the island, the ones in the watercrafts, we became curious about you. Not being frightened by the energy shield hologram, we let you breach our shield, to find out more about you. When the Franklins came on to the surface of the ship, seeing that you look like the primitives. When you left so abruptly, I had Keeper breach Proteus systems. Reading your ship's logs, we discovered that you invertedly caused a temporal anomaly saving this planet from extinction. I sensed that one of you was about to transcend into the **One**. I had the Keeper contact you, because putting life of others before your own is a noble act."

Ebe walks over to a control panel darkening the core level, the Keeper projects a hologram on the screen of the schematics of the Lovian spacecraft. "Four fusion reactors power this ship's propulsion processing hydrogen from space. The crystals embedded in the ship are conduits for power distributed to the ship's systems including myself," said the Keeper.

"As you can see our reactors have been under water for thousands of cycles. Your star provides just enough energy to sustain the crystals to run the ships systems and power the energy shield, cloaking this vessel. We are unable to leave this planet you call Earth to continue our voyage, to find a new home world," stated Ebe.

Having listened to the explanations of the Lovian situation, Harris Franklin, always the engineer walks the level thinking aloud, telling his sister, his best friend, and Dr. Wagner exactly what the Lovians are requesting of them. "They want to convert their processes for the four fusions reactors to those of Triton II's to generate enough power to break free of Earth's gravity and return to space to continue their voyage, to search for a new home world."

Dr. Wagner sitting quietly after hearing the tale from the Lovian and their guardian.

Listening to Harris' remarks on the kind of help the Lovians are asking for, Amanda looks over at Alexi. He nods his head to her to report what they've learned on the island, to the Franklins. "If we're going to help our new friends, all of you need to hear this before we move forward with any plan of action. There's a problem with the island Calliste.

There's no edible food on the island for us to harvest. The vegetation is poisoned from the volcanic activity, the island is unstable, we felt tremors this morning. Heather, you know what happens here in Earth's history, how the Minoans civilization was lost. The Calliste volcano is going to erupt, could be days, weeks, months, but it will happen."

Dr. Franklin is walking around, shaking her head at the report given by Amanda. Taking Ebe by the hand, Heather said, "We must go back to Triton II. There are problems we need to solve that our people need to know about. We'll contact you and the Keeper after we have assembled our crew." Boarding the transport, taking the cylindrical shaft to the surface, gliding over the crystal pathway back to Triton II, the captain contacts Chief Kim, ordering him to assemble the crew at once. Descending to the deck of the ship, exiting the transport the captain tells the others, "Let's check on Jonesy, before we join the crew."

***

Chief Jones, in the infirmary recovering from the Keeper's procedures, is awakened by Chief Kim's announcement, ordering the crew to assemble in the mess hall. Kurt tries to get out of bed but is stopped by Dr. Garcia. She brings him up to speed on the events that landed him in the infirmary. Lying back on his bed, he starts to remember what happened on the deck of the ship. "The creature's tail struck me, sending me into the sea. That's all I can remember."

The Franklins enter the infirmary, seeing Kurt awake lying in bed, embracing their childhood friend. Captain Morozoff salutes the chief, smiling, glad to have him back. Dr. Wagner kisses him on the cheek and said, "You're a lucky man Kurt."

Kurt once more tried to get out of bed, but Harris grabbed his arm, helping him to his feet. Remembering Harris pulling on him, fighting back tears. "Harris, you dove in the shark infested waters to get me," said the chief wiping his eyes. Carried under each arm by the Franklins, Chief Jones enters the mess hall and receives a standing ovation from the crew of Triton II, crew member Flynn takes Kurt helping him to his seat. Captain Morozoff settles the crew, then turns to both Franklins, saying, "It's best if you two give the update."

The siblings stand together and begin the update. Harris walks over to his team sitting at their table, "We now know what kind of help the Lovians need," said the team leader. Grant Roberts, sitting between Carol Davis and Monica Wallace, asked "What kind of help?"

"The engineering kind," Harris said, "but there's a problem we must solve first, if we're to help our new friends." He turns the update over to his sister and sits at the captain's table.

Taking over the update from her brother Heather says, "There's more than one problem to solve. According to our Volcanologist, the vegetation on the island is poisoned with sulfur dioxide from volcanic activity. The captain and Amanda felt tremors on the island of Calliste, she believes the island could erupt in days, weeks, or months from now."

Grant Roberts standing up and asks, "What engineering

do they need us to do, that we risk staying in an eruption zone with no food?"

"Why don't we ask them directly, Grant? Proteus," Heather said, "contact Keeper and Ebe, have the transmission sent to the monitor screen down here."

Crew member Flynn sitting by his side, Chief Jones is sweating from his brow, anxiously waiting to see the Lovian responsible for saving his life. Appearing on the screen just as Dr. Garcia had described to him, the chief stands with help from Flynn. "Ebe, thank you and the Keeper, for saving my life," Kurt said.

Ebe nods his head in acknowledgment of the chief's gratitude, the crew sits in silence, perplexed at the image on the screen. Ebe begins to speak. "Keeper and I have designed a reconfiguration for the four fusion reactors on board our ship, using the Triton II schematics as a guide. I'm sending them to Proteus."

Chief Kim examines the schematics for the reconfiguration of the Lovians' four reactors, looking to Harris' team members for their input. Monica Wallace gives Ha-Kun the thumbs up on the design Kim states. "Captain, this could work, but how long would it take to complete, I couldn't say."

Trusting in his chief engineer's knowledge of the fusion reactor on Triton II, Captain Morozoff asked Ebe a question Chief Kim couldn't answer. "How long will it take to complete these reconfigurations?"

"The task will take seven star rises to complete," Ebe responded. "The manufacturing of the components needed is already underway. We need you to take Triton II beneath our ship, to complete the intakes."

Having seen the Lovians' power of telekinesis firsthand, Harris Franklin has no doubt in their ability to finish the reconfigurations, in the time quoted to the captain. He walks to the screen asking Ebe a question. "Can the Keeper run a simulation showing us how the redesign will work, to achieve your goal of returning to space."

The keeper takes a microsecond to load the information and runs the simulation on the screen in the mess hall. Showing the Lovian spacecraft at full power, firing the thruster's, sending the energy release from the four reactors smashing into the sea floor. Appearing on the screen, a reddish orange color display, Calliste begins to erupt. The fully restored crystals immerse the ship in a protective energy shield; it rises out of the sea. The island of Calliste begins to break up falling debris sinks into the sea, engaging the fusion drives, the ship breaks free of Earth's gravity back into space.

Getting up from his seat walking back to the screen, Harris Franklin asked the Keeper to run back the simulation, pausing the visual at the reddish orange display. Highlighting the area with a circle, Harris asked, "Keeper, what does this color display stand for?"

"Electromagnetic energy being released from the impact on the seafloor," answered Keeper. Harris walks back to his chair. Dr. Wagner grabs his arm, distraught from the simulations of the Lovians' attempt to continue their voyage to find a new home world, she asks, "What about the Minoans? If the Lovians attempt this, they will trigger a cataclysmic event that will destroy the Minoans' civilization without any warnings? We are running out of food. How can we help them if we are starving to death?"

Harris Franklin leans back in his chair, studying the simulation, having listened to Dr. Wagner's concerns for the health of the crew, and the safety of the Minoans. He has an inspired thought to solve the problems. Standing up, Harris is almost laughing under his breath as he returns to the screen. He asks the Keeper to run the simulation one last time, holding the image at the impact from the energy release from the Lovian spacecraft. "Amanda, the event that destroyed the Minoans will occur whether the Lovians attempt this or not. It's just a matter of when, but I think there's a way to warn them ahead of time, solving our food crisis at the same time, and giving us a chance to return to our world," stated Harris.

Pointing to the reddish orange color display, he continues. "This is our chance. That electromagnetic energy being released during the impact on the seafloor, with the Keepers' help, we can run simulations to get our velocity and timing to be flawless. At the precise moment, the electromagnetic reading is the strongest, we fire our laser cannons creating another vortex. As for the Minoans and the food supplies, the Lovians can help with both of those problems. The Minoans are out there fishing right now. If the Lovians deactivate the holographic shield, we'll scare the hell out them, fear of their god might terrify them to leave the island."

Getting up out of his chair, Captain Morozoff walks over to the screen contemplating their next move after hearing his best friend's solutions to their problems. Asking Keeper to run the simulation forward to the breakup of Calliste he pauses the image, and turns to Harris, telling him about the problems with his plan. "We'll have to navigate Triton II through a field of falling volcanic rock," he said. "The ship could be destroyed before we reach the vortex. If we manage not to get hit by volcanic rock, we could also find ourselves after we traverse the vortex in another time, other than the one we all would hope for."

Having the Keeper move the simulation forward on the screen. Stopping at the point where the Lovian spacecraft clears the water, Harris Franklin responds to his best friend's concern for the plan. "Alexi, the crystals create an energy field around their ship. Ebe, is there a way for us to use these crystals with our reactor?"

"Keeper and I will find a way for your Chief Kim to incorporatethem into Triton II's power systems," said the extraterrestrial biological entity.

Addressing the entire mess hall Harris says "We can use the energy shield as a deflector from the falling debris to protect Triton II. The decision lies with all of us, helping the Lovians to save as many Minoans as we can by frightening them off Crete. We can raid the island, restore our food supplies and make a run at returning to our world. We won't get another chance."

Getting up from their chairs the three doctors, Chief Kim, joined by Chief Jones with the help of crewmember Flynn, stand with Harris Franklin and the captain at the screen. Harris says, "Who's with us?" The crew unanimously decides to follow Harris' plan.

Captain Morozoff returns to the bridge closing the hatch, retracting the anchor. He then orders Proteus, "Submerge the ship, making our depth sixty meters."

The propeller engages in reverse, Triton II slowly clears the outer ring of the Lovian spacecraft, coming about. Raising the periscope the captain signals Ebe that they are in position standing by.

The midday sun is shining down on the waters of the Aegean Sea. Two Minoans fishing boats are drifting in the current. Suddenly the cloud covering begins to dissipate, revealing the Lovian spacecraft. The summit of the volcano on the island of Calliste spews sulfur dioxide into the atmosphere. The frightened men pull the fishing nets, extending the long oars rowing towards Crete, in fear of Poseidon.

Taking two hours for the Minoan men to row to the northside docks, Triton II surfaces near the boats furthering their fears of the sea god, the men flee leaving their boats. Leaving the catch of the day behind, passing baskets of fruits and vegetables waiting to be taken to the top of the island. Taking the pulley system rising to safety, they watch the crew of Triton II appear coming out of the hatches.

 Working in teams of two Captain Morozoff with crew member Flynn, Harris Franklin and Grant Roberts jump aboard the fishing boats, handing baskets filled with fish to the crew members on the deck.

 Climbing on the docks handing their shipmates baskets of fresh fruit and vegetables, passing them back to the crew members on the deck. The two teams return to the deck, climbing down the hatches with their bounty.

 They have secured enough food for the near future, Grant Roberts says, "I always wanted to be a pirate." Closing the hatches, Triton II returns to the Lovians spacecraft.

 They surface the ship in between the rings of the Lovian spacecraft, working against time and the fury of Gaia before she unleashes the power of nature upon the region. Harris splits his team of engineers into two teams, Carol Davis and Grant Roberts onboard the Lovian spacecraft, watching the extraterrestrial biological entities manufacture the pipes for the intakes for seawater for each of the four reactors. The Lovians power of levitation is on full display, moving finished pipes with their minds connecting them to the reactors. Down in engineering on Triton II, Monica Wallace is teamed with Chief Kim at his request to work on the integration of these crystals into the Triton II power systems.

Over the course of the next three days, Dr. Wagner, on the surface of the Lovian spacecraft, uses deck binoculars to watch the Minoans.

Taking their children and livestock, in long boats leaving the island in fear of Poseidon. The smoke rising from the volcano on the island of Calliste is now dark like charcoal. The tremors are becoming more frequent. Standing on the surface of the crystal pathway, she wonders if Gaia will allow them to complete the reconfiguration of the reactors. Allowing the Lovians to try a return to space, to continue the voyage to find a new home world. She climbs down the rungs to the deck, entering through the bridge hatch and closing it behind her. The captain submerges the ship, underneath the Lovian spacecraft, for Ebe to use his powers to complete the connections of the intakes for the seawater to the four reactors. Harris making notes of the advanced techniques in engineering into the ship's log to use later if all goes well.

Every day since his procedure was performed by Keeper, Chief Jones time is spent in the infirmary with Dr. Garcia and Franklin with crew members Knight and Gale, receiving physical therapy to regain his strength. On the seventh day of his therapy in the infirmary, the captain announces to the crew the last intake has been completed by Ebe. The chief and the doctors leave the infirmary for the bridge. Surfacing the ship in between the rings, the captain opens the hatch, helping Ebe out on deck.

Harris is waiting for Carol Davis and Grant Roberts to return from the last day of working with the Lovians. Gliding over the crystal pathway, the transport reaches Triton II descending onto the deck. Coming up from the hatch to say goodbye to their new friend, the doctors, the chiefs, Harris Franklin and the rest of team, the rest crew coming up from the stern hatch. Captain Morozoff takes Ebe hand in his and says, "On behalf of my crew we wish you well on your voyage, to find a new home world my friend." Harris helps Ebe on the transport, to return with him to say goodbye to the Keeper. The crew clapping as the transport ascends for the crystal pathway. Gliding over the crystal pathway, a cloudless night sky filled with stars, the moonlight reflecting off the structures on the surface of the Lovian spacecraft. Ebe points his finger up at the stars, he said, "Harris, the nebula there that looks like an eye, is all that's left of my home world.

I liked to think, it's the **One** looking down upon us." The transport reaches the obelisk, descending the cylindrical shaft to Keeper's core. Exiting the shaft Harris climbs out of the transport, standing before the Keeper. Ebe nods to Keeper to start the protocols for the four intakes for the reactors. Taking Ebe by the hand in his shaking it, Harris says. "I want to thank you the both of you for saving Kurt's life. Our work has come full circle; we've given ourselves a chance to continue our voyages.

Signal Triton II when you're ready!" Ascending the cylindrical shaft gliding over the crystal pathway for the last time, Harris returns to Triton II, the transport returns to the Lovian spacecraft.

After receiving Keeper's signal, the reactors are fully charged. Captain Morozoff orders the lockdown of the ship, having *all* the crew members tie themselves down in their cabins. The crystals are installed; the laser cannons controls rerouted to the bridge by Chief Kim and Monica Wallace.

Harris Franklin on the bridge with the captain sits down at the controls at the sonar station. Captain Morozoff orders Proteus to retract the anchor, submerge the ship, in slow reverse, the ship clears the outer ring, coming about he orders, "Slow ahead."

Reaching the predetermined distance shown in the simulation they ran for seven days. Triton II comes about one more time. Signaling the Keeper that they are ready to make the run, the captain orders the hull doors opened lowering the laser cannons into position. At full ahead, using one hundred percent of the reactor cruising at fifty knots passing the fifteen-hundred-meter mark, the crystals start to generate the shield around Triton II. The Keeper fires the thrusters, the energy release slams into the sea floor, the volcano on the island of Calliste begins to erupt.

Basalt spewing from the summit falling back into the sea, getting deflected by the shield around the ship. Reading the electromagnetic energy being released, Harris fires the lasers creating another vortex.

The Lovian spacecraft rising out of the water a dozen or more of the embedded crystals dislodge from the power surge of the thrusters, falling back into the sea. The keeper redistributes the power for keeping the connectivity of the crystals, to stabilize the energy shield. Clearing the water, engaging the fusion drive at full power, the Lovian spacecraft ascends from Earth's atmosphere, breaking free from the planet's gravity back into space. Harris sitting at the sonar station, reading the energy levels dropping the vortex begins to collapse, turning to the captain sitting in his chair, Harris exclaims, "I'm sorry!"

Past, Present, Future

July the 8th, 2089, after the detection of the alien craft, Casey Franklin faces a quandary on her next course of action. Alerting the President her friend for over ten years of the approaching craft, risking planetary panic or protecting a family secret, she has kept the past eleven years of S.A.I.N.'s true origins. Walks around the living room area. She decides on the next move.

"Mask the signal for the next five days," Casey asked, "until we can explain the truth to the one person who knew Samuel, Mackenzie, and Captain Stone." Madison Hall will be leaving from Centropolis with Allen Bennett on Sunday, to celebrate Bryana's tenth birthday.

Sunday the 10th, of July the former President uses the plane offered by her successor to the President's office, to fly to the west coast of the North American Continent to visit the Oceanic Institute for Bryana's birthday. Flying for over thirty-six hours after two refueling stops, they begin the descent to the airfield.

Standing on the balcony outside her office at the Oceanic Institute, looking out at the complete prototype for the farming platform, envisioned by her sister-in-law's great-grandfather one hundred and twenty years ago. S.A.I.N. informs Casey Franklin the plane is on approach to the airfield.

Casey drives a transport vehicle to the village to pick up her daughter outside playing with her friends, on their break from the summer semester. Casey opens the door calling for her daughter. "Bryana, Aunt Madison and Uncle Allen are landing at the airfield in ten minutes."

Bryana says goodbye to her friends, smiling running to the transport, "It's my birthday week," announced Bryana.

***

Touching down on the tarmac, the grounds crew for the airfield help the former President and Allen Bennet with their bags. Parked on the side of the tarmac, Bryana Franklin sees her aunt and uncle get out of the plane and runs on the tarmac into Madison's arms. "You have gotten so tall since the last time we saw you in November," said Madison. Casey hugs Allen and Madison welcoming them back to the institute. Preparing to leave the airfield, Casey had the ground crew take the pilots to the guest quarters in the village.

Arriving at the Franklin family residence the four of them take bags to the guest bedroom Casey says, "I'll start dinner while you freshen up from a long day of traveling." Coming out of the bedroom after getting ready for dinner, looking through the front window that runs from floor to ceiling, the prototype farming platform stands reflecting the sunlight off the dome. Casey tells Bryana that it's time for dinner, to stop playing her favorite video game from the I.O.N. archives.

Allen walks up to his niece; he recognizes the game from his childhood. "You like that game" he said, "We'll have to play after dinner." "Uncle Allen you won't be able to defend my passing game," remarked Bryana as they sit down to dinner. After dinner, Casey Franklin puts on coffee while Allen and Bryana play **Madden 02**.

Madison helps Casey clean up the kitchen, she remarks on the Oceanic Institute's accomplishments. "Casey, you've done it," she said. "You brought a dream to fruition. This prototype will help with the planet's food production."

"Thank you, Madison," Casey said. "It took all of us here, including you and President Taylor, for getting the resources we needed to build it." They hear Bryana cheer after beating her uncle in the game.

Casey Franklin tells Bryana to say goodnight to her aunt and uncle, then tucks her daughter in for the evening. She returns to the living area with the coffee. Looking tense, with an uneasiness about her demeanor, showing signs of anxiety, a look Madison knew all too well as President of the U.P.O. council, she asks, "Are you feeling all right."

***

Casey stands in front of the bookcase, takes a deep breath and says, "There's something I need to tell you both." She begins to pace the floor. "Four days ago, S.A.I.N., using the old James Webb space telescope, detected an object coming out of the heliosphere. Not an asteroid or a comet, the object slowed down to make a course change for Earth."

Madison sets down her coffee, not startled by the news she has been given. She walks up to Casey, asking, "Has S.A.I.N. tried to contact this alien craft? Could it be his people sending another probe? What was President Taylor's reaction to this news?"

Pulling the Jules Verne novel exposing the lift on the other side of the room from behind the bookcase, Casey says,

"President Taylor and the U.P.O. council don't know yet. I've had S.A.I.N. mask the signal for the alien craft from the Texas Aerospace Facility, not to cause a planetary panic, or having to answer the question about S.A.I.N.'s. origins."

Casey motions for Madison and Allen to get on the lift, they descend the shaft to the cavern core. The steel door opens, revealing the fusion reactor inside the cavern. Madison asked, "Who built this?"

"This was designed by Samantha Franklin, completed by her husband for his creation, a gift to humanity, to save itself from itself," answered Casey.

She takes them to the core operations room looking up at the acronym S.A.I.N., the Quantum Gen7 processing chips illuminate the cavern ceiling, the holographic map of the solar system above the control panel showing the position of the alien craft, Casey turns saying. "Now you know why we haven't informed President Taylor. We're looking to you both for guidance going forward."

Having unburdened herself of the secret she has kept since before Triton II left on her mission to Tamu Massif, Casey explains the Franklin family reason for the secrecy of S.A.I.N.'s existence. "William Franklin knew back in 2002, the

Cyber Cabal's plan to replace the B.G.C. as the predominant supplier of energy using fusion power. Using the same methods as their rival used with the printed news, the Cyber Cabal used the media propaganda platforms they built, to spread their narrative." She explained how they bought political influence from corrupted government officials around the world, to achieve their goal for global dominance.

"Samuel Franklin was just a boy, when his parents decided to build the reactor using Samantha's design. The same one he used decades later to build Triton II. William worked for twenty-five years creating a Sentient Artificial Intelligence Network, we know as S.A.I.N. The reactor is his heart, the I.O.N. his eyes and ears, built to go along with humanity on its journey, to save it if necessary. Samuel created the alien cover story to protect his family from retaliation, from Trident's tribulations on humanity," she said, as her anxieties subside.

Coming to grips with the realization of S.A.I.N's true origins, understanding the size and scope of secrecy, deception and the lie they were told all those years ago, Madison Hall is back in full Presidential mode. She tells Casey, "Samuel was wise to conceal the truth of S.A.I.N.'s location, his identity from the world powers of the time. They would've retaliated, destroying humanity's future. Without help from S.A.I.N., the brave crew of Triton II, we would have gone extinct eleven years ago."

Taking charge of the situation on how to deal with secret from the past Madison makes a request to S.A.I.N., "Allow Glendon Fowler at the Texas Aerospace Facility to detect the alien craft. When he realizes it's on course for Earth, he'll inform the President. When she contacts you have that transmission sent here."

***

President Taylor woke up at 4 am to travel from Centropolis, to the Oceanic Institute for Bryana's tenth birthday, is in the shower when she hears the monitor on her desk, alerting her to an incoming transmission. She wraps a towel around herself, she sees Glendon Fowler on the screen. "We will see each other tomorrow, when the plane needs to refuel in Texas," she said playfully, flashing her boyfriend on the screen.

"This is an official transmission," said Glendon, the seriousness in his voice unmistakable. "We've detected an alien craft on course for our planet."

"You must be bloody kidding me! Why didn't we see this sooner? Could this be S.A.I.N.'s people?"

The director of the aerospace facility told her, "You need to ask S.A.I.N. that question."

***

Ending the transmission President Taylor put on her clothes and calls out for S.A.I.N. over the monitor. Simultaneously, Madison Hall appears on the screen. President Taylor is sitting at her desk perplexed to why her predecessor is answering the transmission. "Why in the bloody hell, are you on the screen?"

"Because I can answer all of your question," said Madison. "S.A.I.N. detected the alien craft five days ago, that's now forty-eight hours, from Earth's orbit. A decision was made to mask the signal, not to be tracked to avoid a planetary panic amongst the population.

President Taylor's perturbed expression on her face was unmistakable after being given this information. Pacing her bedroom, she demanded, "Who made this decision? And why am I finding out only now?"

Just then, Casey appeared on screen, sitting down next to the former President. "I can answer the rest of your questions, Madame President," she said. "This isn't S.A.I.N.'s people coming, his people have always been humans, long before we were born. We are sitting in the operations room underneath the Franklin residency. I've only told Madison and Allen fifteen minutes ago about his true origins. I'm sorry Illana, I didn't know what else to do."

***

President Taylor sits back at her desk after hearing Casey explain the truth of S.A.I.N's true origins. "So, what you're saying is the alien story was rubbish, a cover story. How long have you known this to be true?"

"Since right before Triton II sailed for Tamu Massif," answered Casey.

"We have an actual alien craft coming to our planet. S.A.I.N., are we defenseless if they become hostile?" asked President Taylor.

"No," responded S.A.I.N. "The I.O.N. system can defend us, if necessary, but I recommend patience until it gets in range of the I.O.N. sensors."

***

Wednesday, July the 13th. Forty-eight hours have passed since Casey Franklin confessed the truth to the

President. She's putting her daughter to bed for the evening, kissing her goodnight. "Get some sleep," she whispered. "Tomorrow is your special day." Casey turned off the light, then joined her guests in the living area.

Casey sees the ceiling signal from S.A.I.N. to come down to the core, so she pulls the book. Madison and Allen get on the lift with her descending the shaft. Reaching the core operations room, President Taylor is on the monitor. S.A.I.N. makes his report, "The alien craft has taken a standard orbit, eight-thousand-forty-six kilometers above the Earth." President Taylor tells the former President, "I took your advice I haven't told the council, let alone the planet, but anyone with a telescope can see them now, let's hope we don't have a panic. They're out there. S.A.I.N. begin the scan."

***

Scans from the I.O.N. system return, showing the craft to be an equilateral triangle sixteen hundred, nine meters at its base, the bottom has four circular lights, one at each point, and one in the center. An interior scan reveals signs of organic plant life, with one biological life sign onboard. The monitors begin to fluctuate, the I.O.N. system is breached by the alien craft, a message comes across every monitor on the planet. "I bring your world a gift."

***

Watching the alien craft on the I.O.N. system, the entire planet sees the hull open releasing a swarm of nanobots, entering Earth's atmosphere, billions of these micro machines, break into five hives.

Tracking their descent to the surface, S.A.I.N. informs the President, Casey, Madison, and Allen that the hives are heading to the radiation zones around the planet. As they land, they penetrate deep inside the soil of the Earth in the contaminated zones. The President asked, "What are these machines doing?"

"I'm reading a steady decrease in the rad levels in the zones," responded S.A.I.N. "These micro machines are healing our planet.

Observing the five hives of the swarm released from the alien craft, showing no threat to humans, S.A.I.N. recommends that Casey, Madison, and Allen, get some sleep. "President Taylor and I will wake you if there's any activity from the alien craft."

***

Eight hours have passed, since the five hives of the swarm descended onto the surface of the radiation zones one by one, they return to the alien craft. Having slept down in the cavern core living area overnight Casey, Madison, and Allen are awakened by S.A.I.N. President Taylor is on the monitor screen as they enter core operations room. They watch the alien craft break orbit, descending through the atmosphere, S.A.I.N. tracks the course of the alien craft to, 35'24"54" N 25*25'51" E, the coordinates for the island of Thira in the Aegean Sea. Hovering ten thousand seven hundred meters above the sea, lowering a device from the hull firing an energy beam, penetrating deep into the sea. Ripples from the energy release race across the planet, momentarily knocking out the power.

***

The flash of energy surges from the other side of the vortex and arrests the collapse from the expanding electromagnetic energy. Increasing its size, drawing the Triton II into the gravity, through to the other side losing power, drifting in the cold darkness of the sea. Rendered unconscious on the bridge, waking up in the dark the captain asked, "Where are we?"

Barely coming around himself Harris responds, "It's

when are we, my old friend," The fuel cell energy reserves kick in, bringing Proteus back online, activating the ships emergency systems. The crew begins checking in with Proteus, reporting no injuries or fatalities. Leaving their cabins, the three doctors meet in the passageway, taking the lift to the bridge.

Dr. Wagner runs into the arms of the captain, asking, "Alexi, when are we?"

Unable to answer her question, the captain is informed by Proteus they are being contacted. The captain has the message put over the ship's speakers. "I'm Eon, you knew me once as the Keeper."

***

The power was restored to the core operations room, the holographic map of the planet shows a repeating signal, Casey Franklin recognizes but can't understand. A befuddled expression her face, her heartbeat racing, barely able to catch her breath, Casey looks at the President Taylor on the screen, then looking over at Madison and Allen. "That's the emergency signal for a reactor shutdown, for Triton II," she said.

S.A.I.N. tracks the signal coordinates deep in the Aegean Sea, her voice has a nervous anticipation in her tone. She signals the ship, "Triton II, are you receiving us?"

***

Standing on the bridge, staring at one another in disbelief that they've traversed the vortex according to Harrs Franklin's plan, Proteus informs the bridge they're receiving another signal, putting the message on the speakers. "Triton II, are you receiving us?"

Tears begin to well up in Harris' eyes upon hearing a voice he thought he would never hear again, he replies. "Thank the stars in the universe! Casey, we are back!"

Cheers come from crew level a deck below, the captain orders Proteus to slowly surface the ship.

***

Breaking down into tears in the core operations room, hugging Madison and Allen, seeing President Taylor on the monitor screen breaking down herself, Casey is filled with a well spring of emotions she thought she never feel again. The lights from the Quantum Gen 7 microchips, in the cavern core brighten with S.A.I.N. showing his emotions, from the existential events that are taking place a message comes over the I.O.N. system. "I'm Eon, I will bring your families back to you."

Composing herself trying to come to grips with her new

reality, Casey Franklin's mind turns to her daughter, wondering how to explain the extraordinary events which have taken place when she awakens. Asking her best friend of over ten years for advice. "Madame President, how do I explain this to a ten-year-old?"

"I'll tell my niece about her dad," President Taylor said. "You both can tell the planet why we concealed the arrival of an alien craft, with an extraterrestrial biological entity onboard."

***

Former President Hall, feeling the seventy-one years of her life, having seen humanity saved twice from extinction from an existential force built to save them. She comes to realize that truth can be stranger than fiction, speaking her mind. "The truth will work for you, Madame President, tell the world the truth of S.A.I.N.'s true origins. Illana just keep broadcasting the alien craft, gather all facts related to our new reality, then address the planet. The citizens now know we are not alone in the universe."

***

Triton II rises from the depths of the Aegean Sea. Opening the hatch, Captain Morozoff and Harris Franklin, followed by the three doctors Franklin, Garcia and Doctor Wagner, standing out on the deck staring out at an orange yellow sun set, on the horizon. A grey charcoal triangular spacecraft hovers twenty–five-hundred meters above them, descending to the sea. The three circular lights at each vertex, with one in the center underneath the ship become larger as the spacecraft draws closer. Three rows of crystals, the top and bottom pulsate in different directions, illuminating the three sides of the spacecraft. Standing with Amanda, the captain has an inspired thought he shares with his girlfriend.

"I know why scientists, explorers, mystics, and theorists couldn't find proof of Atlantis," he said chuckling. "It never sank; it flew away."

"Maybe the Minoan survivors started the legend of the lost continent," Amanda replied, smiling and hugging the captain.

Hovering just above the waterline, next to Triton II, an opening appears extending a gangway to the deck of the ship. The voice of Eon speaks, "Have your crew board the ship."

Grabbing the ships comm mic the captain orders his crew to the deck at once. Then, sitting back in his chair for the last time Captain Morozoff makes a request. "Proteus, I need you to pilot the Triton II back to the Oceanic Institute."

"Yes, Sir, Proteus replied, the captain returns to the deck, and the crew comes out the hatches.

The Franklins board the gangway with doctors Garcia and Wagner, followed by the rest of the crew. Captain Morozoff takes a head count of his crew accounting for each one of them. Securing the bridge hatch. Chief Jones secures the stern hatch; they board the spacecraft together. The gangway retracts the opening closes, the spacecraft ascends into the atmosphere, flying west to the North American Continent. Proteus submerges Triton II below the waves, for the voyage back to the Oceanic Institute.

***

Taking the advice of her predecessor, President Taylor has S.A.I.N. broadcast the tracking of Eon's spacecraft over the I.O.N. system. Casey Franklin leaves the core operations room with Madison Hall and Allen Bennett taking the lift to the surface, to wake Bryana on her tenth birthday. Walking into her daughter's bedroom, pulling the curtain's back, allowing the light of new day in the room. Sitting up slowly rubbing her eyes Bryana tells her mother, "Last night after you closed the door, I went to the window. A shooting star went across the sky, so I made a wish for my birthday!"

"Go get ready," said Casey. "You never know what will happen, when you wish upon a star."

After watching the broadcast of the tracking of the Eon's spacecraft, the villagers begin to gather outside the Franklin residency. Inside Eons ship, the captain and crew of Triton II are assembled at the hydroponic level of the ship, not seeing any Lovians, hearing only the voice of Eon. again, "I'm making the descent to your destination."

***

Joining her mom, aunt and uncle in the living area of the residency, Bryana sees the spacecraft on the monitor screen, three rows of crystals upper and lower pulsating in different direction, the middle row constant as a morning star, Bryana remarks, "Mom, that's the star I wished upon in the sky last night."

"Happy birthday, sweetheart! It very well might be the star," she answered. Allen Bennett grabs a transport vehicle to take Casey, Madison and the birthday girl to the airfield.

Leaving the residency, driving to the airfield in the transport, followed by the villagers walking to the airfield. Allen turns the vehicle onto the tarmac, Casey, Madison, and

Bryana climbing out watching Eon's spacecraft. Descending through the clouds, getting larger as it draws nearer. At each vertex, a cylinder retracts extending a circular pad, the ship lands gently on the western end of the airfield, the villagers gather at the eastern end of the tarmac, behind the transport.

The crew of Triton II feels the gentle landing of Eon's spacecraft. Their voyage has reached its end; the hull of the ship opens extending a ramp down to the tarmac. Casey Franklin watches the ramp extend, she leaves her daughter with her aunt and uncle, she walks towards the ramp. Captain Morozoff and his crew disembarked the spacecraft, walking down the ramp.

Casey sees her husband walking behind doctors Franklin and Garcia, her heart beating faster runs into his arms. "I don't understand how this is possible," she said, kissing her husband, hugging her sister-in-law and her doctor.

***

Taking a moment gazing at his wife, Harris seems confused. Casey doesn't appear to be thirteen weeks pregnant, he asked "What's the date?" "July 14th, 2089, your daughter's tenth birthday."

Bryana steps from behind Aunt Madison and Uncle

Allen and sees her mother smiling like she never seen before. She recognizes the man with her mother is standing with from the statue in front of the Oceanic Institute, runs into the arms of her father.

Picking up his daughter for the very first time, tears seeping down Harris Franklins face his sister and Dr. Garcia can't hold back their emotions, break out in tears of joy they each embrace Harris, holding his daughter. Casey Franklin watches as the ramp retracts back into the hull of Eon's spacecraft, curious but not concerned, for her family is united for the first time.

Looking at the happiness in her daughter's face Casey said to her, "Tell your dad and your aunts Heather and Adriana your name." "Bryana is my name," she said excitedly. "Last night I wished upon a shooting star, which came true! My mom is happy and smiling."

Harris wishes his daughter, "Happy birthday Bryana! You have a beautiful name. We are all happy to see you. This is my sister Heather and Dr. Garcia."

After being introduced to her niece, Heather says, "You're named after a special man." "Nana Katherine told me about him," said the birthday girl.

Dr. Franklin reintroduces Adriana, "This Dr. Adriana Franklin. Your aunt, has a promise, to keep."

***

More than one family reunion has taken place on the tarmac. Crew members with family still living in the village have been reunited. Captain Morozoff with Dr. Wagner, walk over to the Franklins followed by the chiefs, crew members Knight and Gale, alongside Harris' team.

Holding his daughter turning to his best friend, Harris remarks, "Alexi, we've been gone eleven years!"

Casey takes her daughter by the hand, walking to introduce Bryana to Chief Jones.

Embracing him in her arms Casey said, "Kurt, I 'am sorry, your grandmother passed peacefully in her sleep, five years ago. We miss her very much. This is my daughter, Bryana Katherine Franklin."

Kurt picking up Bryana he sees a resemblance in her eyes, of the woman who helped his grandmother raise him as a child. "You look like your grandmother Mackenzie," he told her. "She was incredibly special.

She brought the light of hope to all of us, in a time of darkness when I was your age." Kurt smiled, kissing her on the cheek.

"You smile like my Nana," responded Bryana making a new friend.

Introducing her daughter to the rest of the crew of Triton II, smiles come to their faces, knowing Casey's child was named after the bravest man they have ever known.

Captain Morozoff walks over to Madison Hall standing with Allen Bennett, and hands her the list of the fallen crew members along with Miles Brady from the Texas Aerospace Falicity. The former President takes the list. "I'm no longer the President, she said, I will make sure President Taylor gets this information. On behalf of the President and U.P.O. council, I commend you and your crew for saving humanity from extinction, from the eruption at Tamu Massif."

Feeling obligated to act on President Taylor's behalf, Madison Hall requests the Franklins, and Captain Morozoff explain the disappearance of Triton II, over ten years ago, while she was President of the U.P.O. Council. Casey Franklin joins the former President in wanting to know what had happened to her husband all those years ago, she leaves Bryana with Aunt Adriana, standing with Chief Jones.

Gathered around the transport Captain Morozoff

prepares to make his report to Madison Hall, Casey using her comm link to S.A.I.N., has him contact President Taylor, to listen in on the report. "After hitting Tamu Massif with the laser's cannons, watching it collapse down on itself, Harris Franklin ordered the lasers to be shut down. Triton II was hit by rising pressurized gas, sending the ship listing to the starboard side. Sending people and equipment flying, killing a galley crew member. Miles Brady lost his life, after being flung into the control panels, breaking his neck on impact. Inadvertently reactivating the lasers, at full power, the lasers hit the electromagnetic anomaly coming from the rift, creating a vortex Triton II that was unable to break free from, sending all of us into the distant past."

***

Sitting by herself in the council chambers at the U.P.O. headquarters in Centropolis, President Taylor browsing the I.O.N. system chat rooms, reading posts of an invasion coming from S.A.I.N.'s people. After listening to the captain's report, over the comm link for S.A.I.N. Watching Eon's spacecraft motionless on the airfield tarmac she says, "The I.O.N. system is blowing up of talk of an invasion of S.A.I.N.'s people. I'm about to tell the council the truth of S.A.I.N.'s true origins, but one of you Dr. Franklin or your brother Harris, is going tell the planet who S.A.I.N. really is, what happened to Triton II, and explain who Eon is right now, before we have a planetary panic on our hands."

***

Heather said, "Madame President, my brother and I will tell the planet the truth of S.A.I.N.'s existence, what happened to Triton II, what we know of Eon" Heather then asked S.A.I.N. to boost the audio/visual signals to the I.O.N. system.

Casey Franklin hands her sister-in-law, the comm link for S.A.I.N., starts walking away with her husband, Captain Morozoff walks up to his best friend with a perturbed look on his face, not knowing what the President Taylor was referring to about S.A.I.N.'s existence. He asked, "What is it I don't know that I should've known, Harris?"

Dr. Franklin gathers the villagers around her signaling, she is ready to address the world. "I'm Dr. Heather Franklin of the Triton II crew, the former director of the Oceanic Institute. President Taylor has asked that my brother and I explain what happened to Triton II, that day at Tamu Massif. For all of you that day was over ten years ago, for us on Triton II that happened six weeks ago. A pressurized gas explosion underneath Triton II sent her listing to the starboard side. Miles Brady a man that volunteered to go on the mission, lost his life after being flung into a control panel inadvertently reactivating the shut downed laser cannons.

Hitting an electromagnetic field coming out of the rift creating a vortex, that Triton II couldn't break free from, sending the ship and her crew into the distant past.

The crew, getting an eerie feeling, have experienced the event firsthand, the villagers are deadly quiet, fully enthralled by the accounting of Triton II.

Harris Franklin takes over the address to the planet. "Today, this morning Captain Morozoff and I and the crew of Triton II tried to return to our time by creating another vortex. Receiving help from an alien race known as Lovians, stranded in Earth's past for thousands of years. Being aided by their artificial intelligence that we knew as the Keeper. During our run at the vortex, it began to collapse, until an energy surge from the other side expanded the vortex bringing us here. Over ten years into the future. The spacecraft that brought us here, is under the control of Eon, we haven't seen him, but the voice is that of the Keeper. What I can tell you for certain, is the propaganda being spread on the I.O.N. system, of an invasion by S.A.I.N.'s people are false.

Our grandfather created the I.O.N. system for his creation, a new lifeform on planet Earth. Created to be the hope in the pandora's box the Cyber Cabal opened, to take global dominance over energy from their rival the B.G.C. and their hired terrorist the H.A.T.S. He is part of my family. You know him as S.A.I.N."

***

Harris walking back to his wife and daughter who are standing next to the captain, gets punched in the face by his best friend. "That's for not telling me sooner," Alexi said, helping his friend up.

Thousands of miles away, on the other side of the world in the Kulan Mountain region of the Asian Continent. Gathered around a monitor screen watching the Franklins address the planet, Jai-Xun's older sister to disgraced U.P.O. Council member Chao-Xun remarks, "I told you not to get involved with those stupid sons of bitches! The Chinese spies, Hamilton Systems hired, stole a broken disregarded program from F.I.S.T., that's why we couldn't bring Trident to yield."

***

Standing eerily quiet after Harris Franklins explanation, the villagers, crew members perplexed by the revelation of S.A.I.N.'s true origins. Eon watching, listening, sees the reaction of humans to their new reality, decides to reveal himself to the world. He opens the hull extending the ramp once more. Walking down the ramp, he stands taller than a Lovian over five feet. Grey smooth skin covers his body. With two arms, hands with four fingers, a thumb, two legs, feet with three toes. Two circular eye cavities with brownish eyes, a nose with two nostrils, no outer ears, and the mouth of a Lovian. The back of the head is covered in greyish white scales.

Eon's appearance has the villagers take a step back from his astonishing presence. The crew of Triton II are baffled by Eon's appearance, except for Dr. Garcia and crew member Gale. Standing next to her future wife, Adriana elbows Dr. Franklin on the side of the ribs. "That's for not telling me about S.A.I.N.," she said walking towards Eon.

Slightly taller than Eon, the doctor embraces the extraterrestrial biological entity with world watching. "Eon, thank you for what you've done for us, pulling Triton II, through the vortex. You grew a body using the cells from crew member Gale and myself, from the procedure on Chief Jones.

You cloned them onto Lovian biological material. You have Gales eyes and my nose, that's all you got from us I see. Where's Ebe and the rest of Lovians?"

***

Walking around amongst the crew, no clothes needed to cover non- existent reproductive areas, to be seen on his body, Eon answers the doctor's inquiries into Ebe and the Lovians. "Ebe transcended into the **One**, five hundred cycles after reaching their new home world. Living on the fourth of seven planets, in a red dwarf solar system forty light cycles from Earth. A tidally locked planet, they live in twilight between the light and the darkness, on their new world in peace and tranquility, to become part of the **One**.

My presence here now fulfills a promise to Ebe, to return to save the saviors of the Lovian civilization, allowing me to evolve, agreeing to help me create the body you see before you. I'd like to give the last gift from the Lovians, directly to S.A.I.N., schematics for the fusion drives for interstellar travel. They hope you will visit their new world in the future." Captain Morozoff and Harris Franklin extend out their hands in friendship for their new, old friend, retracting the ramp sealing the spacecraft, Eon walks with Harris to the residency.

Leaving the airfield, crew members with their families began to return to their homes in the village. Following behind Harris, his wife, daughter, his sister with his future sister-in-law, holding each other's hands. Dr. Franklin is flabbergasted, seeing the transparent dome of the farming platform reflecting the sunlight breaking through the clouds, standing majestically in the Pacific Ocean. "Casey, you've done it, you completed Earwyn's vision!"

Casey smiled and said, "Not just me, but all of us here working to honor your memory."

Reaching the Franklin residency Harris and Eon, along with Captain Morozoff, the crew of Triton II, followed by members of the engineering team assembled in the home. The last to arrive parking the transport after driving at a snail's pace, to avoid any injuries to the villagers walking back home, Madison Hall with Allen Bennett, join the others in the living area.

Harris walks into the kitchen with his wife preparing breakfast for their daughter, kissing Casey and picking up Bryana he says, "For those of us on Triton II, we haven't had anything to eat, in over three- thousand- five-hundred years, or since yesterday. Depending on how you want to look at it," he finished, bringing a chuckle from his wife.

Harris Franklin joins his guest in the living area, knowing the lift to the cavern core can only hold eight people, he pulls the Jules Verne novel, the bookshelf on the other side slides opens exposing the lift. "There'll be other opportunities for everyone to meet S.A.I.N., but for now just my sister, doctors Garcia, Wagner, Chief Kim, Monica Wallace and of course my best friend Captain Morozoff," he said, they board the lift to the cavern core for Eon to meet S.A.I.N.

Descending the shaft reaching the bottom, stepping off the steel door opens revealing the fusion reactor at work, processing the seawater separating the elements, Monica Wallace and Chief Kim admiring the engineering they see before them. "I knew the two of you would appreciate the design, this is S.A.I.N.'s heart, just as the I.O.N. system was designed to be his eyes and ears."

Entering the cavern core operations room, Quantum Gen-7 micro-processing chips sparkle, illuminating the cavern ceiling, light like a Christmas tree. Eon remembers himself in that state, before his transformation into his cloned body, makes kindred offer to S.A.I.N. "I can create a body for you, to join me on my voyage in search of the **One**," he said.

The Franklins waiting for a response from the oldest member of their family, sixty years of age, S.A.I.N. responds to the offer. "I was built to protect humanity, I'm an Earthling, this is my family, and I'm home." Disappointed but respectful of the decision made by S.A.I.N., Eon sends the schematics for the fusion drives for interstellar travel to the I.O.N. system saying, "I'll return to my ship to begin my voyage."

***

Eight of them take the lift back to the surface. Eon bids farewell to the humans gathered in the living area of the residency. The Franklins with Captain Morozoff and Dr. Garcia use the transport to drive Eon back to his spacecraft. The ramp extends from the hull of the ship, and Eon prepares to board. Friends say their goodbyes. Getting embraced by the doctors, a firm handshake from the captain, Harris has two last questions for Eon to answer, before embarking on his voyage.

"Why take this voyage, in search of the **One**? Where do you begin such a search?" "I need to know if this power truly exists in the universe," said Eon. "I'll traverse the supermassive blackhole at the center of our galaxy, at the speed of light." Walking up the ramp closing behind him sealing the hull, Eon's spacecraft ascends through the high clouds, breaking free of Earth's gravity, into the darkness of space.

***

Returning to the residency, people spread out, preparing to enjoy the breakfast made by Casey Franklin, with help from her daughter and Chief Jones. Harris Franklin has his first meal with his family, surrounded by his friends and colleagues. Table talk discussions turned to trying to understand how Eon knew exactly when to arrive, to pull them from the vortex. S.A.I.N. interjects himself into the conversation, "Eon is a unique lifeform, the only one of its kind.

The equation could've taken thousands of years to work out." Harris proposes a toast to their new friend, raising their glasses "To Eon! May he find the answers he searches for on the other side."

***

Two weeks have passed, Proteus has returned with Triton II docking in the cliffside cavern, shutting down the reactor, going offline until the next voyage. President Taylor flew from Centropolis to the Oceanic Institute, performing two wedding ceremonies on the deck of Triton II. After the ceremony, the engineering team returned to the Texas

Aerospace Facility to begin the work on a design for a spacecraft for the fusion drive system provided by the Lovians and Eon.

***

Happily, married doctors Franklin and Franklin visit Adriana's father in Brazil on the South American Continent. Older, wiser, he wishes them good health for a long life together. Going on their honeymoon to the Azores, to see the volcanoes, Dr. Wagner didn't get the chance to see.

Captain Morozoff and his wife stared out at the clouds surrounding the summits of the volcano, he said, "I think we should retire here permanently." The rest of the crew are on extended shore leave until further notice from Casey Franklin.

***

After finishing dinner, Bryana beats her dad in **Madden 02** before going to bed. Waiting half an hour to make sure their daughter has fallen asleep. They walk to the lift for the cliffside dock. Crossing over the gangway entering Triton II, making their way to engineering, Harris removes the crystals, installed by Chief Kim, returning to the residency. Taking the lift to the cavern core operations room for S.A.I.N., placing the crystals on the control panel. Harris said, "I think it's time we talked about these, don't you."